DREAMS
of the DARK

**Other *Dark Shadows* books
published by HarperEntertainment**

Angelique's Descent

Dark Shadows

DREAMS of the DARK

STEPHEN MARK RAINEY
AND ELIZABETH MASSIE

HarperEntertainment

A Divison of HarperCollinsPublishers

📖 HarperEntertainment

A Division of HarperCollins*Publishers*
10 East 53rd Street, New York, NY 10022–5299

ISBN 0–06–105752–5

HarperCollins®, 📖®, and HarperEntertainment™ are trade-
marks of HarperCollins Publishers Inc.

Cover illustration © 1999 by Dan Curtis Productions, Inc.

First printing: October 1999

Printed in the United States of America

Visit HarperEntertainment on the World Wide Web at
http://www.harpercollins.com

❖ 10 9 8 7 6 5 4 3 2 1

*To my wife, Peggy, for your unquestioning
support and infinite patience. And to Frank Smith, in
memory of that day in the fourth grade, when ice and snow
sent us home from school early, and because the hill to my
house was too steep, we ended up at your house. At four
o'clock, on went the television to a show called* Dark
Shadows, *which I couldn't watch at my house because we
couldn't pick up that channel. And to that night, when
sleep just wouldn't come because it really was one helluva
dark night and the face of Barnabas Collins kept
appearing in the darkness, and damn,
them were some teeth!*

*To my sister, Becky—Thanks for doing everything
necessary to hang around; you're the best! Now, let's break
out a couple of Hersheyette canes, sing a round of "Winter
Wonderland," and reflect back on the glory days of
"Spatula City." I love you!*

Introduction

*The nosferatu do not die like the bee when he
stings once. He is only stronger; and being
stronger, has yet more power to work evil. The
vampire which is amongst us is of himself so
strong in person as twenty men; he is of cunning more than mortal, for his cunning be the
growth of ages; . . . he can direct the elements,
the storm, the fog, the thunder; he can command
all meaner things; the rat, and the wolf; he can
grow and become small; and he can at times
vanish and come unknown. How then are we to
begin to strike against him?*

—Bram Stoker's *Dracula*

Dark Shadows has played a major part in my life.
When I was a young mother living on a farm in rural
Wisconsin, I dreamed a foolish dream of becoming a
professional actress someday. A succession of seren-
dipitous events led me to summer stock in Con-
necticut and a brief sojourn in New York City, where
I was given the opportunity to audition for a new

soap opera. Miraculously, I got the job. The show had as its dramatic setting a stone mansion with crenellated towers, hidden rooms, cobwebs, and chandeliers. Eerie, silent, remote, perched on a hill in Maine overlooking cliffs that dropped off to the sea, it was the home of one of the Living Dead. Ghosts roamed the corridors, a werewolf howled in the nearby woods, and restless souls hovered over the graveyard.

However, all this magic existed on one floor of a studio on 53rd Street in New York City, where the series was videotaped. The magnificent mansion was a slide photograph, the sets were painted plywood, the gravestones were Styrofoam, and the werewolf was an actor with bits of fake hair glued to his face. It was into this world I came—frightened, anxious, and very excited.

Although I had been in many plays, in both college and community theater, the part of Angélique was my first professional engagement. I remember the whiteout stage fright I felt my first day on camera, filming a steamy love scene with Jonathan Frid, who played Barnabas, the show's leading man. I wore a charming blue-flowered dress in the style of the 1790s, and my hair was piled on top of my head with pinned-on golden ringlets. The part was that of a lady's maid whom Barnabas had wooed and rejected, as he now preferred my mistress, Josette. In the scene, I beseeched him to love me again, and, when he coldly refused, I remember staring into the lens of the camera and thinking to myself, "Hell hath no fury like a woman scorned." It was that evil stare that won me the part.

Soon Angélique was collecting magic herbs in the woods and fashioning fetishes out of clay. It became apparent that this seemingly innocent girl was secretly a witch, and the day she tied a handkerchief around the neck of a toy soldier used to represent Barnabas and began to chant an evil spell, I knew I was playing a fascinating character. For as the noose tightened around the neck of the doll, Barnabas, luxuriating in the arms of Josette in another part of the house, fell into a spasm of agonized choking. So began the struggle which would culminate in Angélique's curse that transformed her reluctant lover into the tortured being the audience both feared and adored: the vampire.

The vampire is the manifestation of our deepest longing and our strongest fear: desire for immortality and horror of the risen dead. The conflict between these two forces, one seductive, the other repellent, was the soul of this television show, which first captured the popular consciousness in 1966 with tales of the supernatural, and which has resurfaced often in numerous reruns and reincarnations ever since.

Looking back, I realize *Dark Shadows* was destined to become a series of novels, if only to release those mesmerizing stories which so enraptured audiences into the imagination of the reader. For as lavish as the settings, as clever as the props, as lovely as the costumes all were, the power of the written word on the reader's dreamscape offers an even more exhilarating experience.

The plots explore universal themes of loyalty, revenge, courage in the face of evil, and unswerving love. They are subjective, deeply emotional, and often irrational, weighing the concepts of individual karma and implacable fate. All the better to embrace these themes, Gothic writing employs language that is extravagant in description and detail, resonating with metaphor, layered with symbolism; it features hypnotic streams of interior dialogue which, like some drug, draw the reader into a deep reverie.

The TV show had its beginnings in the classics of Gothic Romance. The dark-haired governess, hired to care for a young boy who lived in a gloomy mansion, riding a train through the night toward Collinsport, was straight out of *Jane Eyre*. The show had a literary quality; and now, when special effects have gone digital and acting methods have changed radically, it is the stories themselves that still retain their power over us.

One reason is that the Romantic style of the Brontë sisters, Mary Shelley, Johann Goethe, Victor Hugo, Edgar Allan Poe, Henry James, and so many others still holds such strong appeal in today's world—a world virtually bereft of spiritual meaning. So often news stories or the plots of films leave us with a feeling of hopelessness. Our buildings are stark, our music reeks of cynicism, films are populated with computerized creatures, and contempt for any chivalric ideal reigns supreme. The protagonist is often a punk, a loser, or an automaton; and passion has been replaced by "cool," the coveted attribute of the modern personality. Mindless distraction and a kind of smug and sneering send-up of all traditional values are the modern fare. We continually long for something we have lost.

Gothic Romance invites us to escape from this wasteland into a mysterious world—a world of dreams—where what Wordsworth called the "spontaneous overflow of powerful feelings" is encouraged, and where, oddly, morality is no longer sabotaged. Even though the horror genre adopts macabre subject matter, its power to terrify us is absolutely dependent on a deeply held belief that purity and perfect love exist, that goodness shines in the face of evil, and that heroic sacrifice is still a choice.

Not even the most sophisticated production values of today can rival the imagination's prowess in conjuring up the supernatural. Vivid description can take us to landscapes and settings far out of reach of a television camera. And for the devoted reader, knowledge of the TV series is not a prerequisite. These books are self-contained, original stories where complex narrative and inner dialogue can give intriguing psychological insight into the characters' hearts.

This, the second in the series of *Dark Shadows* novels, offers a compelling tale. Once again we follow the journey of a vampire, but this time a new vampire, in a search for revenge that has unexpected, heartstopping consequences. Death is the price of love—this idea is the thematic core of Romantic literature. The vampire who kills the one he loves, and can therefore never love, is the most fascinating symbol of all of "yearning for the unattainable."

If unrequited love—love unfulfilled and therefore unquenchable—is the most pure, and the love of the vampire is the most depraved, then these two forms of love entwined in one story create an ache in the reader's heart that is almost unbearable. The vampire, an immortal who thirsts for blood and longs for intimacy, exists in a limbo of obsessive madness, and as Theseus murmured to Hippolyta in *A Midsummer Night's Dream*:

> *Lovers and madmen have such seething brains,*
> *Such shaping fantasies that apprehend*
> *More than cool reason ever comprehends.*
> *The lunatic, the lover, and the poet,*
> *Are of imagination all compact.*

Not to be ignored in any discussion of the television show is the fact that it retained an air of whimsy, a tongue-in-cheek campiness where the characters were endowed with flaws and idiosyncrasies that made them uniquely human. Most of the actors were from the theater and they played these meaty scenes with complete sincerity, never for laughs. However, the vampire bat which fluttered in the window and dealt Barnabas his damning bite was a little puppet dangling from strings. The mysterious fog which enveloped the graveyard was created by dry ice and an electric fan. And my ability to float through the room as a ghost was merely a trick of superimposed camera shots. The vampire teeth many of us sported were actually porcelain bridges made by a dentist; they required a quick insertion while off camera in order to provide the frightening moment the audience was waiting for—exposed and bloody fangs! Nevertheless, invariably the magic was sustained, and the actors' total commitment to their roles in absurd situations sometimes created an amusing tone for which *Dark Shadows* audiences developed enduring loyalty and affection.

When I left the snowy cornfields of Wisconsin to try my luck as an actress in New York City, I never dreamed that my first job, the role of Angélique, would remain part of my life for thirty years. Writing the initial novel of this series, *Angélique's Descent*, was another first, my first attempt in the role of an author, and it was once again a frightening prospect. Finally, I was able to tell the story I had only imagined while playing the part, of Angélique's childhood, and of her all-consuming passion and heartbreak. But would the novel find readers as the show had found an audience?

Searching through bookstores for my book and always finding one or two on the shelf in the horror section is quite a thrill. Much to my delight, in one very large BookStar, I found twenty books displayed under the sign STAFF RECOMMENDS. The manager of the store, who was once a fan, and who had run home from school to watch the show when he was a boy, had written a very kind review and signed his name. Book signings brought many fans out of the woodwork. The publicity person from HarperCollins who accompanied me to a reading on Long Island was astounded at the turnout. She was even more aghast when one young man appeared with a picture of Angélique tattooed on his forearm, in color! New captives of the magic who had been watching the innumerable reruns and syndications or renting the videos were also reading the book.

With these novels, what the cast referred to as "going back in time," which essentially meant putting on period costumes, can now be a literary escape into history. The reader can journey to Martinique, a beautiful island in the West Indies, during the days of the slave trade, and see Angélique as a child, shut up in a windmill tower on a sugar plantation. He can wander onto a Civil War battlefield, hear the firing of muskets close at hand, smell the gunpowder, and suffer the terror of the wounded. There are many stories to come, with fresh new characters as well as old favorites, and the spinning out of these stories, the weaving of the past and future, promises new tapestries rich in texture and design.

Dreams of the Dark is an intriguing, original story—a delicious twist on the old Collins hubris. A second vampire, Thomas Rathburn, comes to Collinsport to seek revenge on Barnabas, who he believes played a demon's role in his wife's death during the Civil War. Rathburn proceeds to meet and fall in love with the young governess, Victoria Winters. This provocative tale is combined with Angélique's efforts to return to the world of the living. Reaching from the grave, she chooses this vampire, a monster as evil and depraved as she, as her channel. What follows is a struggle for Rathburn's soul.

Riveting indeed is the description of the vampire's hunger, as from inside his tortured mind we witness his wrenching need. We enter Victoria's emotional world, and we experience her secret longing for acceptance and her confusion when she abandons herself to passion. A chapter in which she is so crazed with desire after the vampire's bite that she scratches her arms in a frenzy until they bleed seems so familiar that the reader can almost recall seeing it on the screen.

Dark Shadows, a television show from the seventies, has endured far beyond the expectations of those involved in the creation of the series. And now a series of novels begins where the TV series left off.

It is my fondest hope that these books will cast a wider net and reach an even larger school of readers who were not fans, but who appreciate Gothic Romance, not only as a re-creation of a beloved memory, but also as a journey into a new world of enchantment.

—Lara Parker
June 1999

Dreams of the Dark

Prologue

—∞∞∞—

How I love you, Barnabas Collins. How deeply I've always loved you.

How I despise you. You betrayed me. Abandoned me.

She can feel him, somewhere beyond the blackness which has become her entire existence. If only she could reach him again.

I must be free.

Get me out of this.

By all the powers of Satan. Lucifer. Diabolos . . .

Set me FREE . . .

There is no answer. There is nothing.

Please.

The darkness is complete, deathly silent, maddeningly still. Yet somehow alive.

I am alive.

She can remember the throb of her heart beating in her chest. The sensation of breath in her lungs. She remembers what it was like to touch warm flesh, to taste the sweetness of another's lips.

His lips.

She has been here before. Banished here by those she has served, however faithfully. How can they be so unjust? Yet she knows now and knew then that the magick she has wielded demands a price, one often exceeding any benefit gained by her use of it.

She knew that. She knew that.

Still. They will release her again. They must. She has done so much for them, these unnamable dark forces for whom she has lived—and yes, even died—to serve, to master.

But has she not also disobeyed their calling? Has she not deigned to put her own interests above theirs? How many times, over how many years? But don't they understand? Can they not know what it means to feel?

To love?

No, how could they? The masters of this abyss know only its emptiness and despise it as much as she. That is why they must make use of the living, for what purpose can the darkness have without an instrument—a means to come forth into the world of light? And here, in this timeless netherworld, she can sense a fury in the very deadness around her. *Yes, the darkness wars even with itself!* If only she can discover the proper channels to follow, the right threads to weave, she can take advantage of the chaos within, eventually make her way out.

She must make contact with a strand of power, follow it, master it. Bend it to *her* will, rather than submit to it. Through her own memory, perhaps, she will discover the key. Yes, she can still remember.

I remember life.

She can recall her childhood on the beautiful island of Martinique, all those many years ago. There, she first learned of the existence of the dwellers in the darkness, the powers they enabled—and the tributes they demanded. Oh, but the life she had known! In the guise of a servant girl, she had worked her way into a family with great wealth and respect. A family of means—riches she coveted, intended to possess for herself. She had found ways to use those people for her own gains, for she had been taught by her mother, and the other *obeahs*, the eldritch truths that few ever dared believe existed. By working insidiously from within, one day all that was theirs would belong to her.

Or so she thought.

Then *he* came to Martinique from one of the American territories, with the hope of discovering new wealth for his already rich and influential family. During his stay on the small island, he was successful in his ventures, secured many contacts, even made something of a name for himself among the locals. And there he met the one who was to become his truest love:

Her own mistress.

Josette, the daughter of Martinique's greatest land baron, André DuPrès. The family in which she had established herself. Yes . . . he had fallen in love with Josette, and she with him. What a beautiful future the two of them planned together, a life of wealth and happiness back in his American home.

But the man. *Oh, that man.*

She had been drawn to him the moment she saw him. He was tall and dark-haired, with the most penetrating hazel eyes in all creation. His voice was deep and hypnotic; his hands, strong yet gentle to the touch. Almost regal in manner, lordly in his bearing. Courteous to all, ostensibly humble yet as self-assured and confident as any man she had ever met.

Barnabas Collins.

She cast everything aside in hopes of winning him for herself. She went to him, tempted him. And yes, he noticed her. Even pursued her.

Yes, he had loved her! She had kissed him, breathed his breath, felt his fingertips upon her skin. The moments they shared were beautiful, delirious. And yet . . .

And yet, he refused to turn his heart from Josette, her mistress. Even realizing what she felt for him, he continued to love the dark-haired beauty. *The fool.* How could he smite her like this? Did he not know the things she could do, the powers she could wield with only a thought? No, of course not. So cultured, so modern in his thinking, he could not begin to imagine the lore of centuries she kept hidden in her heart. Yes, she could have bewitched him, *made* him love her. She was beautiful, so beautiful that no mortal should be able to resist her charms, even with all her powers left dormant. But for her to truly understand the meaning of power, she knew he must choose her of his own free will.

Yet he refused her.

The affront. The torture. She had even considered killing him. In a fit of rage, summoning all the forces of darkness at her disposal, she had tied a handkerchief around the throat of a toy soldier that had belonged to him and tightened it. And how the power had flowed—like a bittersweet dirge building to a crescendo in her very blood. So close to death he had come then. At her hand. By her will.

But she could not kill him. Her love for him, her desire, had stopped her before the deed could be finished. Instead she worked her schemes on those around him: on his own love, Josette, on his beloved uncle, Jeremiah. Indeed, for a time her designs appeared to be on the path to success. Because of her, Jeremiah and Josette had wed, never realizing it was she who had ignited the fire of yearning in their hearts. Then in a fit of fury, Barnabas Collins had killed his own uncle, instilling in him a terrible sense of guilt that would consume him all the remaining days of his life. Now, with his lover forever lost to him out of revulsion for the deed, and unable to quench his own earthly desires, Barnabas Collins had come back to her, even married her. Yet in the end, finally realizing that it was her treachery that had led him to the brink of madness, he resolved to end her life.

With a pistol—the very one with which he had killed Jeremiah—he shot her, mortally wounding her.

The pain! But, oh, God, worse than the pain of the bullet piercing her own flesh was the pain of his hatred, his utter contempt for her.

Yet she was no mere mortal woman, and his betrayal could not go unpunished. He would pay. For an eternity he would pay—as she would make any who dared to love him pay. What mortal could even dream of such a love as she had known? What woman could ever understand the depth of her passion, the irresistible longings that only one such as she could experience? Who could *deserve* to possess him, when she could not?

Oh, yes, she had meted out her revenge. Laid upon him the curse of the undead—a curse that to his sensibilities was the most cruel imaginable. A curse to last eons beyond the day when all those he once knew and loved had turned to dust. That was the depth of her agony, the strength of her determination. *He would suffer and suffer and never stop suffering, even as she suffered in this forsaken world of darkness and torment.*

She saw to it that Josette learned the truth about him; and the beautiful young woman took her own life rather than share the terror and revulsion of his new existence. And with his beloved Josette's death, no man's despair could have ever been more complete.

Yet, perhaps the most horrible—or beautiful—irony of all was that the man's own father, unable to destroy the blood of his blood, had imprisoned his cursed son in a hidden tomb, chained him in a lair of the dead for what was expected to be all of eternity. And for so many years he had lain thus, undead, aware and suffering, forced to relive every moment that led him to his prison—unable even to procure the one thing that might enable him to survive outside the confines of the coffin in which he had been chained: the blood of the living.

Over the long years of his imprisonment, she continued to visit her wrath upon members of his family, intervening in their affairs, bringing about the downfall of any that shared his name:

Collins.

Yet even she had been thwarted on other occasions, betrayed by the dark lords displeased with her vain intentions, and seemingly banned to an eternity of darkness.

She wanted to howl with laughter. What knew any of them of eternity? The only member of the Collins family to have the slightest familiarity with its embrace lay in the darkness of a hidden tomb, endlessly tormented by his sins against *her*.

Until by an act of fate she knew nothing about, Barnabas Collins was set free.

And so he again wandered the world of the living, still suffering, forced into a life of loneliness even more awful than the bitter darkness of his coffin. Unable to love or be loved, he was doomed never to find fulfillment, and all too often was responsible for the destruction of anyone who dared get close to him.

Yet the hell she had once wrought for him is not enough. For her it can never be enough. The pain he caused her cannot be assuaged, not until she once again possesses him, heart and soul. But how can she have him, imprisoned in this seemingly infinite purgatory? *Damn them all*, these blind purveyors of chaos, these blasphemous overlords she has served, yet who so jealously hold her in their domain, preventing her from fulfilling her most ardent desire.

She knows the key to escaping this darkness lies in patience and in plotting new ways to please her cruel masters. But how to do it? *How to do it?*

She can still reach out with her mind, quest for those strands of power that run like conduits through her abysmal prison. Her disembodied senses perceive the energy around her as the throbbing of a million distant heartbeats, like a chorale of infinite tormented voices in the night. She seeks just one of them, focuses on it, forming in her mind the shape of a many-spoked mandala, concentrating on its radiating arms, tracing one of them until it can lead her to the outlet she so desperately seeks.

There.

A darkness within darkness, yet so different in nature as to be almost brilliant—blinding. As her senses adjust, she explores the sensations, the revelations it might hold in store for her. She hears its pulse, the fuguelike music emanating from its onyx heart. She listens to the truths there, and begins to see. . . .

Yes.

There are others like Barnabas who must exist in the world of night, forced to subsist on the blood of the living. They are few in number, forgotten or disavowed by those who dwell beneath the eye of the sun. But most important, there are those who have freed themselves of the kind of guilt that plagues him, if for them such guilt has ever existed. Indeed, not all are bound by the same limitations as he; the conditions of their existence are as varied as their number.

What a valuable, if unwitting, ally one of them might make.

Her will is strong, her desire beyond anything even remotely human. She reaches out.

She makes contact.

The result is like something physical, even in this ethereal form she occupies. A rush of hot, orgasmic energy, roiling like a thunderous ocean tide, sweeping over her and carrying her on waves of wondrous, beautiful sensation . . .

Her victim is aware of her ghostly fingers brushing him, but only subliminally. He cannot begin to guess what is about to unfold before him, the purposes for which she will bend his will. He will become hers . . . and draw her from this abyss, open the way for her to once again pursue her deepest love.

Alive and free.

And she will have him again. This time he *will* have her—or the horror of his existence up to now will be a pale shadow of what is to come, relentlessly and without end.

You cannot refuse me.

You will not refuse me, Barnabas Collins.

You will love me again.

I am Angélique.

chapter

1

My name is Victoria Winters. For two centuries the great house of Collinwood has stood high atop Widows' Hill, its rooms and hallways haunted by shadows of a turbulent, fear-laden past. For generations the family who lives there has been similarly haunted, its secrets tumultuous enough to match the storms that constantly batter the bluffs overlooking the sea.

Now, one young woman has been stricken by a terrible fear of night, for reasons she can neither understand nor accept without a challenge. But in discovering the truth behind her fear, she may encounter a danger more pervasive, more menacing than any she has known before. And though she doesn't realize it, soon she will meet a stranger whose mysterious heart may rival the darkness of Collinwood itself.

• • •

"Vicki, Barnabas is downstairs. He wants to see you."

Victoria Winters turned from the darkening landscape outside her bedroom window and looked at the doorway. A young blond woman stood with her brightly painted fingers pressed against the frame. Carolyn was in her early twenties, slender and attractive, with a slight air of haughtiness about her, dressed in an expensive yet casual pair of slacks and a tight red angora sweater. Carolyn always did know how to attract attention. Vicki, on the other hand, thought of herself as plain, with brown eyes, long brown hair, and simpler outfits fitting her position as a governess. She did not polish her nails, she wore very little makeup on the delicate features of her face, and although others had described her as comely, it was a label with which she did not feel altogether comfortable.

"What does he want? Did he say?" Victoria asked softly.

Carolyn shrugged, tossing her long hair back from her shoulder. "I don't know. But I said you'd be right down. You will, won't you? And for heaven's sake, don't talk with him all night. You and I are going into town to have some fun, to shake off the doldrums, don't forget."

Victoria nodded.

"Is that a yes? You'll be right down?"

"In a minute. I'll be right down," Victoria said, then looked back out the window. She could hear Carolyn sigh, then pull away from the door and move down the long hall.

The sun had vanished a short while ago beyond the ridge, fading in the west behind the rim of tall trees; the shadows of twilight had lost their substance, sucked into the vast darkness that was Collinwood.

It was nighttime at last. Her vigil was over.

Victoria rubbed her arms and took a long, silent breath, letting go of the discomfort that had knotted in her chest. Each evening for the last week, she had come up to her room on the western side of the huge mansion to watch the sun go down. It wasn't that she enjoyed the changing colors in the sky, or the shifting temperature of the coastal air, the shimmering of autumn leaves in the twilight breeze, or the onset of the sounds of night creatures—the locusts, the whippoorwill, the owl. But recently she had felt a need to witness the death of day because if she did not see it happen, if she did not watch the encroaching shadows carefully, something might materialize in the dark that could take her by surprise.

Something that could harm her.

By day, she knew it was silly to imagine she had some power over the unseen with her ritual, but when her afternoon lessons with David were done and the day was growing long, the compulsion came upon her again and she was drawn to her room to watch the sun set.

It's like peeking under a bed to chase away the bogeyman, she scolded herself. *It's like crossing my fingers or whistling past a graveyard.*

But the impulse was obsessive. Where the need had suddenly come from, she did not know. And why, she couldn't guess.

Carolyn referred to Victoria's reaction to nightfall as "night jitters." A trite euphemism, Victoria knew, because Carolyn, so independent and outgoing, could never understand how intense the apprehension was—a dread of what lurked after the world had given itself to the mercy of the dark.

Outside, not far from Victoria's window, towering above the October-brown grass of the Collinwood lawn, an ancient copper beech tree stood like a sinister sentinel, watching her through her panes. It was one of the last things visible as night fell. During the day, it was awe-inspiring, its massive branches coiled and expansive, reaching to all sides and to the clouds. But by night it seemed to Victoria to be able to breathe, move, and even think much as a human did—its intent purely malevolent. Sometimes she dreamed that the tree pulled itself up from its ancient roots, clambered across the grass, and reached in with sharp, clutching limbs to catch her around the throat and strangle the life from her.

Victoria put her hand to her forehead; a

headache had begun to throb. She turned from the window, sat on the edge of her bed and slipped on her plain black pumps. She *needed* to go out with Carolyn tonight. It was the normal thing for a young woman to do: just go out and have fun. Night had come; sunset was over. She needed to straighten up, go downstairs and speak to Barnabas, then get into Carolyn's car and head for town.

But fun was not something Victoria was used to. As far back as she could remember, her life had involved work, study, and little more. She had been raised at the Hammond Foundling Home in New York, in a dormitory for girls under the watchful eye of a stern but not unkind housemother. She attended school at the orphanage as well, excelling in nearly every subject but never quite fitting in with the other girls, who, with the onset of adolescence, became gritty and sassy with each other and with adults. Those girls enjoyed the occasional trips off the grounds, flirted with boys they didn't know, and sneaked out to meet them beyond the orphanage gates at night. Victoria, however, never broke the rules. She feared being expelled before she was eighteen, as some of the others had been. She longed to have their strength, their spontaneity, much as she envied Carolyn's now. But many of the other girls at least had somewhere they might go if the orphanage turned them out. Victoria, on the other hand, had been told from as far back as she could remember that she had no parents, no grandparents, no cousins. She was a true orphan. And she'd best learn to make the most of it.

So, she studied to become a teacher. Even after the other girls her age had graduated and left the institution with giggles and waves, bidding the place good-riddance, Victoria had stayed on, content, if not happy, to teach in the little orphanage school in which she herself had been educated.

Now, Victoria rose from the bed and brushed her hair quickly in front of the vanity mirror. Her hair was silky, flowing, the color of chocolate. Sometimes she allowed herself time to sit before the vanity and brush her hair one hundred strokes, as she'd learned was best, imagining that it was someone who loved her holding the brush, smoothing her tresses, and whispering sweetly in her ear. She treasured these daydreams but knew that was all they were, and often chided herself for letting them go on. She knew it was self-indulgent to hope for much more than a warm bed, a good job, and a roof over her head.

"Be thankful for what you have," she said sternly as she gave herself one last perusal in the mirror. What she saw she considered no more than average—slim, medium height, straight, thick hair, a face that reflected the seriousness of life. Her skirt was dark blue, her sweater a black cable-knit V-neck, and her earrings simple, faux pearls. She would try her best to have a good time tonight. "If it kills me," she whispered with a small, uncertain laugh.

In the hall there was a sudden scream, thump, and moan.

Victoria's blood froze. "Oh, my God!" She raced out, nearly tripping in her pumps, to find a small prone body, draped in black and spattered with red. The fingers opened and closed, as if clutching in the throes of death. The eyes were rolled up in the sockets, and hanging from the lips were two protruding fangs.

"David!" Victoria demanded. "What are you doing?"

The eyes in the small boy's head came back into focus, and the small lips spread in a taunting smile, knocking his makeshift wax canines to the carpet. "Gotcha!" he said.

"Get up this minute!" Victoria said. "You frightened the breath out of me!"

Twelve-year-old David Collins hopped to his feet, tangling and stumbling in the black sheet he'd wrapped about himself. He'd found someone's lipstick, Carolyn's most likely, and had streaked his face and the front of his white shirt to look like blood. Where the wax had come from, Victoria couldn't guess. "I'm making my Halloween costume," he said matter-of-factly. "It's at the end of the month, in case you forgot. And in case you forgot, you promised to help me make the best costume ever."

"Yes, I did," Victoria said. "But not tonight. Carolyn and I have plans. I told you I was going out."

David scowled. "Tell Carolyn you promised to help *me*."

Victoria touched David on the shoulder. She hated to put him off. He was her charge, and even though he was exasperating more often than not, she had come to love the boy. "David," she said, "I did promise, and I will help you. But not this evening. I'm sorry. Now, take that sheet and toss it down the laundry chute. It's got makeup all over it."

David stomped his foot. "I'm bored! I want to make my costume tonight!"

"Acting like a brat won't make any difference," she said. "Throw the sheet in the laundry, and if you still have that lipstick, put it back wherever it belongs."

"But I want to be Dracula!"

"And you can be Dracula," Victoria said. "We'll make a wonderful Dracula costume, I promise. But not tonight."

"Then when?"

"Tomorrow."

David stomped his foot, harder. "Not fair!"

Victoria touched his face and he jerked away. "Life's not always fair, David. But I have never broken a promise to you and I won't start now." Without giving him time to come up with another stalling tactic, Victoria walked briskly down the long hall toward the staircase.

She could hear the voices, and she paused on the balcony in front of the night-darkened stained-glass window to regain her composure. From her vantage point at the top of the steps, she could see down into the foyer, where the front door was closed to the porte cochere and world outside. From the center of the foyer's vaulted ceiling hung a massive, ornate chandelier. On the floor beneath it stood a heavy, elegant table that smelled of Mrs. Johnson's expensive wood polish and always seemed to dance in the chandelier's faceted light.

Directly across the foyer from the front doors, another set of double doors opened to the drawing room. It was from here the voices emanated.

"I'll get her, Mother," Victoria could hear Carolyn say in an exasperated tone. "She must be close to being ready, considering there's not much she ever does to *get* ready."

"Please do, Carolyn," came the refined voice of an older woman. "It's not like Victoria to make guests wait. Perhaps something has detained her."

And then a third voice, one she found compelling and intensely attractive, yet for reasons she could not quite understand, had recently made her feel frightened as well. It was the deep, resonant voice of Barnabas Collins. "I do not mean to take much of your time this evening, Elizabeth. In fact, I had not been planning to stop by at all," he said. "But I feel that I should speak with Victoria. Tonight. Before she goes into Collinsport."

Victoria took a deep breath, straightened her shoulders, and walked down the stairs, hugging the wall so she could see into the parlor before her presence was known. Her fingers trailed the wall, passing over the rough texture of the floral tapestry hanging there, and it seemed that the fabric shivered and trembled at her touch. She thought that if she looked at it, there might be twisted, grinning faces within the patterns, staring at her.

"Night jitters," she whispered. "Cut it out now, Victoria, that's enough."

Elizabeth saw Victoria first and came quickly to the door of the drawing room with one hand extended as if to hurry the younger woman along. Carolyn's mother, and mistress of the Collinwood estate, Elizabeth Collins Stoddard was a lady of elegant stature and face, in her mid-fifties, serious and unemotional yet often kind. Her dark hair was pinned neatly to her head, and she wore a tasteful, simple suit with silver earrings and matching necklace. "Victoria," she said, the urgency in her voice barely disguised. "Barnabas is here to see you. He's been waiting."

"Yes, thank you," Victoria said. She reached the bottom step and went to the parlor door.

Carolyn was leaning against an upholstered sofa, picking at the hem of her sweater. When she saw Victoria, she snapped open the mirrored compact from her purse and began to touch up her lipstick with quick little irritated movements.

Barnabas stood in the middle of the room, his shoulders draped in the black caped coat he usually wore, the silver handle of his walking cane clutched in his left hand. The brooding, handsome, dark-haired man had never been anything but gentle and thoughtful to Victoria, and though her heart was drawn to him and urged her to go forward, something in her soul was repelled and forced her to keep her distance. His dark eyes locked on her and did not blink, as if he expected her to speak first.

She did. "Barnabas, you needed to talk to me?"

"Yes, Vicki," he said. "Only for a moment, I promise. Could we speak in the foyer, however?"

Carolyn stood up and began to follow them, but Barnabas turned abruptly and said, "Only Victoria, Carolyn. I will not keep her, for I know you are anxious to get on with your evening adventure."

Carolyn crossed her arms and frowned, then reached for the decanter of brandy on the table by a leather chair. But Elizabeth held up her hand and said, "You don't need that before you drive, Carolyn."

"Tell that to Uncle Roger," Carolyn replied.

"Carolyn, you agreed," Elizabeth said.

In the foyer, by the stairs, Barnabas stared up at the stained-glass window, then brought his eyes down to meet Victoria's. She felt herself shrink at the gaze. It was intimate, imposing.

"Victoria," he said softly, "you must not go out tonight."

"What do you mean?" Victoria managed.

Barnabas's brows furrowed, throwing his eyes into shadows that seemed darker than night. He lifted his cane and planted it back on the floor with a calculated click. "I'm sure this might sound somewhat strange to you, but I sense danger for you tonight. I can't say that I know the source. But evil is brewing, and I fear you may stumble into it."

"Oh . . ." Her heart began pounding. What was this warning? What was his real intention? Surely he was only trying to be a friend, but such a dire remark. "Don't worry about me," she said. "I don't do wild things like some others who live in this house."

"It is your innocence that concerns me," he said. "I beg you not to go."

Carolyn was at the parlor door, hands on hips, the newly applied lipstick several shades too thick. "What are you telling her? Not to go with me? I'm sorry if I might have overheard that part. Are you afraid I'm a bad influence, Barnabas?"

Barnabas's face grew tight and hard. He glared at Carolyn but said nothing. Then he looked back at Victoria, awaiting her reply.

"Barnabas," Vicki began. "I—"

"She *has* to go with me," Carolyn said. "She promised."

"She has a mind of her own," Barnabas replied. "She can do as she chooses."

"And she chooses to go to Collinsport for a little R and R." Carolyn's voice was rising defensively. "We are two independent women who need no one's permission to do as we want."

"That's not quite true," Victoria said to Carolyn.

"Well, I . . . well . . ." Carolyn said, clearly struggling with what to say next. She had often gotten into trouble, drinking, vanishing for prolonged periods, finding company with shady characters. This was the night for her to redeem herself, but she had to have Vicki along to do it. Her mother had told her she couldn't go out without Victoria tonight.

Victoria turned back to Barnabas. "I must go out with her. But I promise I'll be careful."

Barnabas said nothing for several seconds. "Then keep your eyes open, Victoria," he finally replied. "Remember what I've told you."

"I will, Barnabas," Victoria said. "Really."

He stared at her for what seemed like forever, until Carolyn said, "It's getting late. We have a whole night planned, you know!"

Barnabas stepped back, turned to Carolyn in the doorway and gave her a little smile. "Thank you, Carolyn. I've had my say."

"Good!" Carolyn bounced into the foyer, grabbed Victoria by the hand, and pulled open the front doors.

The air that greeted them was chilly, brisk, smelling of autumn and dead things. "We'll be late, Mother!" she called back to Elizabeth. "But don't worry, we'll be good!" Carolyn giggled, locked her arm through Victoria's, and added, "Well, we'll try!"

Carolyn's car was parked beyond the porte cochere, on a graveled side lot especially poured for Carolyn and her often careless parking. As the young blonde unlocked the passenger door and moved quickly to the driver's side, Victoria looked back at the main entrance and the light that poured out in a mysterious, golden haze.

And at the silhouette of the tall man there in the black cape, holding the cane.

"What was that all about?" Carolyn said to Victoria over the roof of the car, and laughed. "Did he want you to stay home and play cards with him or something equally droll?"

"No," Victoria replied. "Don't worry, it was nothing."

Again she looked at the dark figure still watching her, and shivered. And she knew it was more than night jitters.

chapter

⬦⬦⬦

2

Sunset.

To his right, the deepening blue above had begun to smother the Atlantic horizon, destroying the demarcation between sky and sea; to his left, the last rays of sunlight lanced the train windows, prickling the exposed skin of his hands and face. Now and again the windows went dark as the train passed through dense, encroaching forest. In nearby compartments some of his fellow passengers were having their evening meals, reminding him how long it had been since he had fed. How many days since he'd boarded the train in Atlanta? Two? Three? He was somewhere in the state of Maine, running out of distance to cover, still uncertain where the steel rails were leading him, still unsure why he was here.

The low thunder of the heavy wheels on the track had a lulling effect, especially now that his strength had begun to noticeably wane. He rather enjoyed the muted *rumble-clacking* music of the train, for it reminded him of many pleasurable occasions from days long past. In spite of the more advanced means of transportation so readily available, he preferred the slower, more scenic pathway of the railroad, even now not so different than when he had ridden the rails as a youngster, when signs of human habitation were fewer and farther between. But he had never ventured this far into northern territory before, and the new experience pleased him, despite the uncertainty of his destination and purpose.

As the train roared over a bridge, he looked down and could see a stream of gunmetal-tinted water far below, pouring out of the western shadows and widening into a lethargic estuary before merging with the ocean. Shortly, the trees pressed close on either side of the train, blurring into the growing darkness that again reminded him of the hunger pangs that could soon become gnawing.

Rathburn removed his sunglasses and pocketed them, then took off his western hat and laid it on the empty seat beside him, grateful that the blazing light had taken its leave for another day. Casual onlookers might think him odd for wearing the shades and hat and the duster all day, every day, even here in the relative gloom of the train car; they might, had he not willed virtual invisibility, making himself inconspicuous to those with whom he had no desire to interact. As he grew weaker, however, his ability to protect himself diminished accordingly.

He could not deny his need any longer.

Rising from his seat, he glanced into the corridor, knowing that if she remained true to form, his wait for her appearance would be brief. He had noticed her soon after he boarded the train: a lovely young thing, probably thirty years old; a businesswoman on her way to see family, perhaps. She was traveling alone, and seemed to have had little contact with others during her journey. From his reading of her, she was certainly not anticipating any romantic encounter, but would hardly refuse his advances. To her discriminating eye, he would appear attractive, his tall body, finely engraved features, and thick, sienna hair pleasing to her taste. She would want *him*.

At the end of the corridor the door between cars opened and a blond figure emerged, on her way to the restaurant car. She wore a simple, gray knit dress and matching blazer, classy-looking but comfortable for traveling. Rathburn slid back his compartment door and stepped out, blocking her path without appearing threatening. He put on a somewhat abashed expression, his catlike, green eyes gazing deeply into hers, which were a cool sea blue. "Excuse me," he said softly.

"May I help you?" Her voice was a refined, bell-like chime.

"Good evening. My name is Thomas Rathburn. I couldn't help but notice you were alone. Since you and I are both about to have dinner, I was hoping I might convince you to join me."

Her wide eyes flickered between flattered amusement and wariness. "You knew I was going to dinner. You've been watching me."

Rathburn shrugged. "What is your name?"

"Michelle."

"Michelle what?"

"Just Michelle." She smiled cautiously.

Rathburn grinned, showing her he understood the game. "Just Michelle, I suspect you don't usually have strangers on a train asking you to have dinner with them. Want to give it a try and see how you like it?"

Her smile broadened. "You're not shy, are you?"

"Only when I need to be."

For a moment her eyes tried to resist his, testing his will. When she found she could not turn away, her lips parted slightly in surprise. He lifted his hand, expecting her to place her hand in his. A moment later she did.

"Step inside with me, please."

As he backed into the compartment, she followed, her gaze never wavering. Once they were both inside, he closed the door and slowly drew the shades facing the corridor. He could feel her rising fear and anticipation, and drank in the sensation with relish. With a gentle hand he brushed a streamer of silvery blond hair from her slim neck, saw the faint pulsing of her jugular vein, which increased its rhythm with every passing second.

He slid his arms around her and pulled her slowly into his embrace. Her resistance amounted to only a slight shaking of her head, for even though she was aware of her will having been conquered, she half desired the thrill of danger, the uncertainty of what was about to happen to her. He lowered his face to hers, touched her lips with his, imparting comfort to her, sparking her own carnal desire. He briefly drank in her breath, scenting the fear and excitement that blazed through her body. Then his lips moved to her throat.

When he penetrated her, her back arched in his arms. Her breath escaped her lips with a sigh that tickled his ear like hummingbird wings. Her blood flowed in a sweet rush into his mouth, and he swallowed it eagerly, wrapping his arms tighter around her body and drawing from her a soft moan of sheer terror and ecstasy. He drank for several long moments, until the burning of his hunger finally began to cool. Only when he paused to savor the taste of her essence did he look back into her eyes. Her sea blue irises had receded to narrow rings around dilated pupils, and her expression was one of disbelief and yearning, of horror and pure joy.

He knew he must take no more.

He released her from his embrace, holding her steady with one hand on her arm. She swayed slightly, tilted her head back and closed her eyes, drawing in a deep, steadying breath. He could feel her throbbing pulse beneath his fingertips beginning to diminish along with the excitement of the moment.

He needed more.

But somehow he forced down his desire. His hunger could wait. He had waited far, far longer before, and probably would wait so again. In the close confines of the train, draining her completely posed too great a threat. If her disappearance were noticed before either of them reached their final destinations, he might be faced with uncomfortable questions or delays. He had not thrived in society by acting foolishly or impulsively. Her blood should sustain him for at least the rest of the night—he hoped—but his hunger was hardly sated, only whetted.

He touched the wound on her neck and the oozing of blood ceased. He wiped away the crimson streaks and lifted his fingers to his lips for a final taste. Dazedly, Michelle watched him, her eyes wishing he would take her again. He shook his head, leaning close to her and whispering in her ear, "You will remember nothing. You will go back to your compartment and sleep . . . sleep. And when you wake, you will feel refreshed and contented. Do you understand?" She nodded slowly. "Now," he said in a stronger voice, his tone mocking, "go in peace, and may your God go with you."

The blond woman turned, offering him one more longing gaze. His green eyes sparkled, forcing his will upon her yet again. She slowly opened the door and stepped out, swaying down the corridor in the direction from which she had come with the dreamy stagger of one who had tested one glass of wine too many.

Rathburn watched her disappear through the door to her train car, then closed himself back in his compartment. A single drop of blood dotted the floor at his foot. He knelt and wiped it away, studying the crimson spot on his fingertip. This time, he passed his thumb over his finger and the spot vanished as if it had never existed.

He sat down, peering out the window at the dark landscape passing beyond the glass. The temptation to call her back and finish her was strong. The risk factor was not insurmountable. He frequently overcame far more complex risks; such was the reality of his existence. Still, he thought, better to allow the woman to survive, and merely ruminate wistfully on having denied himself the pleasure of ending the life of another senseless mortal.

Such a familiar regret. In Atlanta he could move

freely, taking victims more or less at his leisure. But because he preferred to prey on a higher class of woman than the typical streetwalker, he usually left them only temporarily weakened and dazed, with no memory of what had befallen them, as he had with Michelle. It had been a long time—too long— since he had killed his prey; it was simply not necessary, for nourishment could be taken nightly and in relatively small quantity. And the satisfaction of killing rarely justified the potential dire consequences.

And dear God, no, he never brought them over. He had forsworn such practices long ago, knowing that new initiates to his breed tended to harm rather than strengthen its chances of a prosperous longevity. This age's humans were stupid, arrogant, pathetic things that brought most of their baggage with them when they changed. Virtually all the members of the breed under a hundred years old had been destroyed, usually by their own folly, most in the course of the last decade or two.

On the rare occasion when one of his kind sought to stake a claim in his territory, Rathburn drove him out, and at least once had even destroyed the intruder. He would abide no trespasser on his ground, not when that trespasser represented a threat to his own security. Of the small number of undead individuals that walked the earth, most of them knew of Rathburn and respected him. Though some of them were older than he, few had the resources to pit themselves against him, if confrontation they wished.

Like only a scant few of his kindred, Rathburn enjoyed a special advantage over almost any adversary, living or undead: the ability to move about in daylight. Though painstakingly developed over the years by his own determination, he suspected the trait had actually been transferred to him by the one who originally turned him from human to Vampire. He still required some protection from the sun, or he could be burned or blinded beyond his ability to heal; hence the protective clothing he wore. But unlike most of his breed, he hardly needed to sleep in a coffin by day. In fact, being able to show himself in full daylight allowed him to maintain a lifestyle that placed him virtually above suspicion in those rare cases where the most broadminded among mortals might cast an eye toward the paranormal to explain certain evidence unavoidably left behind.

To maintain his mundane pretense, he had, over the years, acquired a respectable degree of wealth, through various enterprises in which he'd had the foresight to involve himself. Shortly after his Rebirth, he had settled in Atlanta, at first subsisting off whatever financial spoils could be won from his victims; before long, he invested in numerous ventures that would grow on their own. He began, naturally enough, overseeing cotton plantations, which in the First World War provided him with riches undreamed of by most ordinary men. As time went by he participated in industries—virtually always as an absentee partner—that promised future prosperity, such as telephones, electronics, and now mass media publications. He always saw to it that any caretakers of his accounts were entirely loyal and trustworthy; to this day, only one had attempted to embezzle any of his fortune. That man had quietly disappeared many years ago, now forgotten by anyone living.

He lived, not in some dark, forbidding manse, but in an opulent suite, designed to suit his own special needs, in one of Atlanta's premier downtown hotels—of which he was part owner. Out of necessity, he occasionally changed his residence, as his immunity to the passage of years could not help but make him stand out in familiar environs. To this end, legal records would show that he was the sixth in a line of Rathburns bearing the name Thomas; with wry humor, he could claim to be his own father—and grandfather, and great-grandfather before that.

From his position of wealth and power, Rathburn had lived and flourished for nearly the last century and a half.

Outside the train windows, darkness had fallen complete. His eyes, however, could see distant points of light, warm auras, subtle nuances of shadow that no mortal eye could ever discern. A town lay not far ahead, he knew, and something in his blood began to warm, to insinuate that his journey might be drawing to an end. Suddenly, as had happened so many times over the course of the last few days, his vision changed, and in a rapid-fire burst of intermingled images, he saw:

A dark-haired, willowy young woman standing in the midst of tall trees bearing the red leaves of autumn.

A sprawling mansion atop cliffs that overlooked a raging, storm-racked ocean.

A faceless man in a cape, holding a cane with a silver handle in the shape of a wolf's head.

And, then, strangely, he caught the scent of lilac, like a sweet perfume; a distinctly feminine fragrance, obviously not from within the train car, but from somewhere *out there.*

From the same source as the visions themselves?

The frequent recurrence of these images, along with a wholly irresistible compulsion to follow an unclear path northward, had led him to board the train in Atlanta and begin this journey into the unknown.

As his eyes again registered only the dimly lit interior of his compartment, he felt oddly rejuvenated. But in his many years of existence, he had experienced nothing quite like this before. An almost sexual thrill accompanied the revival of his energy, an excitement of passion without any apparent source. It both excited and troubled him. Surely, these images were being deliberately transmitted to him. But by whom? From where?

And then, against his will, old memories suddenly began to surface; memories he had put away long ago, now creeping forth to stab at him from the darkest pits of his psyche, where they belonged.

His beautiful young wife, Elaine, screaming in terror as a trio of blue-coated figures burst through the door of her home, each wielding muskets or machetes. Their two-year-old son, Michael, running and screaming in terror as the men grabbed his mother and threw her brutally against a wall, knocking her senseless.

No, these were not memories. Rathburn had not been there to witness the events as they happened, only the aftermath. Yet the images were as clear and vivid as if he were observing the obscene attack through the eyes of another, someone there in the room.

He saw one of the officers—a lieutenant, from the uniform—raise a pistol, aim at the fleeing boy, and fire. The impact of the lead ball threw Michael forward, onto his face, his little arms flailing helplessly as he tumbled like a broken doll. Within seconds he lay motionless, a vast pool of red spreading from the wound in his back and seeping into the aged hardwood. Then the child-killer turned his pistol on Elaine, holding it to her head while the others stripped her of her clothes, then in turn removed their own trousers . . . each having his way with her as the others watched with demented smiles on their sweating, ugly faces.

They're monsters.

Rathburn's stomach heaved as one by one the marauders wantonly emptied their seed into her. And finally, when the last was spent, one of them—young, no more than eighteen—produced a bayonet and waved it slowly and gleefully before Elaine's semiconscious eyes. Then, with an almost kindly look of reassurance, that no, he would not really harm her, he pierced her chest with the tip of the blade. Elaine gasped in sudden shock, her eyes widening with realization. And slowly, with utmost cruelty, the young man forced the bayonet forward until its point punctured her heart. Her eyes rolled upward and glazed over as she breathed her last and her life's blood gushed from the horrible breach in her flesh, its hot vitality pouring over the hand that still grasped the handle of the bayonet.

The young soldier looked at the death he had so mercilessly wrought with a kind of detached appraisal, clicked his tongue and stood, finally giving his partners a harsh, mindless chuckle.

Rabid dog. Son of a bitch.

The trio then turned their attention from Rathburn's dead beloved and haphazardly went through the house searching for anything of value. His father's gold pocket watch. A silver vase—a gift from Elaine's mother. And then—God, no—the gold wedding band from Elaine's dead finger. Into the kitchen, looking for food. Some dried meat, a few ears of corn soaking in saltwater. And then their madness seemingly passed, each gazing with calm satisfaction upon their handiwork before marching out, the last slamming the door closed behind him, allowing it to bang back and forth on its broken hinges.

As the vision faded, a swirl of sound seemed to rush through Rathburn's ears: a low whisper at first, rising until it became a chorus of screams, an inhuman, hellish cacophony that dizzied him. As the sound faded, lingering after it came the whisper of a name, repeated over and over, but which held no significance for him. None whatsoever. At least not yet.

Collins . . . Collins . . . Collins . . .

What did it mean? Why had these images come to him, so cruel and terrible in their vividness? Why now?

On that awful date, he had come home only a few hours too late, his discovery of those evil deeds sending him screaming from his own home in fury and despair.

God, he despised them. Detested all their kind. He quickly rose to his feet, leaned into the corridor of the train car and focused on the shadowy figures he could glimpse through the windows of the other compartments. What he would give to rampage through the train, take these wretched beings and snap their puny necks, tearing their flesh with his fangs, tossing each lifeless body into a heap and letting the blood flow and flow until it flooded the very train car itself.

All of you. Monstrous. God, I hate you.

And these *creatures*, what few might have an inkling of the existence of his breed, dared apply the label "monster" to the Vampire.

The insanity of them. It sickened him.

Sometimes he had to marvel at his own restraint: that he had developed the control, the patience over his long life span, to suffer the existence of these creatures he must live among lest he jeopardize his own existence. How interesting it would be, he thought, to meet with the descendants of that depraved trio of Union soldiers who had perhaps run into one battle too many. He had sought long and hard—and failed—to find the guilty parties. Even with the heightened senses of his new existence, he had been unable to pick up the trail of the perpetrators, then long gone. There was simply too much blood. Too much blood on the ground.

As the wave of anger passed, Rathburn felt his energy slowly beginning to seep away, forcing him to sit back down, drained and exhausted. Somehow, those events from long ago were being relayed to him by an intelligence, of this he was certain. Intuitively, he felt that the answers lay somewhere ahead, that whatever power had beckoned him northward would reveal some long-hidden truth.

He could feel the train engine decelerating, the rumble of the wheels on the tracks growing deeper and heavier. Through the window he could see lights ahead, and there, around a bend to the right, a train station. As the long metal snake slowed and finally hissed to a stop, the station sign appeared outside of Rathburn's window, and his weary eyes widened with renewed exhilaration at the sight of the town's name:

Collinsport.

Intriguing. If "Collins," the name whispered to him by some disembodied spirit, turned out to be one borne by any of the dogs who had slain his family, and any of their progeny resided in this obscure Maine village, then the wrath that would pour down upon them would be unlike any since the days recounted by the Holy Book of God.

Rathburn rose, took his one bag of belongings from the nook above his seat, and stepped into the corridor, finding that only a scant few passengers—Michelle not among them—appeared to be disembarking at this particular port of call. Excellent. Though he could maintain a low profile of his own devising, he preferred as few potential witnesses as possible seeing him leave the train. As long as he did not know what he faced, he intended to gain any small advantage that might work in his favor.

What he knew he faced most immediately, and with sudden urgency, was his need for blood. *Damn it.* His feeding had not been sufficient to sustain him, and had only catalyzed his hunger. With some concern, he realized that in a place as small as Collinsport, he might find it considerably more difficult to procure prey and remain inconspicuous than in his own familiar territory. But as he moved slowly through the station, noting the pair of bleary-eyed, listless-looking attendants on duty, the tiny handful of passengers coming and going, his mind shifted into hunting mode, his senses becoming attuned to the local auras, the scents, the sounds, any of which might lead him to appropriate quarry.

Setting foot onto the street outside the train station, he found himself facing a crumbling block of a quaint New England village. The small buildings were mostly dark and weathered shanties, but farther up the road he could see a line of colonial houses that looked to have been made into offices of sorts. From somewhere far behind him, he could hear the low susurrus of breakers, the horns of a few distant boats. The main part of town apparently lay several blocks up this avenue, but off to the right he saw two of the most welcome sights he could imagine at the moment.

A large wooden building with white panel siding, apparently well-kept and brightly lit, displaying an oval, hand-painted sign. It read COLLINSPORT INN. At least here he could secure his belongings and acquire reasonably private quarters in which to spend the daylight hours. And just past it, on a small lane that apparently led to the waterfront: a low building with a barely visible placard identifying it as the BLUE WHALE TAVERN.

Wherever there were taverns, there would be drunken mortals, often seeking companionship for the evening.

Wherever mortals sought companionship for an evening, there lay blood for the taking.

chapter

─⚭─

3

The air inside the Blue Whale was warm and thick with the smells of fried fish and spilled beer. Pipe and cigar smoke clung to the beamed ceiling like cobwebs. The patrons sat on stools along the bar, toasting each other and laughing. Two scraggly-bearded fishermen were at the dartboard, trying to hold each other up while aiming the darts in the vicinity of the target. A fire roared in the stone fireplace on the far side of the room, reflecting sparks of light off the shiny, polished surfaces of the numerous fish that had been mounted for decoration on the dark, rough-hewn walls—a swordfish, a tuna, a blue, a marlin—their eyes wide, buttonlike, and very dead.

Victoria noticed immediately that she and Carolyn were the only females in the place except for the waitress, a crusty yet friendly local named Peggy Kaplan. Usually, on a Friday night, there were other women in the place, girls she and Carolyn knew, if not by name, at least by appearance. Perhaps the impending rain had kept them home.

They hung their coats on the corner of a booth and slid in, Carolyn facing the door and Victoria the fireplace. Carolyn picked up a sticky, laminated drink menu from between the salt and pepper shakers, then crammed it back. "I know what I want," she said. "How about you?"

"Oh, I think I'll just have a white wine," Victoria replied. "And perhaps a slice of pumpkin pie."

Carolyn waved Peggy over, gave the order, then ran her fingers through her hair and put her chin in her hand. "You look good in that sweater," she said matter-of-factly. "Sexy. You're going to attract attention."

Victoria looked down at herself. Sexy? She hadn't thought she looked sexy.

"If this was New York City," Carolyn continued, "I bet we'd have quite a selection tonight."

"Selection of what?"

Carolyn smiled and thumped Victoria on the forearm. "Men, of course. New men. Interesting men. Good-looking men."

"There are some nice-looking men in Collinsport."

"Sure, I guess so," Carolyn said. "But we know them all. There's not much left to the imagination. I'm talking about new blood."

Victoria nodded toward the bar, where a particularly weather-beaten sailor was holding a serious conversation with the stuffed eel mounted over the rack of glasses. "He's new blood," she said. "Never seen him before. Call him over?"

"Shut up!" Carolyn said, exasperated. "I don't mean sailors. There's always a new batch of them coming and going, like migrant workers. I mean intriguing men, elegant, romantic . . ."

"Hello there, Victoria, Carolyn."

They turned to see a tall, dark-haired, handsome young man standing by their booth, slipping out of his coat.

"Chris," Victoria said. "Hi, we didn't see you here."

"Just came in," Chris Jennings was a resident of Collinsport, someone in whom Carolyn had had an on-again, off-again interest. "Wind's picked up a lot out there. I think it's going to rain, and hard."

Carolyn immediately slipped over next to the wall and patted the bench. "Sit down! Come on, Vicki and I just ordered wine."

"Well," Chris said, "actually . . ."

"Actually, you just got here and you want to warm up before you decide," Carolyn said. "No problem. I can keep you warm. And we're in no hurry, are we, Vicki?"

"Not really," Victoria said.

"You see? You can take your time." She patted the seat. "Sit!"

Chris grinned, clearly flattered. But he shrugged and said, "Actually, I'm waiting for someone."

Victoria could see a slight grimace at Carolyn's mouth, though her voice didn't let on. "Oh? Someone we know? He can join us, too, can't he, Vicki? The more the merrier!"

"It's not . . ." Chris began, then gestured toward the door, where a pert, curly-haired girl had just come in wearing tight jeans and a New England Patriots jacket. "I'm meeting Patricia. You know Patricia Harmon?"

"Sure," Carolyn said. "Isn't her father Joseph Harmon? The mechanic who was caught stealing petty cash from the owner of the garage? Didn't Sheriff Patterson have to arrest him? Isn't he still in jail?"

Chris's smile faded. He ignored the dig. "Patricia's a senior at Rugby College, and she's home on fall break."

"Hmm," Carolyn said, touching her lip with her finger. "Just watch your own pockets, Chris. Like father, like daughter, I've heard."

Chris turned abruptly and walked to the bar, and he and Patricia quickly found a table as far from Carolyn and Victoria as possible.

"That was cruel," Victoria said.

"Not really," Carolyn replied. "I was just teasing. He knew that."

Peggy brought the glasses of wine, a bowl full of

fat, salted pretzels, and a large slice of pumpkin pie with a dollop of whipped cream. Victoria cut off the tip of the pie and put it in her mouth. It was warm and sweet, and she let it dissolve on her tongue, savoring the flavor.

"Good?" Carolyn asked.

"Wonderful," Victoria said. She took another bite, closing her eyes and chewing slowly. At last, she began to feel more relaxed. The anxiety that had become so much a part of her existence began to loosen and flow away.

I'm stronger than my fears, she told herself. *I'm bigger than my worries.*

"Wine's not bad, either," Carolyn said. "I'll have to ask exactly what brand this is. I should get some to take home, and . . . oh, my God. Don't look."

Victoria's lids snapped open. Carolyn was facing her, but her eyes were focused to one side and locked on something that had her full attention.

"Who is it?" Victoria asked, beginning to shift in her seat. But Carolyn's hand shot out and grabbed her arm.

"I said don't look! At least not now, not yet. Give it a second. I'll tell you when."

"But who is it?"

"A man. And God must have heard me, because this is no local yokel and certainly no fish-gutting, floor-swabbing deckhand!"

A man, Victoria thought. *Of course, what else?*

Carolyn's voice fell to a whisper. "He's coming this way."

A country tune began to play on the jukebox. The dart game was getting more rowdy, and Bob Rooney, the bartender, was threatening to throw some of the men into the street. Nearby, a chair scraped the floor as someone pulled it out from a table to sit down.

"Okay," Carolyn whispered.

Victoria looked over. The man, who was perusing the drink menu at the table not five feet away, was clearly a newcomer to Collinsport. He was striking, with locks of light reddish-brown hair pouring from beneath a wide-brimmed western hat, a long gray duster that reminded Victoria of something from the Civil War, and a pair of dark glasses. He put the menu down, removed his hat and then his glasses, placed them on the chair next to him, and then turned slowly to stare directly at her.

Oh, my God.

The gaze was almost painful in its intimacy, a steady, unflinching stare that made her wonder for a moment if he knew her, or if she was supposed to know him. His eyes were green, and the smile on his face easy, comfortable.

But Victoria felt anything but comfortable. She wanted to look away, to return to her wine and pie. But she couldn't. Not yet. Not quite yet . . .

"Hello there!" Carolyn said. "Are you from out of town?"

"Good evening, ladies." The man's voice was as mesmerizing as his stare. It was soft, deep, and rounded with a smooth southern drawl that hinted at education and an aristocratic station. "I am indeed new here. And I seem to have found a very charming town. To whom do I have the pleasure of speaking?"

"I'm Carolyn Stoddard," Carolyn said, laughing lightly. "I don't suppose you know who I am?"

The man shook his head slightly. He put his elbow on the table and put his cheek in his hand. Victoria wondered what it would feel like to caress that cheek, and the thought embarrassed her. She was glad it was dark in the tavern, or the man might have seen the blush that had risen to sting her face. "I can't say I do."

Carolyn rolled her eyes, as if finding it incredible that her family's fame might not extend beyond the limits of the tiny Maine village.

"My name is Thomas Rathburn," the man said. "And what is your name?" He was looking again at Victoria.

She managed, "Victoria Winters." She was suddenly very conscious of the clothes she was wearing, the low-cut sweater that Carolyn had dubbed "sexy." She felt uncertain and exposed.

"Won't you join us, Mr. Rathburn?" Carolyn asked. She slid over and patted the side of the bench. Victoria cringed. At times, she wanted to be as outgoing as her friend, but at other times she was glad she was not so brazen. They did not know this man, nor he them. It might be better to end the conversation and return to the relaxing evening she'd come into town to find.

Thomas Rathburn stood but did not join Carolyn on the bench. Instead, he pulled his chair to the end of the booth. He sat back and folded his hands on the tabletop. "I suspect you don't usually have a stranger sitting down to have a bite to eat with you. Do you recommend the pumpkin pie, Miss Winters?" He was staring directly at her again, without hesitation. His green eyes seemed to glow, but Victoria knew it had to be a reflection from the fire.

"Very highly," she said.

"I see."

Carolyn touched Rathburn on the arm, drawing his attention back to her. "Are you in Collinsport on business, Mr. Rathburn? My uncle is the most important businessman in the area. His name is Roger Collins."

Thomas Rathburn raised an eyebrow.

"Oh," Carolyn said. "Do you know him, then? Did you come here at his request?"

Rathburn shook his head. "No, actually, I happened upon this town somewhat by chance. I'm up from Atlanta. I'm the publisher of *Southern Culture* magazine, but I've decided to take an extended holiday for myself. Thought I'd take a train as a bit of nostalgia. I haven't traveled in a long time." He smiled slightly. "I'm finding that New England towns have such a different, distinctive ambiance. What a discovery, this village. Rather charming and quiet. It seems just the place to relax and forget one's responsibilities and troubles."

"Oh, it's that!" Carolyn said. "Quiet, I mean. Charming, maybe. That will be for you to decide." She grinned broadly and wrinkled her nose.

Rathburn said, "I hope to," then shifted in his seat toward Victoria. Her breath caught in her throat. What was it about this man that so disturbed her, someone she'd never met and would likely never see again after tonight?

"And you, Miss Winters? Are you also related to Roger Collins?"

Victoria didn't want to tell him that she was not a member of the Collins family, just an employee. How much better to have a fascinating story to make an impression. But as she looked into the man's eyes, the feeling came over her again that he knew her, or thought he did, and on the heels of that, a warm and dizzying sensation ran through her veins, and she found herself unable to lie. "No," she said. "I work for the Collins family. I'm the governess for Roger Collins's son, David."

"Interesting. Do you enjoy the job?"

"A great deal. I've never had a family of my own, and the Collinses have been very kind to me."

Thomas Rathburn nodded. Her dizziness increased, and Victoria prayed he would look away. "Are you originally from Collinsport, too?"

"No, I grew up in New York."

"Where are you staying, Mr. Rathburn?" Carolyn asked, and his eyes turned back to regard the young blonde. He picked up a pretzel without looking at it, rolled it between his fingers, then put it on the table in front of him.

"I have a room at the Collinsport Inn," he said. "I would think you know the place?"

Carolyn and Victoria nodded.

"It was reasonable enough," Rathburn said. "Clean, rustic, with a genuine charm of sorts. No privacy, of course, save for a tiny little room and a chair, but I don't think I have many options, do I?"

The man's eyes seemed to narrow a fraction, as if the smoke from the fireplace and the cigars had become uncomfortable, but Carolyn was now the full focus of his attention. In response, she blinked rapidly and blurted, "I just remembered the guest cottage! Back at Collinwood, our estate, there's a little house that's been vacant for some time. It's not elegant or anything, but it has privacy, not like one of the inn's rooms. I'm sure I can convince Uncle Roger to lease it to you for as long as you'd like to stay. I mean, if you think you'd be interested."

"Indeed?" Rathburn said. "That is more than generous, Carolyn. I wouldn't want to be an inconvenience, but it sounds like an agreeable proposition. If you can arrange it, of course."

"Good, then!" Carolyn said, picking up her wineglass and taking a sip. "Here comes Peggy, Mr. Rathburn. You really should order this wine, it's marvelous!"

Victoria took a long drink from her own glass, her gaze flitting from Carolyn to the pie plate to the pretzel bowl to the floor. Her arms were shaking beneath the sweater, in spite of the heat in the room. *What is Carolyn thinking?* she wondered. They knew nothing about this man. His name, yes, and his occupation. But otherwise they knew nothing, and here Carolyn was inviting him to take up temporary residence at Collinwood.

But then Victoria looked at him once more, and she felt the excitement he had stirred in her rise again, and knew that in fact she was glad that Carolyn had made the offer. He would be close, only a short stroll from the mansion. And she might have the chance to get to know him the way he seemed to know her.

But I think I do know him, somehow, she thought. *It makes no sense, but I feel like I do.*

The sensation was both exhilarating and terrifying.

chapter

4

Victoria Winters.

Without question she had been the one in his visions. Even before he allowed her and her companion to perceive his presence in the bar, he had begun exploring her psychic vibrations, and like a raiment, she wore the aura of having been brushed by the supernatural in the past. Could she be the one actually projecting the images he had experienced? If so, what was her motive? Victoria was in some strange fashion unreadable, as if her own life, her own personality, was a mystery even to herself. This one certainly warranted further investigation.

And he knew, too, that he would enjoy delving deeper into her heart and soul. A fascinating and most appetizing creature, young Victoria.

Her friend Carolyn was a pretty thing; he could envision her as most satisfying prey—perhaps even as a useful source of information. She appeared transparent, one he could easily hold in his thrall to use as he saw fit. With the slightest psychic nudge she had extended an invitation to him to take up residence on the Collins estate. He fully planned to accept as soon as the invitation was offered by this Roger Collins. And offer it he would, Rathburn thought with some amusement. He would see to it.

But Carolyn could be at best only an unwitting accomplice in his quest, and possibly a victim in the end. She, too, seemed to possess some link with a supernatural presence; her mind was tractable, as if it had been invaded and used by another sometime in the past. Yet it was obvious she was scarcely capable of transmitting telepathic visions. Still, he was certain the sender was female. He could not forget the scent of lilac perfume that accompanied the spectral visitations. He could almost smell it now. But it was just a memory, an insubstantial reminder of something itself without substance. But for now he had to force his mind away from the mystery of his presence here to the matter of survival in a strange and possibly hostile environment. There was blood in the air, beckoning him.

He had positioned himself in a shadowy corner outside the tavern, observing those still coming and going at this late hour. The Blue Whale appeared to have little competition in this community, but even so, commerce was relatively light, given what he was accustomed to in Atlanta. Most of the patrons traveled in pairs or groups. While inside, he had seen some fishermen at the bar who appeared thoroughly engrossed in their own solitude. They would be easy enough quarry; however, they would probably be the ones closing the bar for the night.

At last, the door opened and a young, attractive redhead appeared, staggering slightly, obviously under the influence of spirits. Rathburn remembered having seen her in the company of a young man, the one he overheard Carolyn and Victoria call "Chris." The girl's perturbed expression told him everything. She swayed up the sidewalk in the direction of town, turning left at the next block onto a narrow lane that he assumed led to a residential neighborhood. Dark; few streetlights. Excellent.

Then the Blue Whale door opened again and an indignant-looking Chris Jennings appeared, heading in the same direction as the girl. If he'd been drinking, his coordination had scarcely been affected; his deliberate stride carried him quickly after the redhead. Sure enough, he turned down the same side street, and Rathburn knew his prey had found an unwitting reprieve.

Damn it.

Now he could feel his eyes radiating the fire of his pain, and his retractable fangs had fully extended of their own accord.

Oh God.

He was completely in the grip of the blood lust; there could be no disguising it. He realized that water had begun to fall from the sky, chilling his skin. Within moments the drizzle became a torrential downpour, clattering violently against the rooftops and windows of the nearby buildings. The door to the Blue Whale opened, then closed again as a rain-shy patron decided to wait until the storm let up, and perhaps use it as an excuse to have that final drink. Rathburn groaned in frustration, falling back into the shadows under the dripping eaves of the tavern.

Down by the waterfront he spied a few dilapidated fishing shacks by the rickety-looking wharves. Pulling his coat around him, he staggered down the cobbled walk toward the first of them, slammed his fist against the door and shattering the lock. Falling inside, he shoved the door closed. Outside, the wind rose to a mocking wail, while the waves pounded at the docks and shook the aging walls of the feeble shack as if attempting to rout him out.

God almighty, this is hell. Perhaps he should have risked draining on the woman in the train after all. For the moment, he had to recover himself before he could venture into the night again without risk of exposure. This far gone, it was hard. *Too damned hard.*

He slid to the brine-stained plank floor amid a number of bundled fishing nets, seeking desperately to regain mastery of his body. His right leg began to throb—a sensation he hadn't felt in count-less years. The pain brought with it yet more long repressed memories; this time, true recollections, not spirit-induced visions from some unearthly realm. He could hear the distant sound of voices, some shouting, some crying out in pain and terror.

Voices from the past.

The cannon exploded with a horrific *boom*, sending up a swirling pillar of flame and smoke, the debris of both machine and men flying in every direction. Rathburn dropped to the ground just in time to avoid a hunk of shrapnel that whirled past his head with the sound of a screaming banshee. As the thun-der of the explosion trailed away, it was replaced by the cracks of nearby gunfire and the distant thuds of Union cannons discharging across the wide grassy fields. He scrambled toward the shelter of a nearby tree, trying to gain his footing but failing, a sudden pain in his leg forcing him to crawl on his belly. As he slid into a depression at the base of the huge trunk, he glimpsed the reason for the pain and his inability to rise: the haft of a bayonet protruded from his upper right leg, just above the knee; the blade sprouted through a jagged tear in his trousers on the other side, its gleaming tip dripping blood.

"Oh, Christ," he groaned, realizing that shock from the wound had prevented him from feeling its impact. The bayonet must have been blown off a rifle during the explosion and hit him just as he avoided the shrapnel that would have taken off his head. Now conscious of the injury, he felt the first waves of pain beginning to creep up his leg, moments later sending him into uncontrollable spasms, drawing the first scream of agony from his lips. He didn't dare try to remove the blade; he was liable to bleed to death the instant he tugged it from his flesh.

For a few moments the battle seemed distant, part of a different world that meant little to him. He could see gray-coated figures crouched behind trees at the near end of the field, lifting their rifles and firing, great clouds of smoke quickly obscuring them from view. From somewhere else he heard the pounding of horses' hoofs, the shouts of desperate men as they began a charge across the field. Rathburn could not see which side was advancing.

He lay back, as much in anger as in pain. The men of his company, of the 39th Virginia Regiment, had scattered, and without his firm hand to guide them, were likely as not to get themselves killed in a courageous but foolhardy assault on the enemy. Damn kids, most of them hardly old enough to tie their shoes without their mothers showing them how. He gingerly touched the haft of the bayonet, winced as the slight pressure sent a hot wave of pain up his leg and back. Even if he survived, he'd be lucky as hell to ever walk again.

"Son of a bitch."

The words came softly from somewhere to his right. He turned his head and suddenly felt a cool splash of water in his face, a gentle hand stroke his forehead, brushing his hair out of his eyes.

"Jesus, Thomas, you're in a world of hurt. Stay still. Don't try to move."

Rathburn nodded as the face of Lieutenant Phillip O'Conner, his second in command, appeared and hovered over him. The fair-haired young man looked him over with deep concern in his pale blue eyes, then poured another few drops of water from his canteen over Rathburn's parched lips. "Hold still now," he said. "This is going to smart." He tipped the canteen and let the water pour over the wound, holding onto Rathburn's hand as his back arched in a paroxysm of pain. In a moment the agony subsided enough for Rathburn to speak.

"It would be you to find me like this."

"You couldn't be in better hands."

"Damn you. Get the hell out of here before you end up worse than me. I expect I'm gonna die here anyway."

O'Conner looked at him thoughtfully, then at the smoke-shrouded field that still teemed with scurrying figures. The sky was rapidly darkening as the sun fell toward the western horizon. "You have a point, Captain. Not a good point, but a point nonetheless."

"The Federals are charging, aren't they?"

O'Conner nodded grimly. "Yes, sir."

"Then get the hell out of here. That's an order."

"In a minute, in a minute." The lieutenant grabbed Rathburn under his arms and began to pull him farther into the cover of the trees, the movement sending a new wave of pain up Rathburn's leg. The shadows finally concealed them from the view of anyone at the edge of the field. "Wouldn't you rather die a bit more peaceably?"

"I hadn't anticipated going out like a crippled mare." Rathburn saw the trail of blood in the grass where he'd been dragged, which caused his stomach to heave. "Phillip," he said, the effort of speaking now taking a greater toll on his energy, "I want you to leave me alone. Get out of here."

"In a minute."

"Listen," Rathburn said, grasping the other's arm as he lowered the canteen to his lips again. Then he spoke with great effort: "As long as you're waiting around to die with me, I never told you . . . how deeply sorry I am. I never meant . . . never meant to hurt you."

"I know that, Thomas." O'Conner's eyes gazed back impassively.

"You could have transferred out at any time. But you stayed with me. Why?"

"Because I know you didn't mean to betray me. Neither did Elaine. I saw the way it ate you up. Because of that, I knew you were a decent man."

"She belonged to you . . . first. A lot of men might have looked to kill me."

"I am not one of those men."

While visiting O'Conner's home in Richmond in the earliest days of the war, Rathburn had fallen in love with his comrade's sweetheart, Elaine—and she with him. Shortly, they had married, leaving Phillip heartbroken. Yet the young lieutenant refused to leave Rathburn's company, and, even while still hurting, offered his best wishes to the newlyweds. Phillip remained stoical, gracious, generous.

On the battle ground, Rathburn nodded weakly to the young lieutenant's response. O'Conner was indeed unlike any man he'd had known before. Sometimes he wondered if O'Conner was even entirely human. Some of the troops whispered that the lieutenant had made deals with the devil. Others said he had books of black lore that "good Christian men" would have shunned in horror. Whatever the reality, Rathburn knew that Phillip O'Conner fulfilled his duties with a competence and coolness few could match. And whatever his men thought of his personal beliefs, they followed him with unwavering loyalty. Some probably even feared him.

Rathburn respected the younger man, liked him. He was a brave and dutiful soldier, with a somewhat somber but generally amiable disposition. He had known O'Conner going on four years now and could say with certainty that there was nothing about this man to fear—unless you wore a coat of blue.

Rathburn felt his consciousness fading, but he dared not allow it, knowing he might never wake again. "Tell me," he said to the lieutenant. "Tell me why you don't hate me."

"I already told you."

"That can't be all of it."

O'Conner knelt, leaning close to him. "Thomas, I know in those days Elaine loved me. Yet when she met you, she became enamored of you in a way she never was with me. That meant you had a power of sorts. I wanted to learn from you."

"You . . . from me?"

"You are a great leader. You inspire your men." O'Conner seemed to choke. "You draw others into your presence."

"I betrayed you."

O'Conner's eyes gazed inward, back at some hidden past. "One sometimes does these things, despite his best intentions. If one is to be forgiven, he must also forgive."

The young man seemed to have more he wished to say. But at that moment he rose and drew his pistol from his holster. "You may not die like a crippled mare after all."

Rathburn swiveled his head to see a number of blue-coated figures rushing into the trees near where he had first hidden. He reached for his own .44 Colt, checked the chambers to make sure the balls were still seated. Only two shots left.

A chorus of pistols boomed from near at hand. The deeper roar of rifles sounded from the field, followed by a chorus of agonized cries. The Yankees were overrunning the company's fortifications. Rathburn could feel the end creeping closer, advancing like a slithering viper. He raised his pistol and aimed it at the nearest of the approaching enemy. They had not yet seen him or O'Conner. He squeezed the trigger and the gun thundered, spewing a plume of thick gray smoke. His target staggered, gazing toward him in bewilderment and disbelief, then fell forward, his head hitting the ground with a nauseating crack.

That was it. The rest had seen them now. O'Conner's pistol fired, taking down another. Rathburn saw three more men, some twenty yards away, moving through the trees toward them, each carrying an Enfield rifle that would be brought to bear at any moment. He glanced back into the darkness of the trees, then at O'Conner, who still knelt over him, taking aim at one of the figures. "Phillip," he groaned a final time. "You can get away into the trees. For God's sake, leave me and get out."

"That's your guilt talking, Captain." O'Conner's gun unleashed another ball, and another man fell.

With a shaking hand, Rathburn raised his pistol

for what he knew would be the final shot he ever took. Drawing an unsteady bead on the nearest target, Rathburn fired, and his last ball slammed into the Yankee's chest, hurling him backward, the man's rifle flying uselessly into the underbrush. Simultaneously, O'Conner's pistol spoke, its shot catching the falling man squarely in the forehead, opening flesh and bone and sending a thick spray of blood over the lush greenery. The body disappeared behind the tree where he had sought cover.

"I'm out," O'Conner said.

"So am I," Rathburn replied, his voice now a hoarse whisper.

Suddenly, the last of the Yankee soldiers leaped from his protective cover, rushing forward with bayonet leading the way. O'Conner stumbled backward, his retreat blocked by the trunk of a tall poplar. Realizing the Yankee was going for the man still standing, Rathburn somehow summoned a superhuman burst of strength and rose to his feet, his hand grasping the haft of the bayonet still protruding from his leg. Jerking it free with an agonized cry, he swung the blade forward, catching the surprised attacker in the hollow beneath his sternum. The tip sank deep into unprotected flesh and, in an almost mindless fury of pain, Rathburn tugged the bayonet through the man's abdominal muscles with all his strength, spraying himself with blood. The force of the body impacting his almost sent him reeling, yet, miraculously, he managed to keep his footing.

But Rathburn's steadfastness proved to be his undoing. Braced by the body of his killer, the Yankee, in one final, desperate act, plucked a dagger from a sheath on his belt and drove it upward, catching Rathburn in the right side, its blade scraping over his ribs before driving deep into his lung. With a gasp of shock, Rathburn toppled, the body of the dead Yankee collapsing on top of him.

Now, endless waves of pain were all he knew. Even when O'Conner knelt to grasp his hand, he could no longer speak, only struggle for one agonized breath after another. Through a haze of red, he saw his lieutenant silhouetted against a twilight sky crisscrossed with spidery tree limbs. He felt the weight of the dead man being lifted from him.

"Don't try to talk," came O'Conner's voice. "I don't know if I can save you. But I will try."

O'Conner reached toward the body of the Yankee. A moment later his hand reappeared, now drenched with crimson blood. The Lieutenant bowed his head over the dead body, whispering words that Rathburn had never heard before. "*Iä, iä,*" O'Conner intoned, "*elohim el shaddai. O elohim, el shaddai.*" The chant droned on for several moments, becoming more and more energetic, building to a crescendo that rang like a howl in the darkness of the wood. Then O'Conner lowered his blood-soaked hand to Rathburn's lips, forcing him to taste the essence of the man he had killed.

"Drink of this, the blood of your enemy," O'Conner whispered. "Drink, that you may have life everlasting. Drink, that your spirit be not driven from these mortal remains." Unable to do otherwise, he sipped the blood from O'Conner's cupped hand. When it was gone, O'Conner traced the sign of a cross on Rathburn's forehead with his thumb. To Rathburn's surprise, moments later the mark began to burn his skin like virulent acid.

Whispering more of the strange words, O'Conner again dipped his hand into the dead man's wound and bid Rathburn drink of the blood a second time. Unlike the first taste, which almost sickened him with its metallic, salty flavor, this one tasted sweet, almost like honey.

"And now begin anew. May the spirits of the night sustain you for eternity."

Life was escaping from the wound in his side, he could feel it. Only moments remained for him in this world. Struggling for breath, he managed to whisper, "Phillip . . . escape. Now."

He felt his friend's hand take his, squeezing it warmly. In a gentle voice O'Conner said, "You saved my life, Thomas. This is the best I can offer you. It is like nothing I have ever worked before. Know that your past sins against me are forgiven. I pray you will now forgive me, my Captain."

The lieutenant rose, giving Rathburn a long,

thoughtful look. "They will be here soon. I will do as you ordered and leave this place. If they find you, it will be at their peril." O'Conner then came to attention and gave him a respectful salute. "Good-bye, Thomas Rathburn."

O'Conner then disappeared into darkness, leaving Rathburn to face the onrushing void alone. He could hear a roaring in his ears, drowning out the sound of gunfire, which had been drawing steadily nearer. All the pain was gone now, leaving him floating in a sea of warm numbness. He felt his lungs freeze in his chest, his heart beat its last beat. In the endless black before him, a threshold beckoned, sang sweetly like a dark cherub, calling, "Come across."

There was no more time. As all that he was and had been passed from an envelope of flesh lying in the woods of Aiken County, Virginia, on September the 29, 1864, Thomas Jackson Rathburn had no choice but to step through the door that Phillip O'Conner had opened for him; a door leading to a world whose secrets he could neither see nor begin to imagine, even if he'd had a hundred lifetimes to try.

He did not know how many hours had passed when consciousness returned to his body, still lying in the now silent stand of poplars and sycamores beneath a starlit sky. He could hear the sound of crickets chirping, a soft breeze rustling through the branches overhead. No gunfire marred the quietness, no voices or cries of pain pealed in the distance. He felt something crusty at his lips—dried blood, he realized, as he lifted a hand to wipe it away.

The touch of his own hand chilled him. It was as cold as the hand of a corpse.

Wait.

Memory came flooding back to him.

He had died. No dream, no flight of twisted fancy. He had been stabbed, and bled to death. He *knew* he had died.

Yet here he was, in the same grove where he had fallen. The body of the soldier he killed—who had killed him—still lay next to him, where Lieutenant Phillip O'Conner had placed it. He touched the cheek of the dead man. It was icy, even to his own frigid touch.

His forehead burned as if a hot iron had branded his flesh. *The sign of the cross, traced in blood.* He shook his head, trying to flush out the confused impressions that whirled through his mind like a nightmarish cyclone. His leg, where the blade had pierced it, no longer throbbed. The wound in his side leaked no blood, and thrusting his fingers through the rip in his coat, rather than a raw, gaping hole, he found only a jagged scar—a mere wrinkle in his skin, as if it had healed over a long, long time ago.

He rose on wobbly legs and took a deep breath of the cool evening air. To his shock, he realized he had not been breathing. Only when he felt compelled to test the air did his lungs function. But the air itself had become a charged, living organism, full of vibration and sensation, revealing knowledge of his surroundings far beyond the capacity of his ordinary physical receptors. He knew the nearest living human was far away. The stench of death, though, was strong, almost overpowering. He knew that nearby but unseen lay the bodies of countless men and horses; the aftermath of the furious battle.

As his eyes adjusted to the darkness, he realized he could perceive shapes to which his ordinary vision would have been blind. An owl perched on a low tree limb a hundred yards away, its eyes glowing in the light of the moon, now a silvery crescent shining through tangled tree limbs. A slight shuffling sound told him that a fox was hunting in the darkness almost a quarter of a mile away.

Oh, God. What has happened to me?

A sudden jab in his gut startled him, bringing on a strange craving that at first seemed unidentifiable. Then, when the truth of his desire—his need— dawned on him, he choked back a cry of disgust, horrified by his own pernicious longing. A spasm of pure hunger shook his body, and he realized that his teeth ached as if they'd been struck with a hammer. Tentatively fingering his mouth, he found his canines unnaturally long and sharpened. And his fingernails had extended into pointed, glistening claws.

With a strangled cry, he turned and began running through the trees, his legs stronger and faster than they ever could have been before. When he leaped over fallen trunks, he hung suspended for what seemed an eternity before lightly touching down and continuing on his mad flight. He realized as he ran that the feeling was exhilarating.

But the pain . . . the pain of his hunger. It was awful. Like the blade that had pierced his flesh, it bit at him, forcing him to accept the need to do what he must do.

Somewhere, still far away in the night, he sensed a presence. A warmth. *A living man.* He turned in the direction he knew would lead him to sustenance, passing deserted farmhouses, scorched fields, slaughtered livestock—all the handiwork of the Union Army, which in its advance had adopted the tactics of total warfare, destroying not only the military forces it struggled against, but the means for the enemy to sustain itself. A bitter anger now blended with his confusion and hunger. What had he done to himself? What had been done *to* him?

There. Ahead, a solitary figure crept along the treeline at the edge of a burnt-out cornfield. Rathburn finally realized his point of view was from far above the ground. *Good God . . . he was flying.* The revelation almost caused him to grow faint and fall. But he somehow maintained control and descended toward the figure, which stopped moving and stood still, seemingly aware of the rapid approach of death itself.

In a moment Rathburn stood face-to-face with the man who had opened this door for him: Lieutenant Phillip O'Conner. The younger man snapped to attention and gave him a salute.

"Captain," he whispered, his eyes wide with surprise—and something else, Rathburn thought. *Satisfaction*?

"O'Conner," he growled, his nerves tensing, his taloned hands balling into fists at his sides. "My God, what have you done? What have you done to me?"

"It would seem my venture was successful. You live still."

"This?" Rathburn extended his clawed fingers, pressed them to his heart. "You call this *life*?"

"Such as I had to offer," O'Conner said softly. "There appeared to be little choice at the time."

"You could have left me to die with honor. This . . . this is ungodly."

"Thomas, you know nothing of the word. Of which 'god' do you speak?"

Rathburn took a step closer to O'Conner, who did not retreat. "Can this be undone?" he whispered with a dangerous, catlike purr.

O'Conner shook his head. "You must accept your gift in the spirit it was given, Captain."

As the hunger pangs intensified, Rathburn's body became a raging pyre. He clutched O'Conner's coat lapel and dragged the younger man toward him. "A gift! You bastard, you have cursed me! It is horrible. Horrible!"

O'Conner studied the eyes that glared redly back at him. Then, with soft sadness, he said, "You are in pain, Thomas . . . I didn't know. I swear, I didn't know."

A stab of silver fire racked his body, and he hurled O'Conner backward into a tree. "Then let me show you pain!" he growled. Lunging forward, he lifted the young man until his face hung close to his own. "Is this 'gift' of yours my punishment for taking Elaine from you? How long have you been plotting this against me?"

O'Conner shook his head, still maintaining his composure even in Rathburn's deadly grip. "No, you're wrong. You will come back to yourself, Thomas. You will realize."

But now, tortured beyond endurance by the inferno inside him, Rathburn tightened his grip around O'Conner's throat and pulled the young man's head back with his other hand. Almost with a life of their own, his new fangs ripped into the soft skin of O'Conner's neck, puncturing his jugular vein. Warm, rich blood poured from the jagged wounds, and Rathburn's tongue extended to meet it, the honeylike taste almost immediately assuaging the conflagration inside him. Unable to stop himself, he pressed his mouth over the wound and sucked hard, drawing out the blood in a smooth, satisfying draught. O'Conner did not so much as protest as his life's essence flowed from his body, his eyes gazing skyward as if contemplating its deepest secrets.

For an interminable time Rathburn drank at the gushing fountain, each swallow a panacea for his inhuman hunger. As the ache subsided, his rational mind finally began to reassert itself, and the realization of what he was doing caused him to release his captive with a gasp of surprise and self-loathing. "Oh, God," he groaned. "What am I doing?"

O'Conner gazed weakly back at him, his eyes betraying the rapid ebbing of his life. In a whisper he said, "This is what you are now, Thomas. You must accept it."

"Oh, no, Phillip," he said. "I didn't mean to . . . I'm sorry. Oh, God, I'm so sorry."

"If I die from your bite, I will become as you," O'Conner said softly. "Tell me what you feel. What is it like?"

A flash of rage flickered inside him. "Hell, you son of a bitch! It is hell!"

"I did not intend to see you to suffer, Thomas. I swear it."

Rathburn nodded. "Good Christ, look at you. I have to help you, somehow."

O'Conner shook his head. "Too late. The best you can do is end this for me. You gave your life for me on the battlefield. Now take mine, before this can't be undone. Don't be afraid."

"Damn you, Phillip. Damn you. I didn't want this. Not for you."

"I know. End it, Thomas. Now. There's no time left."

Rathburn saw the last glimmers of life in O'Conner's eyes. Knowing what he had to do, he leaned forward and kissed his friend on the forehead. "Again, I ask for your forgiveness. I'm so sorry."

Then, in a smooth motion, he twisted O'Conner's head and snapped his neck, letting the body fall slowly through his arms to the ground. His friend's face wore the same look as when Rathburn had broken the news about his engagement to Elaine. A look of deepest grief, which Rathburn had before glimpsed only briefly, for O'Conner had buried it quickly and fully. Yet afterward, he continued to call Rathburn "friend."

My God, the man had never had a friend in his life who accepted him for the strong soul that he was, Rathburn reflected, rather than as an eccentric with a predilection for dabbling in the occult. What had Phillip been hoping to do? Conquer death? He had done that, in a way—but not for himself. He'd been a gentle spirit attempting to manipulate forces greater and far less benevolent than he. And now Phillip O'Conner lay dead at his feet.

"You poor fool," Rathburn whispered, kneeling and placing O'Conner's hands over his chest, gently tilting his head back from the awry angle at which it hung. The blood on his lips tingled, and he touched them with his cold fingers. What incredible arcane energy had flowed through his friend's veins? O'Conner's blood was now a part of him, and he could almost hear his lieutenant whispering, "Use your power wisely, my friend. I tried, but I failed."

Leaving the body where it lay, he turned to the night once again and flew, spurred on by pure grief and rage, not knowing what to do, where to go. An instinctive horror of the sun's rays catching him unprotected told him he needed to find shelter before the first light of day. As far as the army was concerned, he was missing in action, presumed dead. Captain Thomas Rathburn no longer existed. He was now a dark spirit, a wild creature of the night, terrified and terrifying. Panicked and alone.

Only one rational thought managed to intervene between the pangs of despair and loneliness that overwhelmed him. He must find someplace safe, somewhere secure and familiar.

Home. He had to get back home. Quickly, while he retained control of his faculties, his blood lust.

Back to Elaine.

I live, Rathburn thought, rising from the tangle of fishing nets, his memories fading away like dissipating smoke from a gun. *I will live. No hunger will stop me. I will not be manipulated. I will not be controlled. Not by lust, not by spirits. I will kill to live.*

No wonder so few of his kind existed. What sort of being could withstand the violent, constant extremes that dominated this existence? Pleasure and pain taken to their ultimate limits; the way of madness. How many initiates to the breed, once realizing the path that awaited them, threw themselves into the deadly light of the sun rather than face a future of endless isolation and bloodthirst? Far from the soulless creature of legend, Rathburn thought wryly, the Vampire possessed passions unlike any that could be imagined—or tolerated—by simple mortal minds.

Someone was moving outside the fishing shack. He could hear the sound of shuffling footsteps, smell the blood in the air. Blood that would be his. It *must* be his.

He threw open the door, startling an ancient figure in a rain-soaked slicker, holding a bottle of whiskey in wrinkled, shivering hands. "Who that?"

came a coarse growl from beneath the brim of a floppy hat. "Benny?"

Rathburn did not give the old fisherman a chance to even react in shock. In a heartbeat he had snapped the old man's neck and bent it to angry fangs that sought his blood. They rent the old man's flesh and spilled the elixir of life, now useless to the shell Rathburn grasped in taloned hands. Dragging the body into the shack, he drank and drank again until the corpse had shriveled into a withered husk that stank of alcohol and sweat. Eventually, Rathburn regained control of his body, and he could retract his fangs and dim the burning of his glaring eyes. Outside, the rain had stopped. He let his every sense explore the atmosphere, to verify that he was indeed still alone in the night.

Clear.

He opened the door and dragged the body to the end of the long pier. With one effortless motion of his foot, he kicked it over the edge, a moment later hearing it splash into the foamy waves below. The corpse floated for a few minutes, its arms outstretched as if it were trying to remember how to swim. The current swelled around it, dragging it steadily out to sea, until the weight of the water filling it dragged it at last into the depths and out of his view.

Forgiveness was something he no longer sought. There was no point in it. Too much blood. Too much blood on his hands.

"Adios, amigo," he said softly, then turned his back on the ocean, refocusing his mind on the matter at hand: determining who or what had led him here, and how to deal with forces he did not know but that apparently knew him.

chapter

∞

5

Victoria stood in the large garden behind the Collinwood mansion, watching a hawk circle in the air high above the world, seeking its prey somewhere among the distant trees to the west. It was a solitary creature, single-minded, and Victoria wondered what it would be like to have such a distinct and simple purpose in life.

The morning sky was clear and blue, all traces of storm clouds chased away by the sunlight. Puddles lay scattered on the stone walkway. Raindrops sparkled on the small green leaves of the boxwood hedge and on the barren branches of the maples and lilacs. Red and burnt-orange leaves had been tossed by the wind against the stone wall and clung there, as if painted with a wet, brilliant brush. Victoria had plucked a single purple New England aster blossom, one of the last of the season. Most flowers were long gone now, with only the occasional, determined dandelion showing its ragged, yellow face amid the cracks in the stone walk.

A moment of solitude, like that of the hawk, Victoria thought, drawing the damp flower petals along her chin. *A moment to feel, to imagine, to dream. This is heaven.*

The call came from outside the garden near the gate, shrill and loud. "Vicki, are you in here?"

She didn't answer at first. Perhaps Carolyn wouldn't find her and would go away. *That is selfish,* she chided herself. *But I do so want to be alone right now.*

Then, "Vicki, you're in here, aren't you?"

"Yes."

The voice was coming closer from beyond the turn in the garden. "I talked to Uncle Roger! Where are you?"

"Here," Victoria called. She let the aster fall to the grass. Her moment of solitude was over.

Carolyn came around the boxwood hedge, her face lit up and flushed. "I told Uncle Roger about Thomas Rathburn. I asked him if we could offer the man the cottage for his stay."

"And he said no," Victoria said. "I could have told you that. I gave it a lot of thought last night after we got home. We don't know the man at all, Carolyn, only that he looks good and seems nice enough. There isn't a women's magazine on earth that would advise you to offer an invitation to a stranger that would allow him to take up residence on your property."

"You're wrong, Uncle Roger didn't say no," Carolyn said with pursed lips. "He said he wanted to meet Thomas and then decide."

Victoria's heart jumped with unexpected excitement. She said, "Your uncle doesn't read many women's magazines, does he?"

Carolyn ignored this. "Uncle Roger said he would call Thomas at the Collinsport Inn to offer an invitation to dinner tonight."

"And did he?"

"No," Carolyn said. She picked up the flower Victoria had dropped and rolled it between her hands. Petals fell like rain. "I offered to make the invitation in person. I said it was more polite. I'm going to drive down there now!"

Victoria had tried not to think much about Thomas Rathburn after they left the tavern last night, his beautiful and commanding eyes, his strong face, his masculine and elegant manner. On the drive home she had watched herself in the side-view mirror as the rain pelted the glass, and she saw the plain, simple girl she was and no more. She had felt pretty just a half hour before, but it had faded with the distance they'd put between themselves and the Blue Whale. A man like Thomas Rathburn would not be interested in her; it had been her imagination, fueled by the warmth of the tavern's fire and the white wine.

But now, hearing Carolyn speak his name aloud, Victoria was caught off guard with a need to see him again, in the daylight. To see if it had been her imagination or something more.

"I'll go with you," she said suddenly.

"Oh . . ." Carolyn's smile faded. "No, you don't need to do that. You seem to be having a nice morning here in the garden, and I don't want to disturb that."

"It's not a disturbance," Victoria said. "It's Saturday, I don't have classes with David today, and I would be happy to keep you company. You've always been after me to come with you into town for this or that, and right now suits me just fine. Besides, if Mr. Rathburn turns out to be dangerous, you will have me to protect you."

"He's not dangerous, Victoria. I know that. You know that."

"I'll come anyway."

Carolyn took several breaths, dropped the flower stem, now barren of its petals, and said, "Well, all right, sure."

They walked toward the garden gate together, then Carolyn turned to Victoria, raised one finger and added seriously, "But *I* get to do the talking!"

The Collinsport Inn was the sole establishment in Collinsport, not counting several bed-and-breakfasts, that catered to visitors—not tourists, but visitors. Victoria was aware that the town's size, location, and often unpredictable weather didn't draw in many out-of-towners looking for a relaxing weekend. Visitors to Collinsport were most often men and women on business or those who had come to see family for a few days.

Tourists, like Thomas Rathburn, were a rarity.

The inn had done little remodeling since its last make-over in the fifties. There was no elevator, as the inn was only four stories high, and the stairs ran up the wall just past the desk. Keys were keys, not electronically coded cards, and they were nestled in cubbies behind the desk. Off the lobby was a diner-style restaurant, complete with soda fountain, linoleum flooring, kitchenlike chairs and tables, and weary waitresses.

The proprietor of the inn, Mr. Wells, stood at his usual post behind the desk, as much a fixture here as the old sofas and whaling prints. He was a balding man with a hawkish nose, in a brown corduroy jacket with patched elbows and a bow tie, and holding a half-smoked cigarette between two fingers. A pack of breath mints peeked from his shirt pocket.

"Miss Stoddard, Miss Winters," he said politely as they stepped through the door and Victoria pushed it closed against the cold sea air. "Good morning. How may I help you?"

Carolyn put her hands on the top of the desk

and nodded politely. "Mr. Wells, good morning. You're looking well."

"Thank you," Mr. Wells replied, his words coming slowly. Like most people in town, he knew Carolyn could be full of mischief. "And you, too."

"Listen." Carolyn leaned in. "You have a guest, a man from Georgia, and I need to speak with him. It's very important."

"Would that be Mr. Rathburn?"

"Yes. I'm delivering a message from my uncle."

"I see," Mr. Wells said. "Should I call him to come down?"

"Oh, no. If you'll give us his room number, we'll just go up. He's expecting us."

"Is he?" said Mr. Wells, who had lived in Collinsport long enough to know that one didn't often argue with members of the Collins household. The family owned just a bit too much of the town to rock the boat. "Fine, then." He ran his finger down the register. "I've put him in room 213. Near the end of the hall upstairs."

Carolyn went up the creaking, carpet-covered stairs ahead of Victoria. A fading oil painting on the wall along the steps caught Victoria's attention, and she paused to stare at it.

A twilight seascape showed a rocky shore, a dark lighthouse, and seabirds circling above a patch of ocean. A pale wash of light from the setting sun threw distorted, elongated shadows through the rock-clinging trees and out onto the waves, making it seem as though black, angry claws had ripped across the painting, tearing the approaching night apart. And striking the shore were two green, foamy splashes, looking very much like two glowing eyes—fixed, unblinking, cold.

Night jitters, Victoria thought. She rubbed her arms. *Someone has painted night jitters.*

"Come *on*!" Carolyn called, exasperated, from the top of the stairs.

Outside the door marked 213, the two hesitated, looking furtively at each other and up and down the dingy, wallpapered hall. Victoria felt like a teenager ready to pull a prank, and she whispered, "Perhaps we should have called first. I don't know about you, but I'm feeling pretty silly."

That was all the prodding Carolyn needed. She pounded on the door.

They listened. There was only silence.

She pounded again, and again, but they heard only the sound of Mr. Wells downstairs, coughing around his cigarette and saying something to himself.

"I wonder if he's gone out?" Carolyn said.

Victoria shrugged. She hoped he had gone out. And she hoped he was still there.

The doorknob jiggled then, and the door pulled inward. The room beyond was jet-black, and no one could be distinguished in the darkness. But the voice was familiar, and its reverberations drove into

Victoria's blood the sudden heat of excitement she'd felt last night at the tavern. She was instantly aware of the beating of her heart.

"Good day, ladies," Thomas Rathburn said. "What a pleasant surprise to see you both this morning. Please, won't you come in?"

"Sure!" Carolyn said.

The door opened wider. A figure stepped back farther into the shadows, and Carolyn and Victoria had only the light from the hall to show them the way.

"Were you sleeping?" Victoria asked in the vicinity of the man in the dark. "I apologize if we woke you. Perhaps we should have had Mr. Wells call up first."

"No, I was not sleeping," Rathburn said. Victoria's eyes had begun to adjust to the darkness. She could see the tall man standing near the bed, sunglasses obscuring his eyes.

Carolyn saw Rathburn then, too. "Why the sunglasses, and inside for heaven's sake?" she asked with a surprised chuckle. "You in the witness protection program or something?"

"As a matter of fact," Rathburn said, "I suffer from a condition known as iritis, which renders my eyes hypersensitive to sunlight. I try to give them a rest as much as possible, you understand."

"Of course we understand," Victoria said. It was rude of Carolyn to make a callous joke. Such a condition would be dreadful. She wanted to let him know she sympathized, but the words that tried to come out seemed overwrought or childish, so she kept them to herself.

"Uncle Roger would like to invite you to dinner this evening," Carolyn said. "He wants to meet you and have the opportunity to verify your credentials before agreeing to lease the cottage."

"Certainly," Rathburn said, removing his glasses and slipping them into his shirt pocket. He opened a valise on the nightstand and withdrew a piece of paper, which he handed to Victoria. His thumb brushed hers briefly as she took the page, and an electric shiver passed clear up to her shoulders. "This is a list of names and phone numbers of individuals and companies in Atlanta with whom I do business and with whom I keep in touch, even on holiday. Please present this to Mr. Collins and let him know I greatly respect a man who is cautious and careful in his dealings."

"Great!" Carolyn said, tugging the list away from Victoria and folding it in half. "There will be a car here to pick you up at six-forty-five. Now, won't you join us in the restaurant for a cup of coffee or some breakfast? We had so little time to actually talk last night, what with the drunken sailors and the general hubbub. My treat."

"Thank you, but I must decline," Rathburn said. Victoria had become aware of his eyes, the green visible in the faint hallway light, yet seemingly with concentrated pinpoints of light of their own. He was staring at her. She felt her knees tremble. "I am still weary from my travels, and would like to be refreshed before arriving at Collinwood tonight."

"Oh," Carolyn said, her voice not hiding the disappointment. "Well, sure, that's fine."

"Good day," he said.

"Good day," Victoria said.

In the hall, after the door had closed behind them, Carolyn clutched Victoria's arm and leaned into her with an air of conspiracy. "Isn't he amazing? And absolutely gorgeous?"

"He is at that," Victoria admitted. *And more than that, so much more than that.*

Down in the lobby, Mr. Wells was in a serious discussion with a pudgy man in his early fifties, dressed in a uniform shirt and tie. Sheriff George Patterson's brows were drawn up with concern, and Mr. Wells was shaking his head.

Patterson turned as the two women reached the bottom of the stairs. "Good morning, young ladies," he offered with a slight nod, though the scowl on his face didn't falter.

"Is there some trouble?" Victoria asked.

"I swear whatever it is, I didn't do it!" Carolyn joked.

"Sad business last night," Patterson said seriously. "We had a fisherman disappear on us. A crewman on a fishing vessel, name of Jack Howard. He was last seen near the Blue Whale around the time of the storm."

"So what are you thinking?" Carolyn asked.

"Nothing yet," Patterson said. "I'm just questioning anyone who might have seen him. His wife's beside herself. He likes to go out and drink with his pals, but at least he always comes home. Last night he didn't."

"That's too bad," Victoria said.

"I'm told you two were at the Blue Whale last night."

"Yes," Carolyn said. "Vicki and I had a few drinks. And we saw plenty of fishermen. But we don't even know who Jack Howard is, or what he looks like. So we couldn't say."

"Mr. Wells here tells me that an out-of-towner with a southern accent registered last night, and that you two had in fact come to see him this morning. True?"

"Yes," Carolyn said. "That's true, Sheriff. But he's no suspect in your possible crime. He's a businessman from Atlanta, educated, quite refined, and as a matter of fact, will most likely be moving into the vacant cottage on our estate."

"Is that so?"

"Yes, of course it is."

"And is Mister . . ." The sheriff glanced over at the register and put his finger on a finely penned

name. ". . . Mr. Rathburn awake this morning? I
need to speak with him, regardless. All routine, you
know."

"He's not in his room," Carolyn said. Victoria
glanced sharply at her friend, surprised at the ease
of the lie. "We knocked and knocked, but nothing. I
suppose he's gone out walking, taking in the
scenery." She gave the sheriff a coquettish smile.

Sheriff Patterson looked at Mr. Wells. "Did you
notice the man leave?"

"Ah, come on, George," Mr. Wells said. "I take
time out for coffee in the restaurant, I don't watch
the desk every second."

The sheriff looked at Victoria then, his eyebrow
going up as if seeking confirmation of Carolyn's
statement. And to Victoria's own surprise, she
found herself saying, "The man's not here, Sheriff. I
suggest you look elsewhere."

As the sheriff turned and left the hotel, and Mr.
Wells returned to the magazine he was reading, Victoria wondered to herself, *What have I just done? Why
should I lie to protect a man I don't even know?*

chapter

◆◆◆◆◆

6

Mr. Rathburn? I'm Jake Stiles. Mr. Roger Collins sent me to collect you."

The driver was a coarse-looking young man with longish auburn hair, thick lips, and narrow eyes, wearing a neatly pressed if well-worn gray suit. Rathburn greeted him politely and followed him through the lobby to the car parked outside: a black Bentley, obviously the property of a wealthy owner. He slid into the plush leather rear seat as Stiles got in behind the wheel and asked Rathburn if the temperature was satisfactory.

"It's fine," he said, glancing at the golden sunset in the west. For the moment he was still forced to wear his hat and sunglasses, but he would be able to lose them by the time he reached the estate. The driver made an unnecessarily fast turn out of the parking lot and headed south on the road leading past the train station where Rathburn had arrived. Stiles appeared to be an untalkative sort, which suited Rathburn fine, as he preferred to devote his attention to orienting himself with his surroundings.

Braithwaite Road, which appeared to be a main thoroughfare through the village, took them past a number of local businesses housed in the ubiquitous, aging, colonial-style buildings. Then they turned west onto Collinsport Loop Road, which led to U.S. 1 Alt, ten miles away, the only significant commercial artery running anywhere near the town. Rathburn noted with interest the almost complete lack of familiar franchise names, giving testimony to how isolated a place this truly must be. Only a half mile or so out of town the businesses gave way to a few private residences, all tucked far back from the road, and finally to grassy fields and pockets of dark woods with only the occasional house to indicate human habitation. After so many years of living in a metropolitan area, Rathburn found the scarcity of population pleasing, reminding him of the countryside where he'd been raised so many distant years ago.

About five miles out of town they turned left onto a narrow lane, identified by a tiny sign as South Beach Road. And after another half mile of thick pine forest on either side, Stiles slowed and turned left into an almost hidden driveway, through a high stone gate adorned with a warning sign that read, *Private Property: Trespassers Will Be Prosecuted.*

Stiles glanced back and said, "Here we are, sir." And Rathburn sensed that he was entering a place different from any he had experienced before, a place isolated from the rest of the world by more than just distance. An odd, unidentifiable aura hung over the dim landscape like a vast silken web, striking a chord of both strangeness and familiarity—as if here, indeed, lay the source of the visions that had been visited upon him.

For a good quarter mile the winding drive led through dense deciduous woods that were losing their leaves, finally opening to an expanse of wide, well-tended lawns bordered by linden, oak, and maple trees. Finally, on his right, Rathburn could see a crumbling brick building half obscured by twisted vegetation. Stiles noticed his look of curiosity and said, "That's the old swimming pool. It hasn't been used in years. Lotsa old structures on the estate, mostly just wasting away now. Over there"—he pointed past the natatorium toward a long, metal framework building—"that's the greenhouse. Used to be pretty impressive. Just junk now."

"So I see," Rathburn said, removing his sunglasses now that the fiery ball of the sun had passed from view. To his left he could see through some broken woods the distant edge of the Atlantic, trying to hide beneath the cloak of rapidly settling darkness. For a moment he glimpsed the roof of an apparently large building or house, but it was quickly obscured by another stand of tall trees, here mostly juniper. Ahead he could see a few lights along the driveway, leading up to a dark, hulking structure that dominated the landscape like a medieval castle rising over ancient, blood-soaked moors. Its chimneys cut jagged teeth marks in the deep blue sky, and from its far side a prominent but unlit tower rose above the rest of the house like an uneasily sleeping sentry. Only a few lights burned in the house's myriad windows.

"Welcome to Collinwood," Stiles said softly. "I'll drop you at the front door."

The Bentley came to a stop in front of a porte cochere, and Rathburn climbed out with his hat in hand, giving Stiles a curt nod as the young man drove off to park the car. He took a quick look around at the nearby grounds, the tall bushes that grew around the sides of the porte cochere, the gray stone walls rising high above him. His senses absorbed the atmosphere, the scents and sounds in the air, at last detecting a subtle but unmistakable vibration, coursing through the very essence of this baronial estate: *danger*. He straightened his tie and stepped up to the broad wooden front door, sharply rapping the door knocker.

After a few moments the door was opened by a dark-haired woman in her fifties, wearing a black dress and white apron. She evaluated him with a stern glare, but in a not unpleasant voice said, "You must be Mr. Rathburn. Come in, please." He stepped inside and at her invitation handed her his coat and hat, which she hung on a rack just inside the entryway. "I'll tell Mr. Collins and Mrs. Stoddard that you are here."

"Thank you," he said as the woman, obviously the housekeeper, turned and disappeared down a dimly lit hallway to the left, her footfalls echoing sharply on the polished stone floor. He found himself standing in a grand foyer with a vaulted ceiling, illuminated by a chandelier that hung over an ancient, hand-carved wooden table. Against the far wall a fine old grandfather clock tick-tocked noisily, its chimes suddenly coming to life to peal the seven o'clock hour, their mellow ringing finally fading into the unknown corridors of the great mansion. To his right, a stairway climbed to a balcony that clearly led to other areas of the house, the wall above it dominated by a huge stained-glass window that would surely appear impressive when backlit by the sun—or even the moon. To the right of the grandfather clock, a set of closed double doors would open to what he guessed was the living room or drawing room; to either side of the doors stood a pair of carved stone busts on tall pedestals. He recognized the figures as George Washington and the Marquis de Lafayette.

"Those were sculpted by Horatio Greenough in 1832." Hearing the low, silky voice, Rathburn turned to see a distinguished-looking, blond man with a stern demeanor extending his hand. "Mr. Rathburn, I presume. I am Roger Collins."

Rathburn accepted the proffered hand and returned a firm handshake. The other man flinched at the coolness of his skin but made no remark. "Thomas Rathburn. I'm very pleased to meet you."

"We don't often have visitors from out of town," Collins said. "You must have made quite an impression on my niece for her to have invited you here. I must say it is an honor."

Rathburn smiled. Roger Collins had apparently done some research into his background. As he expected. "You have a most impressive home, Mr. Collins. Very beautiful indeed."

"The mansion actually belongs to my sister," Roger said with a faint scowl. "So, you are looking to retreat to some out-of-the-way spot, is that it? I must say, you picked the most out-of-the-way of them all."

"Well, I'm not sure yet. But it is a possibility. I've been a city man for quite a long time. I think a change would do me good."

"You're much younger than I expected. I can't imagine Collinsport would offer you anything of the lifestyle you're accustomed to."

Rathburn took a breath and sampled the atmosphere, finding the scent of Victoria Winters strong in this place. "On the contrary. You have no idea how appealing that sounds," he said with a smile.

Just then an elegant, dark-haired woman appeared from the hallway that the housekeeper had earlier taken. She wore a satin dress of pale gold and a sparkling pearl necklace that looked to be of great antiquity. Her smile was cautious yet pleasant, clearly well-practiced in social situations. "Good evening, Mr. Rathburn. I'm Elizabeth Collins Stoddard. It's a pleasure to meet the man my daughter carried on so about last night."

Rathburn chuckled. "I'm glad I made such a positive impression. I was just telling your brother what a fine home you have. I want to thank you for having me to dinner. It's nice to feel welcome when in a strange place."

"A man of your means will surely find Collinsport a dull and ordinary place," she said, echoing her brother's sentiments. "But please accept our hospitality. We'll be having dinner in just a few minutes. I'm sorry, but we didn't ask if you require any special diet."

"Not at all," Rathburn said. "I'm looking forward to whatever your hospitality offers."

"Then let me offer you a drink," Roger Collins said, opening the doors to the drawing room, which was ornately furnished, with a number of portraits adorning its walls. A broad fireplace occupied the far wall, while to the left, a large bay window revealed a wooded portion of the grounds outside.

Roger chose a decanter from a table on the left. "If you like brandy, this is Hennessy cognac. Or, if you prefer, we have bourbon or scotch."

"Brandy is fine, thank you."

Roger poured three snifters, handed one each to Elizabeth and Rathburn, then took a swallow from his own. "The cottage that Carolyn told you about is on the northwest corner of the property," he said.

"So it goes," Rathburn said, taking the tiniest sip of his drink. The cognac tasted sweet and not unpleasant, though its alcohol would scarcely affect his system. As he drank he let his hypersensitive receptors absorb the psychic emanations from Roger Collins, who would be quite unaware he was being so thoroughly scrutinized. Rathburn quickly decided that this man had no close involvement with any supernatural force, at least not that might concern him. Whereas Roger perceived himself as a complex, erudite individual, Rathburn perceived him to be simple and conceited, more proud of his family's history than his own accomplishments. *And what of your family's history?* Rathburn thought. *Were your direct ancestors murderous animals who took everything I held dear?* Whatever secrets Roger Collins hid, they might be ugly but were certainly insignificant.

But Elizabeth ... she concealed many secrets; deep and puzzling ones. It would take more than a cursory exploration of the reverberations from her psyche to determine whether she might be connected to his visions. She presented herself as confident, but there was great insecurity lurking behind the forced facade.

And what of Victoria? He hoped she would appear soon, for she certainly was the most enigmatic, most alluring, creature he'd encountered in a long, long time.

"I'll have Stiles drive you to the cottage after dinner, if you don't care to walk," Roger was saying. "It's not that far, but you have to either go through the woods or take the road around them, which is out of the way."

"I don't mind walking," Rathburn said. "In fact, I would enjoy getting a better feeling for the grounds. How much land does the estate include, if I might ask?"

"Something over two hundred acres," Roger said. "But we also own a great deal of real estate in the surrounding areas. Elizabeth looks after that end of the family business. I manage the cannery in the village. You might be interested to know we're still Collinsport's biggest employer, after well over two centuries in the business."

"I see," Rathburn said, abruptly turning as he sensed the arrival of a new presence in the room. He felt a twinge of disappointment when he saw that it was Carolyn. The young blonde wore a tight-fitting, short knit dress of dark blue that accentuated her gold hair. She beamed unashamedly at him, obviously smitten by his manner. Yes, her unfettered lust could be useful to him, he thought, though for a moment he again detected a vibration that suggested she might have been similarly utilized in the past by another.

An avenue worth exploring.

"Good evening, Thomas," she said, giving him an openly seductive grin. "How nice to see you again."

"Hello, young lady," he said, adopting an intentionally paternal demeanor. "I must thank you for the invitation. Your mother and uncle have made me feel most welcome."

Carolyn appeared to bristle at the idea that he more readily identified with the older generation. "We always expect our guests at Collinwood to enjoy themselves. I hope you brought an appetite with you."

"Indeed I did," he said.

And then . . . he felt her. She was somewhere just beyond the drawing room doors. She was nervous. But she wanted to see him. Her scent was everywhere, unmistakable. He could not stop himself from going to the doorway to greet her as she came down the stairs.

Victoria looked radiant in a black, low-cut dress, her dark hair cascading elegantly over her slim shoulders, her face bearing only the faintest traces of makeup to highlight her natural beauty.

Christ. He had seen beautiful women, *fed* on beautiful women countless times over countless years, yet nothing and no one had moved him as this one did. Perhaps it was having seen her in visions long before actually meeting her, intensified by some effect worked by the unknown sender. Or perhaps the mystery behind the psychic waves she exuded lent her an attraction to which he was entirely unaccustomed in a mortal. He offered her a polite smile of greeting, which she returned, then shyly lowered her eyes. But as he was about to speak to her, he saw over her shoulder, on the foyer wall, a portrait he had not noticed when he first entered.

"Excuse me," he said, stepping around her to view the painting. It was of a dark-haired man with a rather gaunt, sad-looking face, and deep-set, hypnotic eyes. But what had caught Rathburn's attention was the fact that the subject held a cane with a silver wolf's head in one hand, the forefinger of which was adorned by a huge, onyx ring. *Beyond a shadow of a doubt, the man from his visions.* "I find this portrait fascinating."

"He is an imposing figure," Elizabeth said, following Rathburn into the foyer. "That portrait is of Barnabas Collins, who went to England in the year 1796."

"And what you may find most interesting," Roger added, stepping up beside him with drink in hand, "is that his namesake, a distant cousin of ours,

lives on the estate as well. There is a rather remarkable resemblance between the two."

"Interesting indeed," Rathburn mused. Then,
turning to Victoria, he said, "Forgive me, I didn't
mean to be rude. I just had the distinct impression
that I have seen the man in this portrait at some time
or another."

"That doesn't seem likely, since you just arrived
in town," she said.

"Quite, quite."

Victoria had appeared oblivious to the sugges-
tive tone in his voice. If she had been the one to tele
graph the psychic images to him, he doubted she
would be able to conceal it so well. He noticed Carolyn studying him, and sensed her jealousy at his
obvious favoring of Victoria. But before he could say
another word, the housekeeper appeared and
announced that dinner was ready.

"Ah, thank you, Mrs. Johnson," Roger said.
"Come this way, Mr. Rathburn."

"Thomas, please," he said. "No point in standing on formality."

"Of course," Roger said, turning right out of the
drawing room to lead them down the hall toward
the dining room at the far end.

Rathburn found himself again in a room of
unabashed opulence and cultivation, illuminated by
candles on the table and on the mantel over the fireplace, which occupied the long wall opposite the

entry. The polished oak table was fully ten feet long, meticulously laid out with fine china and silverware. Patterned glass bay windows with window seats overlooked the lawns at either end, indicating the room occupied the entire width of this wing of the mansion. Roger gestured for him to have a seat next to Carolyn, across from Victoria, while he and Elizabeth took their places at each end. Then, an approaching patter of footsteps announced a new arrival. Rathburn saw, with some consternation, a brown-haired lad about ten years old enter the room and take his place next to Victoria with an inquisitive look at their dinner guest.

"Thomas, this is my son David," Roger said. "David, this is Mr. Rathburn. He is interested in renting Matthew Morgan's old cottage for a time."

"That's a creepy place," the boy said, obviously nonplussed by Rathburn's presence. "You won't like it there."

"Well, perhaps I can give it a much needed cheering up," he said pleasantly. "Assuming your father is of a mind to lease it to me."

"As you might expect," Roger said, taking the cue, "I checked on the references you sent this morning. I must say, you certainly are a man of substantial means. And I received a rather glowing personal recommendation from the management of your hotel residence. You seem to have the city of Atlanta in the palm of your hand, Mr. Rathburn . . . er, Thomas."

"I've always tried to do my part to improve the economic standing of Atlanta's citizens. Myself included," Rathburn said with a grin.

Roger chuckled. "I think it's safe to say that Elizabeth and I both approve if you actually want to rent the place. It's furnished, and certainly habitable, though I expect it needs a thorough cleaning. You'll want to look it over before making a decision, I'm sure."

Rathburn nodded as Mrs. Johnson brought in a cart loaded with steaming dishes of vegetables and a covered meat tray, which she opened to reveal a huge roast of prime rib, swimming in fragrant juice. As they were served, Rathburn sent Victoria an almost conspiratorial smile, as if to say he would much prefer to be sharing a quiet dinner somewhere alone with her. She smiled back, but couldn't hide the blush that followed. Nor could any at the table miss seeing it, especially Carolyn.

"So what's it like in Atlanta?" Carolyn asked in a voice harsher than necessary. "I've been to Boston and New York, but I've never traveled anywhere in the South."

"It's grown a lot in recent years," he said, his smile cooler than the one he'd given Victoria. "It's nowhere near as big as New York, but it's one of the most prominent financial centers in the country. It's all the more remarkable when you consider it was destroyed by General Sherman in the War Between the States and rebuilt to become what it is today. It's treated me very well over the years."

"Have you lived there all your life?"

"Most of it," he said carefully. "Certainly since long before you were born."

Carolyn frowned and sighed softly, apparently finally accepting that Rathburn hardly considered her a suitable candidate for courtship. He turned his attention to his dinner, which he sampled with as neutral an expression as he could manage. The beef blood was succulent, the meat itself tender, but the vegetables were intolerable. Still, he forced himself to swallow them without betraying his distaste. It was a masquerade to which he was quite accustomed.

After a time he said to Roger, "Tell me . . . your cousin, Barnabas Collins . . . does he live in this house as well?"

"the estate," Roger said, his expression hinting that he held his cousin in no greater regard than he did the rest of humanity. "The place we call the Old House."

"Collinwood was built by Joshua and Jeremiah Collins, two brothers, in the late 1700s," Elizabeth said. "The Old House is not as large, but dates back almost one hundred years earlier. It was the home of the original Barnabas, until he went to England. The present Barnabas has restored it and has been living there since he came here, oh, quite some time ago."

"Perhaps I'll have a chance to meet him during my stay," Rathburn said.

"Cousin Barnabas doesn't get out very much," Carolyn said in a bored tone. "He keeps to himself in the daytime and only visits occasionally in the evening. He seems to enjoy his privacy."

"Oh, I see." Rathburn could hardly keep from laughing aloud. "He sounds like an interesting character."

"He can be very charming," Victoria said, her gaze drifting from Rathburn to some point in space, as if she were suddenly reminded of something she had forgotten. "He always was."

The others seemed taken aback by her remark, but no one said anything. Rathburn searched his psychic receptors and understood that something was indeed tearing at this girl, something that involved Barnabas Collins. She could barely hide her own confusion from the others of her kind, and to his heightened senses, it fairly screamed at him.

As dinner came to a close, Rathburn asked to be directed to the rest room. "Of course," Roger said with a nod. "David, would you please show Mr. Rathburn the way?"

"Yes, sir," the boy said sulkily, but got up to lead Rathburn down the hall to a door on the left. He flipped a casual hand at the door. "Here it is."

"Thank you, David," he replied, barely concealing his own distaste for the human child. He detested the creatures, considering them little better than howling monkeys—and hardly immune to his appetite, when circumstances permitted. As he entered the bathroom and closed the door, he received a quick flash of a tiny figure suddenly picked up and hurled into the air by a gunshot, his little arms and legs flailing before smashing to a blood-soaked wooden floor. Rathburn's knees almost gave way then, and a stab of century-old pain in his chest caused him to double over.

Oh God, my son.

He was just a little boy.

He had to take a moment to compose himself. When he lifted his head again, he realized his eyes were wet.

No. They're just howling monkeys. He himself had preyed upon them.

"Damn it," he whispered to himself. Whatever was happening to him, it had affected him more deeply than he cared to admit. He had buried all remorse for his actions, for his feelings, a century ago; yet, however briefly, David Collins had called to mind his long dead son. He could not—would not—allow guilt to surface and derail him now. He resolutely wiped away the traces of any tears, then leaned over the toilet bowl and quietly regurgitated his undigested meal. Once he'd flushed the remains away, he washed thoroughly at the sink and popped a breath mint from his pocket as a finishing touch.

Finally feeling more himself again, he made his way back to the dining room to find the party beginning to break up.

"Thomas, would you care for an after-dinner drink?" Roger offered.

"Or coffee, if you'd prefer," Elizabeth added.

"Actually," he said, "I was thinking I might take a look at the cottage this evening. I wonder if Miss Winters wouldn't mind walking with me to point me in the right direction."

Victoria said, "I'd be happy to. That is, if it's all right . . ."

Elizabeth studied Rathburn thoughtfully for a moment, as if deciding whether or not his interest in Victoria was acceptable to her. "Of course. Don't worry about David. I'm sure Carolyn can see him up to bed when it's time."

"I'm sure I can, too," Carolyn said with a resentful sigh, looking longingly at Rathburn again, as if begging him to change his mind about her. Realizing that her effort was in vain, she bade him good night and sulkily led David to the stairs while Rathburn walked with Victoria toward the front door.

Just then David Collins leaned over the rail and called, "Looks like you've been taken in by the southern accent, Miss Winters. Y'all come back now, ya heah?"

"Oh, you!" she cried after him, with obvious affection for the boy, irritating though he might be.

"I don't want a bad report from Carolyn or you'll be on the next train south yourself."

As Rathburn slipped into his duster and helped Victoria on with a short wool jacket, Elizabeth approached him with a set of keys. "Here, in case you want to go inside. But let me warn you, the electricity is turned off. We'll have to have it turned back on for you. If you'll wait a moment, I can get you a flashlight."

"No need to bother, Mrs. Stoddard," Rathburn said. "I'm sure I can manage. Just a quick look is all I require. Thank you for dinner. It was delicious."

"Our pleasure," Elizabeth said. "But do be careful. It's a dark night."

A moment later Roger reappeared with an after-dinner brandy, his eyes showing the slight haze of intoxication. "Thomas, it's good to have met you. And it is nice to see our Miss Winters in the company of someone other than our illustrious cousin."

Rathburn could not suppress a sudden smile. Victoria Winters and Barnabas Collins, apparently in a closer relationship than he might have anticipated. What a wealth of information yet to be gleaned from this delicate creature at his side.

"I won't keep Miss Winters very long."

Roger Collins smiled wryly. "Think nothing of it, Mr. Rathburn . . . Thomas. It isn't as if we're her doting parents."

Rathburn chuckled inwardly at Roger's callousness as Victoria lifted her head to give him an abashed, apologetic smile. He opened the door to the brisk ocean air and stepped into the night with her, taking in the scents of the outdoors, the light but distinctive lilac perfume she wore—the same as he'd smelled on numerous occasions before, or different?—and most intensely of all, her sweet blood, throbbing with anticipation she didn't even realize she felt, and evident in the almost imperceptible pulsing of the jugular vein at her lovely, slim throat.

7

The evening air was not kind. What had been a cool and mild afternoon had evolved into a night of biting cold, punctuated by fingers of icy wind that taunted Victoria's face and neck and tugged at her hair. She pulled the pair of knit gloves from her jacket pocket and slipped them on as she and Rathburn stepped onto the driveway. She was not going to mention the weather and ruin an evening that had left her so unaccountably excited.

She shivered and tucked her chin into the collar of her jacket. But it wasn't just the cold that had her shaking. She was alone with Thomas Rathburn. Alone with this man and with her night jitters.

Good Lord, she thought. *What a combination.*

"Chilly?" Rathburn asked her as he adjusted the collar of his own duster.

"Just a little," she said, with a laugh she hoped

sounded casual. "But you can't live in Maine for long without making peace with the temperatures. Or at least a truce. October isn't too early for snow, you know. Sometimes you can smell it coming for days."

"One reason I love the South," Rathburn said. "Rarely a snowflake to be found. Although I do find the cold here to be most invigorating."

They passed out of the glow provided by the mansion's windows and into the shadows of the lane. The sudden rustling of some night creature in the nearby trees gave Victoria a start, and she pressed herself closer to Rathburn.

I think Thomas likes me, she thought. *This is incredible. I think he likes me, but I'm trembling like a leaf. Get hold of yourself, Vicki. All you need is just a fraction of Elizabeth's or Carolyn's self-confidence. Get hold of yourself, Vicki.*

"The estate has quite a history," she said, breaking the silence.

Rathburn turned to her, his face awash in wind-tossed moonlight. "Indeed?"

"It does," she said. "I could show you a few of the more interesting spots if you'd like, before we go to the cottage. If the Collins family is ever in a need of money—although I can't imagine that ever happening—this place would be a marvelous tourist attraction. What Collinsport doesn't draw in by way of vacationers, Collinwood could, with its incredible history. The Ladies' Historical League of Maine

would fall over themselves to get a foot into
Collinwood. High schools would bring busloads of
students on field trips."

"I see."

"I'm teasing."

"I thought so."

"But only about the field trips. Not about the
intrigue."

"Well, then," Rathburn said, "I must be given a
tour of this fine estate. Lead the way." He smiled. It
was beautiful.

Victoria felt her heart pick up speed, but she
pressed on, looking up the lane toward the rocky
cliff in the distance. "A . . . very odd history, disturbing at times, sometimes quite remarkable and quite
romantic."

"Romantic?"

"Yes, well . . ." Victoria said. She cleared her
throat and then wished she hadn't. It sounded so
insecure. "I'm sure a family member could tell it better, but I sometimes feel that I belong here and that I
know the place as well as any Collins."

The trees along the lane opened to reveal a wide
stretch of wind-ravaged grasses and thistles sil-
vered by moonglow, with a barely visible path leaving the lane and winding through the weeds out to
a huge outcropping of rock and the sheer drop
beyond it. Halfway up the path Victoria began to
slow down. This place had always disturbed her.

Why had she brought Thomas here? There were enough other places to share—the old stable, the old swimming pool, even the Old House that Barnabas occupied.

But here? She stopped and pretended to adjust her gloves. She didn't want to go much closer. From here, over the repeating song of the owl and the whistling of the wind through the grasses, she could hear the roar of the ocean below the cliffs. She could taste the salt on the air.

"What is it, Victoria?" Rathburn asked. "I sensed your fear before we even left the lane. What is this place?"

"Widows' Hill."

"An ominous title."

"An ominous place," Victoria said. "I don't want to go much closer, if you don't mind."

The man took her elbow. She felt an indescribable feeling surge through her body; not warmth, but something as powerful as a blow. She found herself leaning into him to keep from toppling over.

"Thank you," she managed, although she knew it was he who was making her feel weak. Weak, yes, but not bad.

Not bad at all.

"Why is it called Widows' Hill?" Rathburn asked. She could smell his aftershave and soap. She felt the solid strength of his body. For a moment she had to think to herself, *breathe*.

"Because of the women who died there," she managed. "They killed themselves, jumping off the rocks, to be smashed between the tide and the granite. So sad, so incredibly sad." She could feel the hand on her elbow caressing lightly, encouraging her. "Wives of sailors mostly, who had gone to sea and never returned."

"I see."

"Love ending in tragedy. Love ending in nothing but heartbreak and disaster."

"Yes. Tragic, indeed, untimely deaths."

"Mr. Rathburn—"

"Thomas."

"Yes, Thomas," Victoria said. She did not want to look at him directly because there were tears brimming her eyes, tears for ancient pains and torments she knew intimately, some that made sense and others that made no sense at all, and her tears would embarrass her. They would make her feel vulnerable when at this very moment all she wanted was to be strong. But her head turned up on its own accord as though commanded. She saw his eyes, was locked in his gaze, and the words spilled out as if he had reached in and squeezed her soul.

"Thomas, do you believe it's possible to have a connection to the past? I know we all have connections, family, ancestors, and such. But I mean a firsthand connection. Do you believe it's possible to have actually been somewhere in the past, to have gone there and experienced what is there, as surely as you and I are standing on this knoll?"

"Go on."

"I've had hallucinations, strange memories, of having been here at Collinwood in the distant past." She broke away, moving back several feet. This was all too intense, too intimate.

But he stepped up to her and touched her shoulder. "Yes?"

She had no choice but to continue. "I don't mean dreams, mind you, but recollections so real that sometimes I remember a taste, a smell, a touch as if it were happening again. They are frightening memories and they are sad. If they are even memories."

Rathburn nodded. The moon above was swept behind a cloud on the cold wind, and his features disappeared, yet still she could see his eyes. His green, almost surreal eyes.

"Do you think it's possible for someone to have lived in the past for a time? To have known people of the past as surely as I know Elizabeth and Roger and David? Or do you think I'm losing my mind?" Suddenly the rim of tears in her eyes were floods. They spilled down her face. She had never spoken these things aloud before.

"Victoria," Rathburn said, "in all my life experiences, I've never found reason to rule out the extraordinary."

"No?"

"No. And you have no reason to cry. What is, is. Questioning, wrestling with it, trying to make what is real unreal is a waste of effort. Here . . ." He wiped her cheeks with his ungloved hands. There was a rush of blood in her head, as loud as the rush of the sea, drowning out her thoughts for a moment. It was a blessing. "There is more you want to tell me," he said.

There was, though until this moment she did not know she would say it. "This morning at the inn, the sheriff was looking for you. He wanted to question you about something. About . . ."

"About?"

"Well, certainly nothing that would have any validity, of course," she said. "But a man disappeared last night, and being the small community that we are . . ." She hesitated. She didn't want Thomas to think poorly of the citizens, regardless of the way they were often suspicious of new things, new people.

"What is it?"

"Sheriff Patterson wanted to talk to you, to question you about a man who went missing. An old fisherman."

"Sheriff Patterson," Rathburn said, as if tasting the name in his mouth. His expression didn't change, but one eyebrow went up. "And what did you tell this member of Collinsport's finest?"

"I lied to him."

A smile. Unreadable, but enough to make Victoria feel he knew her thoughts. *You remind me of someone I've known before,* she thought. *Someone who bears the weight of the years on his shoulders. Who do you resemble? Who are you, Thomas Rathburn?*

She continued, "Well, Carolyn told the sheriff you weren't in, although we had just left your room. And I backed up her story."

"Why did you do that?"

She shook her head, only able to say, "I honestly don't know. I don't lie. It's not like me to tell things that aren't true."

Rathburn looked off for a moment, past her to some distant point. He said, "I wonder. After your conversation with the sheriff, do you believe you have reason to distrust me?"

"Oh, no," she said.

"Are you quite certain, Victoria?"

The sound of her own name on his lips made her breath catch. She felt unsteady again.

"Victoria?"

"I . . ." she began, but couldn't finish. Why did she feel so strange around this man? Why did she feel wonderful and nervous at the same time? Was this what it felt like to fall in love? She couldn't remember ever truly falling in love before. There was one man, Burke Devlin, whom she'd known for a while when she first arrived in Collinsport. Had she loved him, and he her? She thought maybe they would have come to that had he not been killed in a plane crash. And then there was Barnabas. She knew full well he had a romantic interest in her. But although there had been a time earlier when she might have felt the same way, something had happened, something she couldn't clearly recall, that left her feeling uneasy and had made her withdraw from him. As sad as it was, there was nothing she could do about it.

"Victoria, are you all right?" He was looking at her again.

She nodded slightly. "I think I am. Certainly, of course I am."

"I should like to look over the cliffs," he said. "I'll be just a moment." He strolled toward the rocks, leaving her alone in the rustling grasses and the rattling thistles. Rathburn stood with his back to her, staring out over the sea. The long coat billowed in the wind, his arms reaching out as if beckoning for something to come to him.

Come to me. Come to me.

The voice that spoke in her mind was masculine and overwhelming. It had no familiar human tone, but resounded with an ancient power that was both ultimately desirable and terrifying. It was a voice of her longing, a voice of her greatest fears. Deep within her chest she felt her lungs lock in cold, frozen dread. Deep within her she felt the burning fire of urgent desire.

Come to me.

She began to walk toward Thomas.

Who is speaking? What is happening?

And then there was a shadow moving above, streaking the grass and path with its quick, fluttering motions. Victoria glanced up.

"A bat," she said.

Rathburn turned back to look.

The bat was large, dark, and, but for the leather beat of its wings, silent against the night sky.

"Just a bat," Victoria said. "A large one, but it's no harm. It just startled me."

But Rathburn moved quickly down the path to where she stood, his face set and grim as if there might be true danger. He put his arm around her shoulder and glared up at the agile animal.

"It's only a bat," Victoria repeated. "Collinwood has a lot of them. Some nest in the old carriage house, others in the eaves of the old swimming pool. I'd have thought they would be hibernating by now, as late as it is in the year, but I'm not surprised there's a holdout. One who will wait till the last minute. It's nothing to be concerned about."

"I'm sure you are correct," Rathburn said. "But it's cold and I feel you shivering. Shall I take you back to the main house and see the cottage on my own?"

"No, I'll show you. But let's walk quickly, and not on the lane but across the lawn and through the old orchard to outrun Jack and his frosty knives."

"Such a saying."

"We used to say it back home at the orphanage. The heating system in the old dorms was poor, and the girls used to tease each other at night when it was time to get into bed. 'Jump, quick, onto your mattress before Jack can catch you with his frosty knives!'"

"Charming."

"Not really. Scared us to death, thinking of something in the dark coming at us to kill us."

"But you're an adult now."

"Yes," Victoria said. "Well . . . and Jack is nothing more than ice on a car windshield or a frozen skim on the top of a pond."

"Then lead on. I'll trust you to take me where we need to go."

They walked back to the lane, through a narrow line of trees and onto the wet grass of a vast, sloping stretch of lawn.

"There are no snakes this time of year," Victoria said. "Don't worry, they should be hibernating by now, not out on the prowl looking for ankles to bite or pant legs to run up."

Thomas laughed. "I'm not worried."

Victoria was keenly aware that she was walking with her arms to her sides. Drawing on every ounce of courage, she reached out and slipped her arm through his.

"Thank you," he said.

"Really?"

Rathburn nodded.

Victoria laughed, shook her head and said, "You're welcome, Mr. Rathburn."

They walked in silence for several moments, until Victoria heard the fluttering sounds again. From above. They were faint, but they were close.

"What . . . ?" she began, jerking her head back to see.

The huge, black bat nearly brushed her face as it dove between her and Rathburn and then darted up again. She jumped backward, flailing her arms to keep it away. "Dear God!" she cried. "What on earth is wrong with it?"

"I don't know," Thomas said coolly.

The bat arched the air, then hurtled down again, and with what sounded like a hiss lashed its wing-bound claws at the couple on the ground. Victoria ducked, and Thomas raised his hands above her head to protect her. The bat dove again, coming within inches of the two, then up again, then back down, close enough for Victoria to see the glint of cold red in its eyes.

"Thomas!" she screamed.

"Stay still!" Rathburn ordered.

The bat circled above their heads, and then, in an eye's wink, vanished into the black shadows of the trees back by the lane.

"That was incredible," Victoria said, her hand to her throat, staring after the creature and breathing heavily. "I've not had that happen before! Are you all right?"

"I'm fine," Thomas replied, lowering his hands and holding one out. Victoria took it and held it, more tightly than she intended. "And you?"

"Oh, yes, yes," she said, aware that her shaky voice betrayed her. "Though I've not witnessed it myself, I've heard tell that late season animals sometimes lose their senses and go a little batty." She tried a smile. Rathburn didn't seem in the mood for humor.

"Victoria, let's go back to the manor house," he said. "You are cold and we both were startled. I don't need to see the cottage to decide I want to lease it. I'm sure it's fine."

"You don't? But it might not be at all what you have in mind. You may take one look and realize it is too much to straighten up, too much to dust, perhaps too small. The Collinsport Inn may seem like a great deal once you see the cottage."

But Rathburn took her chin in his hand and said, "Let me just say this. Tonight I have realized there is nowhere I'd rather stay but here on this estate. I'd settle for the old stable if I had to."

"Yes?"

Rathburn nodded.

"And what should we tell Elizabeth and Roger?"

"That it was too dark to see inside. That it looked fine from our vantage point, that it is all I need and I'll be most comfortable."

Victoria grinned widely. "That we shall tell them, then!"

Rathburn nodded, and the two turned back toward the mansion up the long slope. But for a brief moment Victoria noticed Rathburn's interest shift from her to the line of trees where the bat had flown. And the cold, grave expression on his face made her think he was watching the retreat of a hated enemy.

8

A gust of frosty wind swirled in through the front door as Rathburn escorted Vicki back into the house, a few stray leaves following them inside. He felt a little swell of satisfaction in finding that she still held his hand, which meant he had gone a long way toward earning her trust. He released her hand to help her off with her jacket, which he hung on the coatrack for her.

"Did you get to take a look at the cottage, Mr. Rathburn?" asked Elizabeth, who appeared in the drawing room doorway, holding a cup of hot tea.

"As you said, it was very dark down there. But what I saw of it looked to suit me just fine. I can move into it tomorrow, if that's all right with you."

"Of course. I'll have a copy of a standard lease agreement made for you so it will be ready tomorrow morning."

"Wonderful."

"I hope you two enjoyed your walk. It's beginning to get quite chilly at night, but it looks like a nice evening."

Vicki nodded. "Yes, it is." She gave Rathburn a smile.

Elizabeth nodded. "By the way, Mr. Rathburn, since you don't have a car here, would you be interested in using one of ours? I can include it for a very minimal fee. It would certainly be more convenient than renting one from the village."

"I'd hate to put you out any further."

"Nonsense. We have one that is seldom used, so it would be no bother."

"Well," Rathburn said, pleased to have seemingly won over the Collins family so readily, "it would be handy. I doubt I'll be out and about all that much, but it would save me from having to make other arrangements anytime I want to go somewhere."

"Indeed. It has a good many miles on it, but it's in excellent condition. I'll get the keys for you and you can take it tonight, so you can use it to help you move in at your convenience."

"That's very kind, Mrs. Stoddard. Thank you."

Elizabeth left in search of the extra car keys, and Victoria turned to Rathburn and said softly, "I enjoyed the company, Thomas. Very much. Thank you."

"It was my pleasure."

"Do you have to leave now?"

"I really should be going. But as of tomorrow, I'll be your neighbor. I'm sure I'll be seeing much more of you. In fact, I'm looking forward to it."

"That sounds nice."

Moments later Elizabeth reappeared with a set of keys, which she handed to Rathburn. "The car is parked in the drive behind the house. It's the beige Buick."

Just then, a knock sounded at the front door, and Rathburn was surprised to see Vicki flinch nervously, a dark shadow of apprehension falling over her features. When Elizabeth went to answer, Vicki backed away slowly toward the drawing room and took a deep breath, as if she dreaded seeing whoever might be at the door. Rathburn felt a charge in the air, an electrical current building in intensity as Elizabeth reached for the handle and pulled the door open, revealing a solitary, hatless figure, his face hidden within the darkness of the porte cochere.

The caller stepped inside, and Rathburn felt a peculiar mélange of both trepidation and almost ecstatic fascination. *The man in the portrait, come to life.* He wore the now familiar black Inverness coat and held the same silver wolf's-headed walking stick that Rathburn had glimpsed in his visions. On the forefinger of his right hand he wore a large, onyx ring with a gold band. His deep hazel eyes were hidden beneath a prominent brow, over which his dark hair fell in several comma-shaped locks. He smiled warmly at his cousin and said in a low but sonorous voice, "Good evening, Elizabeth. I didn't realize you had company tonight. I hope I'm not intruding."

"Not at all, Barnabas." She motioned to Rathburn and said, "This is Mr. Thomas Rathburn, from Atlanta, Georgia. He is going to be staying on the estate for a time, in the old guest cottage. Mr. Rathburn, this is our cousin, Barnabas Collins."

"I gathered as much," Rathburn said, extending his hand and taking the other's in a firm grip. *Cool skin.* "I was told you resembled the portrait of your ancestor. I should say you do."

Barnabas Collins gazed impassively at him. "So I've been told." He turned his attention to Victoria, who still stood at the drawing room entrance wearing an expression of ill-concealed alarm. Barnabas's own face clouded with concern. "Good evening, Vicki."

"Hello, Barnabas," she said quietly.

From the drawing room, Roger Collins appeared behind her, holding a refreshed glass of cognac. "Good evening, Barnabas," he said with an air of vague annoyance. "I thought it might be you, at this hour."

"Hello, Roger. Perhaps I've come at a bad time."

"Well, no worse than any other. I don't suppose you would care for a drink, would you? No, I didn't think so."

Barnabas smiled with some amusement, apparently accustomed to his cousin's acerbic demeanor. "So, Mr. Rathburn, what brings you to Collinsport?"

It was difficult to resist the temptation to say, *Why, you do.* "Well, I'm taking an extended holiday from my business and doing some traveling. I came upon Collinsport, and I've so far found it to be a most hospitable little town. It makes the idea of early retirement not altogether unappealing."

"I see," Barnabas replied, a flicker of wariness in his eyes. "There isn't much in Collinsport to occupy a young man such as yourself, I wouldn't think."

"I keep hearing that. But believe me, it may be just the change I am looking for. I'm not as young as I look." Rathburn gave the other man a wry smile.

"If you'll excuse me, I'm very tired," Victoria said. "I think I'm going to go upstairs to bed."

"I trust you're feeling all right?" Barnabas asked, his face again filled with concern.

After a moment's hesitation, she said, "I'm fine. It's been a long day, and David was a handful, as usual."

Rathburn decided to tempt fate. He stepped up to her and said, "I enjoyed the evening very much. Thank you for being so gracious."

Her smile to him was warm, if still nervous. "I had a nice time, too."

"Could I interest you in having dinner with me tomorrow night? I'm sure it would do us both good to get out, wouldn't you say?"

He noted that she consciously kept her eyes averted from Barnabas's. With a nod, she said, "That sounds nice."

Rathburn broke into a broad grin, aware that Barnabas Collins was watching him with rising disapproval. "Good. Seven o'clock suit you?"

"That'll be fine."

He took her hand and gave it an affectionate squeeze, though this time she did not return it. Watching after her as she went up the stairs, he felt the dark eyes behind him boring into his back, which only intensified the feeling that he'd been triumphant in this round. *Excellent.*

There was one other matter he needed to take care of before he left. As he turned back to the others, he focused on Elizabeth and *pushed* with his mind. *Success*, he thought, for after a moment she blinked her eyes in bewilderment and took a faltering step forward.

"Goodness," she said. "Suddenly I'm feeling rather faint."

Before the others could react, Rathburn stepped quickly to her side and took her hand, guiding her slowly toward the drawing room while Roger and Barnabas followed. As he helped her sit down on the velvet-upholstered divan in front of the fireplace, he gazed deeply into her eyes for a second, just long enough to get what he needed without being obvious. He kept hold of her hand for a few moments, rubbing the back of it with his own.

"Are you all right, Mrs. Stoddard?"

"What's wrong, Elizabeth?" Roger asked, all brotherly concern, putting his drink down and kneeling before her.

"I'm all right now," she said, rubbing her forehead. "Thank you, Thomas. I just felt a little unsteady there. Silly of me."

"You're probably overtired," Roger said.

"I hope I haven't caused you too much trouble tonight," Rathburn said, feeling a measure of satisfaction at the scene he had wrought.

"No, no, of course not. Think nothing of it, I'm fine."

"Still, I can't help but feel responsible."

"Don't be silly. Roger, would you get me a cup of tea, please?"

"Of course," Roger said. But before leaving the room, to Rathburn's surprise, Roger shot an accusing glance at Barnabas, as if Elizabeth's sudden spell might be his cousin's fault. Barnabas appeared oblivious—or apathetic—to the affront.

It's getting better all the time.

When Roger returned with Elizabeth's tea, Rathburn said, "I should leave now. I don't want to tax your energy any further."

"Your concern is most kind, but I assure you I'm fine now," Elizabeth said, rising from the couch. "I'll at least see you to the door."

Barnabas now stepped in and took her arm, making sure she was steady on her feet. They walked with Rathburn to the door, where he retrieved his hat from the top of the coatrack. He shook hands with Roger and gave Elizabeth a grateful smile. "Thanks again for your hospitality. I'll stop by tomorrow for the lease, but it may be in the evening, if that's all right."

"Whatever suits you best. Good night, Thomas."

Rathburn then extended his hand to Barnabas. "Mr. Collins. It was a pleasure to meet you. I'm sure I will be seeing you again."

"I think we can count on that," Barnabas said, shaking his hand while eyeing him as if sizing up a potential rival. "I'm sure you have many interesting tales to tell. About life in the South."

"Yes, I'm sure we could learn a lot from each other. Until another time, then."

"Good night, Mr. Rathburn."

As he opened the door and stepped out into the night, he turned back briefly and said, "Oh, and feel free to call me Thomas. All my friends do."

"I'll remember that," Barnabas said.

The door closed behind him and Rathburn set off along the flagstone walk that led to the back of the house, where he would find his newly leased car. The evening had been eventful, he thought. Stimulating. He had now made contact with the two key figures from his visions. And though he could prove nothing yet, he suspected there was far more to Barnabas Collins than anyone else—save perhaps the sender of his visions—could possibly begin to guess.

Somewhat disappointingly, his exploration of Elizabeth's psychic potential during her "faint spell" had turned up a dead end. She was certainly a woman who hid many fears and strange secrets, some of which seemed to revolve around Victoria, though none was relevant to his own situation, as best he could determine. She had been highly vulnerable to his supersensory influence, and was obviously quite incapable of having contacted him telepathically.

He found the car parked in a small circular lot a short distance behind the house, from where he could see the extensive stable complex a few dozen yards to the southeast. In the moonlight the gray shingled roof of the main stable building gleamed a phosphorescent silver, and he could hear the faint snuffling of horses within, undetectable to ordinary human ears. Before getting into the car, he looked around, listened, and scented the air, just to verify that he was alone in the darkness. For the moment all was clear.

He slid behind the wheel, started the engine, and pulled the car out of the lot onto the narrow gravel back road that led toward the cottage. To the right, he could see the massive dark house looming over him; to the left, dense woods led down a steep embankment toward the mouth of the Narraguagus River, a half mile or so distant. He drove slowly, his headlights wavering erratically as the car bounced along the deeply pitted road. A few hundred yards farther on he saw the shadowed hulk of the old, original stable building, half crumbling and ravaged by invading vines and creepers; and just past it, the gnarled limbs of dozens of barren apple trees in what had once been a lush orchard. And then, ahead and to his left, hiding amid the overhanging limbs of many tall oaks, the northwest cottage, dark and deserted, seeming to lie in wait for him with an air of expectation.

He turned into the short gravel drive that led down to the cottage's side door and shut off the engine. The house was two stories, but still quite small, with a steeply sloping roof and a small veranda facing the road. As he got out of the car he paused, hearing the chattering of night life as he hadn't heard it in a long, long time. The erratic rhythms of the crickets, owls, and whippoorwills reminded him of his simple youth when such sounds were commonplace. Yes, for all its potentially direful secrets, this place had its pleasant side, especially in that it had introduced him to the lovely and mysterious Victoria Winters.

He unlocked the cottage door and stepped inside, the odor of age and mildew washing over him in noisome greeting. He took a moment to let his eyes adjust to the almost total darkness, his supersensitive night vision beginning to take in his surroundings with a clarity that in some ways surpassed his eyesight in the light. Augmented by his keen hearing, his perception of distance became more acute, with objects assuming crystalline shadow patterns that defined space as clearly as if under direct sunlight.

He stood in a small living room with sparse furnishings: a couch and wing chair before an almost disproportionately large fireplace, a pair of end tables, a serving bureau and a bookcase, all covered with a thick layer of dust and spun with cobwebs. The walls were bare, any decorative items that might have once hung there long since removed. Through a door at the far end of the room he found a small kitchen, also choked with dust, and a door that opened to a stairwell, with flights running both up and down. Taking the one leading down, he found himself in a tiny basement with no windows; just a water heater and a few old boxes. An ideal place to put a cot where he could sleep during the day.

Upstairs he found a single bedroom and bathroom, neither of which would serve much purpose for him. But for appearance's sake he would have to give them, like the rest of the house, a thorough cleaning at the earliest possibility. Going to the grimy window, he found himself looking out at the small front yard and his parked car. On the other side of the gravel road, under the pale moonlight, he could see the scraggly apple orchard and the lower lawn of the estate, which climbed to the right and out of sight beyond the nearby woods. The grim old mansion with all its secrets hid behind the trees, all except for the apex of the unlit tower, which peered over the treetops as if seeking a glimpse of the unfathomed newcomer to its domain.

Rathburn tugged the window open and leaned out, glancing up at the waxing sickle of the moon. He could feel Victoria Winters across the vast space between them, almost catch her now familiar scent on the breeze that swept lightly across the lawns and through the trees. Something in his blood stirred, something that seemed to him as long forgotten as the ancient pain of the bayonet that had come back to stab him while in the throes of blood lust. It was a throbbing heat; a heartfelt longing to unite with the soul of another, more powerful than any since his passionate love for Elaine, back in his days of human mortality with all its inherent frailties.

A condition to which he could not return. Nor did he desire to return to it, ever again.

Yet Victoria Winters stirred him, moved him to see her as something other than prey or blood slave, unlike any woman he had known in countless years. Long ago he had forgotten loneliness, having been forced to leave that baggage behind in order to survive. But now he remembered the burn of the perpetual isolation he was forced to endure, the emptiness of long years with no one to share his soul on equal terms. Yes, he desired her for more than her blood; he desired her for her spirit. She was a beautiful creature, somehow innocent and unblemished when viewed against the backdrop of the abhorrent race to which she belonged. And to find her tortured by some unidentifiable dread, some spiritual pain inflicted by the unseen hand of another . . .

It angered him.

It was more than just the effect Barnabas Collins had on her. This feeling for her . . . had it truly come from his own heart? Or was it simply another of the orchestrations from *out there*, like those damned visions and the incomprehensible urge to travel north? The very idea of being played like a puppet sent him slamming down the window and turning to the darkness of the room in disgust, clenching his fists at his sides.

He must have complete trust in his own resources, in himself. The one thing he could never forget was that powers existed beyond his understanding. His very existence was due to such a power. Anything that could subvert his spirit and awaken ancient weaknesses could prove fatal. That *something* possessed such a disturbing ability had been proven by his reaction to David Collins. Now more than ever he needed to keep up his guard.

He returned to the downstairs and walked through the house, checking the ground floor for any means of ingress that might need to be fortified in case of unwanted visitors during his more vulnerable hours. Despite being filmed over with grime, the windows all appeared secure, the door sturdy, with both a dead bolt and a chain. Satisfied the cottage afforded him a reasonably safe haven, he dusted off the wing chair in front of the old fireplace and sat down, staring into the darkness, contemplating the subtle vibrations from the past that coursed through the empty abode like brooding, ghostly sighs.

This place was no stranger to dark happenings, he thought.

These were events long past. But was his sense of old danger and fear in some way portentous? What dire events might follow in the days to come that would involve him—and perhaps Victoria Winters as well? He felt his ire rising at the thought, followed by a swell of anxiety for her well-being. He willed it all away, shifting his focus to his own priorities: first, survival; second, comprehension of the forces whose purpose in drawing him here he had yet to determine. And last, but most important . . . revenge.

I did not come here to romance a woman.

Yet the scent of her lingered, if only in his mind,

and his forged steel heart seemed horribly malleable in the hands of an impossible passion for the dark-haired young beauty.

Then, somewhere at the most distant reaches of his hearing, he thought he detected a whisper, one that took several moments for him to realize could only be some kind of false memory, for the voice was one he had not heard in almost a century and a half.

Why impossible, Thomas? After all, your hatred has been alive and well for all these years.

This way, madam, sir," said the hostess with a nod of her head and a gesture of her arm. "You have a table by the window, overlooking the water. The lights from the ships at sea can be quite enchanting at night."

"Thank you," Victoria said. She and Rathburn followed the hostess through the small crowd at the Pennock Supper Club and took their seats at the table-for-two with its white lace tablecloth and fresh rose centerpiece. A delicate hurricane lantern hanging on a post next to the table cast a warm glow over the secluded corner of the restaurant. Across the dining room a fire blazed in a huge stone fireplace, the thick scent of wood smoke mingling with the aroma of spices and cooking meat. The old supper club, reputedly named for a long-dead sea captain of some notoriety, perched on a bluff at Collinsport's northernmost end, its windows facing the small harbor and lights of town a mile or so distant.

Victoria wore a thin, sleeveless black dress that Carolyn had found in the back of Vicki's closet and insisted she wear. The velvet, bead-embroidered jacket Carolyn had selected for her from Elizabeth's wardrobe now hung in the club's cloak room. Although the air in the dining room was warm, Victoria felt chills along the length of her arms. She let her eyes briefly roam around the restaurant, almost wishing she would see a familiar face or two; some of Roger and Elizabeth's business acquaintances, perhaps. Alas. No one that she knew.

I wish the girls who grew up with me could see me now, she thought as Rathburn pulled out her chair. *They would never believe little Vicki Winters was out for the evening with this handsome man. I hardly believe it myself.*

Victoria picked up the wine list and pretended to look it over. Rathburn watched her, his head titled slightly to the side, as if waiting for her to finish so they could talk.

"Nice place, don't you think?" she asked, glancing from the menu and catching Rathburn's steady gaze. "The view must be something in the daylight."

"I think I prefer the night. But you've not been here before?"

"No. I'm not . . . well, no. This is a place for the elite of Collinsport. There aren't a lot of elite, but this is their restaurant. Glance around and you'll see those of the town who have the power, the wealth. Roger and Elizabeth come here. Sometimes they bring Carolyn."

"But not you?"

"Not yet." Victoria shook her head. "But I'm sure they will. They just haven't. Do you want to look at the wine list? I wouldn't begin to choose for you."

"You're having?"

"Chardonnay."

"I'll have the same."

Victoria nodded. She put the menu down on the table. She looked at her fingers, linked on the tablecloth, and suddenly became aware of how utilitarian her fingernails appeared. Though painted by Carolyn in an exotic red, they were short, rounded, filed to a length appropriate for a governess.

She folded her hands in her lap.

A waiter in a white jacket took the wine order and handed them opened meal menus. After he mentioned the specials—poached salmon and blackened tuna steak—Rathburn nodded and told the waiter they would order when the drinks arrived.

"Very cosmopolitan for such a small town," he said with a smile after the waiter turned away. "A pleasant surprise." He was wearing a slate-gray suit with a gray silk tie patterned with tiny threads of red. Gold cuff links peeked from beneath the sleeves of his jacket. His fine, wavy hair caught the light from the lantern on the table. Victoria wondered what he would look like in a casual sweater and jeans, walking barefoot along the soft, warm sands of a southern beach, the sun caressing his face.

"Is there something you wanted to say?" he asked.

Victoria flinched. "Oh, no," she said. She straightened her shoulders and pushed a strand of hair behind her ear. *You need small talk. Carolyn is good at it, you managed last night, so why should the setting make it more difficult? Come on, Vicki.* "So," she said, louder than intended, "tell me about your home in Atlanta. Are you in the city or outside it? A house, town house, castle . . . a brooding mansion like Collinwood?" She laughed softly, hoping she didn't sound juvenile.

"I have several homes."

"Really?"

"A suite in the business district of Atlanta, the top floor of one of the buildings I own."

"*One* of your buildings?"

"Real estate is another interest of mine in addition to publishing," he said.

"Do you like being in the middle of all the city hassle? The crowds?"

"Absolutely. Crowds are essential to my well-being." He winked. "I may seem like a loner to you, but people are very important to me."

"That's good. Liking people, that is." *I wonder if*

he likes me? she thought. *If only he would reach across the table for my hand.*

"I enjoy people a great deal. And I have a lot of respect for Atlanta. It's a friend, a vast and constant companion with much to offer a man like myself."

"You make it sound like it was alive. Like it has a soul." *Like it's aware and conscious, the way you imagine Collinwood to be when you watch the sun go down and the night comes to the estate.*

"Perhaps it does have a soul. An old soul, at that. Atlanta was destroyed during the Civil War, yet the city quickly rose from the ashes. It was reborn, only to become stronger, wiser, more powerful."

Victoria looked past him for a moment at the winking lights through the windows. She became conscious of his persistent gaze again. "Somehow you seem more the country type," she said at last. "Like somebody who would have a lot of land, and spend his free time riding horses."

"I once had a horse farm," he said, with a pleased smile. "I raised Thoroughbreds. But that was a long time ago, before the wa—" He stopped short. "I was much younger. I haven't ridden in years."

She leaned forward with curiosity, wondering what he'd meant to say. "I adore horses. There are several good ones at Collinwood. Since I've been here, I've learned to ride—reasonably well," she added with a grin. "In New York, needless to say, there wasn't exactly a world of opportunity to go horseback riding. But I used to daydream that a horse would find its way inside my dorm room, wearing a big blue bow, just for me. All the other girls would have been jealous, but I would have climbed on and ridden away, never to return."

Rathburn smiled. "I can see you riding."

Before she realized it, she found herself asking, "Would you like to go riding with me at Collinwood? It's the perfect place for it. Two hundred acres."

His green eyes for a moment seemed to flash with a youthful exuberance. But then a shadow crossed his face and the reticence he'd briefly shown before returned. "I'm afraid I can't. My eyes, you see. The iritis prevents me from certain activities during the day. I'm very limited in the amount of time I can spend outdoors."

"Oh, I see," Victoria said, abashed that the thought had not occurred to her. She remembered how he'd been closed up in the dark room at the inn. The idea of riding by moonlight might be a reasonable possibility, but now didn't seem to be the appropriate time to bring it up. He might be more sensitive about his medical condition than she had realized.

"Thank you anyway, Victoria," he said. "I appreciate the offer. But even if I could, it's been so long . . . so long, that I'm afraid horses and I might not exactly get along as we used to."

As she looked at him, she felt a strange heat on her neck. She rubbed the spot, then realized how odd it looked and stopped.

"I guess sometimes it's hard to look back at something you used to enjoy but can't do anymore," she said softly.

"That," he said slowly, turning to look out the window at the black sea. His face was thrown into shadow. "And so much more." These words were soft and almost unintelligible.

"Are you all right, Thomas?"

He looked back at her. "Of course," he said with a nod. Victoria suddenly wondered what he looked like without the suit jacket, without the silk tie and the white shirt. He would be muscular and lean. He would have a chest covered with the same light brown hair as on his head, and it would be soft, sensuous. She could imagine her fingers on his skin, in his hair, moving gently, swirling, probing. Her breath caught in her throat with a soft click.

"Victoria? What is it?"

He can't read your mind. Don't let fantasies get the best of you.

"The wine, here it is," she said as the waiter appeared to pour two glasses. She sipped hers, grateful to have something else on which to focus for a moment. "It's good."

Victoria then ordered a shrimp salad and braised perch. Rathburn ordered only conch chowder, saying he did not have much of an appetite.

"You know," she said in a soft, conspiratorial voice after the waiter was gone. "Some consider conch chowder to be an aphrodisiac."

"Is that right?" Rathburn replied, sitting back.

"Yes, and I can't believe I said that. I'm sorry."

"Don't be," he said with an amused smile. "I like a woman to say what she is thinking."

"You do?"

"Yes. And so, Victoria, I'd like you to tell me about yourself."

Victoria shook her head. "So much time, so little to tell."

"I mean it sincerely. Last night on our walk you told me about the estate. In the car tonight and just now I've been telling you about myself. But what about you?"

"When I was a baby, someone apparently left me at the orphanage with a note saying 'I cannot take care of her.' But someone—I've never been able to learn who—continued to send money for me, every month. Really. So, that's where I was from the time I was a baby until I graduated at eighteen. But I stayed on, teaching the younger girls there at the small institutional school until I received an offer from Collinwood to come and be governess for David Collins."

"Quite a sheltered life you've led," Rathburn said.

"Yes, it has been. But I consoled myself as a teenager by imagining myself as Jane Eyre. Do you know the story?"

"Certainly."

Victoria spread her hands flat on the tabletop and leaned into them. "I felt myself much like that girl, raised without family, stoic, determined, destined for excitement and love somewhere in the not-too-distant future." Victoria stopped. "I can't believe I told you that, either."

"Why not?"

"It's very personal. I'm no Jane Eyre. Life isn't a romance novel. It is life, and that's that. The Collins family has been most kind to me, and in spite of their eccentricities, I care a great deal for them. It's more than most people have, you know? Many people don't have anyone to care for."

"True, true. But why did the Collins family seek you out? Certainly there were young women much closer geographically they could have hired."

"I don't know," Victoria replied.

"You know," he said, narrowing his eyes thoughtfully at her, "it seems to me you bear a resemblance to Elizabeth."

Victoria looked at Rathburn sharply. "You think so?"

"Yes. Don't tell me you haven't noticed, or that others haven't made the same observation."

"Not really," she said. But Rathburn had

touched on something she'd wondered about before. Why, indeed, had the Collins family asked for her, when there were so many miles between New York and Collinsport? Yes, she had registered with New England Home Enterprises, an organization that specialized in placing only the highest qualified domestics, au pairs, and governesses. Her references from the orphanage school were impeccable. *But still*, she thought as Rathburn watched her, *still I dream of a romantic ending, like Jane. I dream that the Collinses are my real family, and that they have brought me home. But if I say it, if I ever say it out loud, the dream will shatter like a mirror on the floor, leaving nothing but jagged shards of a wonderful illusion.*

"Excuse me." Sheriff Patterson stood beside the table, in uniform, a wrinkled coat obscuring most of it. He smelled strongly of cigar smoke.

"Hello, Sheriff," Victoria said, putting down her glass. "Are you stalking us?"

"Good evening, Miss Winters," he said, and gave Rathburn a polite but cool smile. "May I assume you are Mr. Rathburn?"

"You may," Rathburn said with an equally polite smile. "I understand you were looking for me yesterday. I am sorry we missed each other."

"You knew I was looking for you?" Patterson asked.

"Yes," Rathburn said. "I'm told you wanted to question me on something. The proprietor of the

Collinsport Inn told me yesterday evening as I prepared to go to Collinwood."

"What is your business in Collinsport, if you don't mind my asking?"

"No business in particular. Just pleasure." He looked at Victoria and smiled. She found herself suddenly imagining what it would be like to be in his arms at that moment, feeling his body against hers.

"Do you intend to stay long?"

"I'm not sure."

"Mr. Rathburn is a guest of Roger and Elizabeth," Victoria interjected. "They have rented him a cottage on the estate."

"I see," Patterson said. He scratched his nose and rubbed one eye. Maybe he had hoped to have an upper hand here, and it had been taken away, Victoria thought. "Well, Mr. Rathburn, I'm sure you've probably guessed why I came to talk to you. A local fisherman has gone missing, and I had to question anyone of suspicion."

"I was a suspect?"

"I only said 'of suspicion.' Any stranger in town would have fit that category. Got to watch out for our own, Mr. Rathburn." He reached into his pocket and withdrew a faded photograph of a grizzled, ruddy-faced character holding up a mammoth sea bass. "I picked this up since I saw you last, Miss Winters. That's Jack Howard. I don't suppose you would recognize him from the tavern?"

"No," Victoria said.

"Mr. Rathburn? Look familiar to you at all?"

Rathburn raised a brow and shook his head. "Without meaning to be callous, Sheriff, one old fisherman looks much like another. I don't think I saw that one."

"Sheriff," Victoria said, "you don't really suspect foul play, do you?"

"I hope not, Miss Winters. To be honest, Jack's getting pretty feeble, and has a penchant for alcohol. He might well have fallen off a pier and drowned. But his wife insists that I cover every angle. She's pretty hysterical. I suppose some lucky lemon shark could be having his way with the body parts as we speak. Pardon the reference, Miss Winters."

"That's all right," Victoria said, aware that her disgust had been obvious on her face.

"Well," Patterson said. "I don't want to wear out my welcome, and it looks like you two are having a nice dinner, so I'll be on my way."

"I should be most interested if anything new develops in the case of the fisherman," Rathburn said.

"I'll get back to you." Paterson crossed the restaurant, nodding to several patrons on his way out.

"Nothing like having a police officer make a special point of tracking you down to name you an ex-suspect of an imaginary crime in the middle of a first date," Rathburn said with a touch of wry amusement in his voice. "Is this a lovable touch of Collinsport culture?"

"I don't imagine the sheriff gets out much . . . socially." Victoria grinned. If Thomas was annoyed, he certainly didn't show it.

"In the South, tact is a more commonly practiced virtue. Ah, well. There is little that I would let spoil this evening." With that, he took her hand across the table and began to stroke the palm of her hand with his thumb.

His skin felt strangely cool. *So much like Barnabas's . . .*

A strong, electric charge ran from her hand to her shoulder. She flinched and drew back, but he held on tightly.

"Victoria, don't fight it," Rathburn said in a near whisper. "Whatever you are feeling, trust it. Trust me."

Victoria opened her mouth to speak, but only a long sigh escaped her lips. What was this? It was happening again, the same as last night, the sense of drifting, of losing control.

"Tell me, Victoria," Rathburn said, so softly she thought he might only be sending her thoughts across the space of the table and the dancing lantern light. "Tell me about Barnabas."

Her voice came, seemingly from far away. "I don't know what to tell you."

Rathburn's eyes widened, then narrowed, making it seem as though they burned with a luminescence not from the candle but from within. "What do you feel for him?"

"We were close. . . ." she began.

"Yes?"

"Several months ago, things were becoming . . . romantic. But then it changed."

"What do you mean?"

When Victoria tried to pull her hand away, she saw her hand come loose and felt herself jump up from the chair, knocking it over onto the floor. But the action only took place in her mind. Her hand stayed in Rathburn's. She remained seated. And the words flowed from her as though he'd taken a plug from her heart, and they were flowing freely like blood from a wound.

"Something happened that I can't remember. But ever since, I have been afraid of him."

"Roger and Elizabeth seem uneasy around him, too."

"I don't know if it is the same thing, but when he comes near me now, I feel cold. I want to run. I see love in his eyes, but I want to escape as quickly as I can." She lowered her eyes, not wanting to face his penetrating stare. "I'm sorry. I'm embarrassed, Thomas."

"Victoria, look at me."

She looked again. His eyes glowed, swirling with ice blue and blood red, and she felt herself falling under his spell.

Help me!

"Victoria, tell me."

Help me!

And then she was in total darkness, helplessly spinning as if tied to a string and buffeted by the wind. There were voices chattering around her, stinging her ears with their shrillness.

And then there were flashes of memory. They came like frames in a dreadful slide show: close, terrifying, holding but a moment before flicking away to be replaced by another.

A little girl dressed in clothes of an older century, her face twisted with fear, waving her arms as if warning her of danger.

A beautiful blond woman with the smile of the devil, her turquoise eyes dancing with glee, blood on her hands.

Collinwood on a dark hillside with only candlelight in its cold, grim windows.

Help me!

God, help me please!

And then there was something around her neck, tightening, cutting into her flesh, crushing her windpipe, and she was swinging in the wind by a rope, spinning into a vortex of pain and insanity. Blood roared in her ears.

I'm dying!

"Victoria!"

She opened her eyes to find Rathburn standing over her, holding her face in his hands. She coughed, caught her breath, coughed again. The pain in her throat subsided immediately, but the expressions of concern on the faces of the other patrons did not. A woman whispered to her husband from behind her menu, and another raised a cloth napkin to her mouth. A waiter cut eyes at the couple by the window as he whisked trays about.

"Are you all right, Victoria?" Rathburn asked.

"Yes," Victoria said. "Yes, I am." She took a sip of wine. "Please sit down. I never wanted to cause a scene."

"No scene," Rathburn said as he gave her face one last gentle pat and then returned to his chair. "You just seemed to go faint for a moment."

"Did I say anything?"

"A few things. Disjointed things. Nothing was very clear."

Victoria sighed and gritted her teeth. He thought she was unstable. He thought she was touched.

Oh, isn't this just wonderful.

"Ah, our food is here," he said.

The waiter gave Victoria a curious glance as he placed the plates and bowls on the table, but with a curt nod from Rathburn, he left without hesitation.

As they ate, the conversation returned to how fine the food and drink was, and how lovely the view of the village was, and though she was mortified about her earlier behavior, nothing more was said about her episode. Before they left, Rathburn made a brief stop in the rest room.

The drive back to Collinwood was much too quick, and as Rathburn parked his car in the drive and got out to escort her to the front door, Victoria wished there was something she could say to delay the parting. Something she could do to slow down the final minutes.

I may never be alone with him again, she thought as he helped her from the passenger seat and she pulled her coat more tightly around herself. *If he thinks something is wrong with me, this may be the last time we're together.*

He took her arm and they took several steps across the graveled drive.

What can I do? she thought.

But she needed to do nothing, because at that moment, before they reached the pool of light from the fixtures by the door, Rathburn turned to her. He slid his arms around her waist, and before she could think of anything to say, he lowered his face and pressed his lips to hers.

Oh, my God.

She tilted her head back in obedience to his insistent tongue, and opened her mouth to let him explore her. She clung to him, knowing through the fabric of his duster and jacket that his chest was muscular and lean, that his legs were strong.

Dear God!

He kissed her neck, and then her lips again, and she wanted him, she trusted him, and there was nothing else she knew at that moment.

But then he stepped back, took her arm, and without a word ushered her to the door.

"Thank you, Thomas," she whispered. "I had a wonderful time."

"As did I," he said.

She unlocked the door, and when she looked back to where he had stood beside her, he was gone, already in the car, starting the engine. She watched as he drove away, waving hesitantly, knowing he did not see her do so.

I will see him again, she consoled herself as her heartbeat at last began to slow. *He is just a short walk away. He will come again.*

Before she turned to open the door, she heard a fluttering out over the driveway. She squinted into the darkness, and then saw it. A bat, flying on the edge of the shadows as if watching, but this time, instead of attacking, it merely whirled up and into the night sky with a leathery rustle and vanished.

Victoria had begun to open up to him with increasing confidence in his sincerity. That in itself pleased him. But the deeper he explored her mind, her emotions, the more intrigued, the more sympathetic to her—even caring—he became. He refused to consider that there might be more; more was impossible. Unthinkable. Yet this delicate creature stirred latent passions within him, so like Elaine once had. Elaine's memory to him was precious. Nothing could ever change that. And still, her horrible death, and the death of his son, haunted him with an intensity surpassing any feeling he might have for Victoria Winters.

He must cling to this, he told himself. Anger was venom, and venom was power. Controlled and channeled, it was his greatest ally against the dark unknown that still prevailed in this secluded corner of New England. He had been a soldier once, and his solder's discipline still ruled his existence. He could never forget that.

Rathburn drew his 1920s vintage watch from his coat pocket; it was almost one in the morning. By now the inhabitants of Collinwood would almost certainly have retired for the night. There was still a great deal of the old mansion he had not yet seen, and the thought of a clandestine exploration of its many dark rooms appealed to him. No telling what ancient secrets they might reveal. The identity of the killers he had sought for so long, perhaps? From what Victoria told him, much of the house had been closed up for many years, the rooms probably in the condition in which they had been left, complete with old books, photographs, documents . . . any number of clues that might lead him to the end of his quest.

How easy to simply slay them all as they sleep.

Innocent or guilty, at least nothing would be left to chance. Victoria he would spare, even take her back to Atlanta as his bloodmate, willingly or unwillingly. Alas, these people held too high a profile in their community to be eliminated until he was certain of their connection. His trail to Collinsport was traceable, and in the aftermath of such a rampage, the most unappealing alterations to his lifestyle would be necessary.

For now, patience.

He stepped out of the darkness of the cottage

and locked the door behind him. Starting down the
dark back road toward the mansion, he again took
some delight in the musical silence of the night, the
distant whisper of breakers against the rocks, the
calls of frogs and insects that he'd only heard in
memories from a simpler life until he came here.
These had a calming effect on his hypersensitive
nerves, so rattled by the frenzied rush of unfamiliar
feelings and images over the past few days. Happily,
the only discernible hint of human life beyond the
boundaries of the estate was the sound of highway
traffic on the huge suspension bridge over the Narraguagus, some two miles to the north, and even
this he could only detect at the edges of his hearing.
To mortal ears the sound would be imperceptible.

He left the road to cut through the apple
orchard, where the faint aroma of sweet fruit lingered, though only a few small, misshapen apples
remained on the ground. The skeletal limbs clacked
noisily together as a gust of cool wind came rushing
down the hill from the direction of the mansion,
which he could now see vaguely silhouetted against
the starry sky on the hill far above him, all of its windows darkened.

The lower lawn rose steadily toward the house,
the stands of trees to either side pressing closer and
closer together until they almost converged near the
top of the hill. As Rathburn reached the crest, he
found himself at the northwest corner of the man-

sion, facing the dark tower and the terrace that ran along the broad west wing. Directly in front of him a pair of spindly linden trees pressed close against the house, most of their leaves piled at their trunks, but for a few stubborn survivors that refused to depart for the season. To his right, a short distance down the hill, he noticed a towering gray giant, its gnarled branches spreading skyward like massive, beckoning arms. Something about the tree captured his attention; taking a few steps toward it, he focused his senses upon it in hopes of understanding any message it might hold for him.

It was a copper beech tree, two hundred years old or more, with a trunk almost ten feet in diameter, its bark wrinkled and ridged like elephant hide. As he drew near, his hackles rose as if to warn him of imminent danger. He laid his hand upon the age-old wood, and was nearly thrown back with a surge of energy through his fingertips. But he clenched his jaw and pressed into the tree, determined to know.

He smelled the lilac perfume that had accompanied his visions, now stronger than ever before; and at the limits of his hearing were distant voices, not from a far place, but from a far time.

A coarse, male voice, intoning: *"We do what we must for thy sake, in thy name. Amen. Prepare yourself for eternity . . . witch!"*

A female voice crying out in terror or fury, which was suddenly silenced.

And as Rathburn looked up into the ascending limbs, for the briefest moment he thought he glimpsed a figure—female, with golden hair—then it was gone, and only the silence of the present night remained.

But the scent of lilac prevailed. He backed away, both bewildered and excited. Again, he thought, something about this place was different from any other he had known, as if it retained the shadows of past events like a trap, occasionally allowing them to seep out to be received by one possessing acute senses such as he. What if the place itself, rather than some individual, had sent the visions to him all those many miles away?

An incredible notion. But beyond the realm of possibilities?

He could not be sure anymore.

His eye was drawn to the northeast corner of the house. There, perhaps a hundred yards away, he saw a pale white shape, misty, yet distinctly feminine in form, drifting slowly across the lawn toward him. The figure seemed to waver in the darkness, as if some ghostly, translucent veil prevented it from being seen clearly.

Rathburn took a few steps in its direction, but in an instant the figure was gone. As he came upon the spot where it had been, the scent of lilac grew even stronger, and the feeling of having encountered this apparition before, in some fashion or another, struck him with almost as much power as the vision from the tree. The air in this spot was painfully frigid.

He recalled Victoria uttering something during her spell at the supper club about a blond woman with the smile of the devil. Turquoise eyes. Blood on her hands. Victoria had carried on about her as she sat transfixed in her chair, bemoaning that she did not know this woman who surely meant to harm her.

Rathburn wondered if his spectral visitor was the same one who had appeared to Victoria and momentarily thrown her life into such turmoil. If so, it now appeared certain that Victoria's broken memories and his own presence here were connected in a way he could not have suspected, nor yet comprehend. But he knew that *something* was being transmitted to him that was inexorably bringing him closer to understanding.

Nearer to vengeance?

He walked back to the old copper beech, regarding it in hopes it might offer some new insight. But it had fallen silent, having vouchsafed all its secrets, at least for now. And as Rathburn stood there, he once again perceived a movement from somewhere near the front of the house.

This time, however, it was no ghostly apparition, but flesh and blood—or something close to it—approaching from what he surmised was the direction of the Old House.

Rathburn slipped quietly beneath the drooping branches of the nearby linden tree and with a firm, mental *push* scattered his atoms to become a living mist, barely cohesive, but with consciousness and physical receptors wholly intact. Conjuring a low breeze, he propelled himself toward the tree trunk and hovered, eagerly anticipating the new arrival. Moments later Barnabas Collins appeared around the corner of the house, complete with Inverness coat and walking stick. The dark figure strode toward the linden trees without hesitation, seemingly confident he was alone in the night. But then he stopped and glanced around suspiciously, as if aware that some-one had passed recently. He did not seem to notice the mist clinging to the trunk, however; and finally he moved beneath the windows near the tower, gaz-ing up at the one that Rathburn intuitively guessed opened into Victoria Winters's room.

He watched as Barnabas focused on the win-dow, eyes gleaming with something more than reflected moonlight. A low, animalistic snarl came from his throat.

That's what I thought.

Since Victoria had spent the evening with him, Rathburn knew that Barnabas would want to glean from her any information about him that he could. If Barnabas were able to summon her hypnotically, he might be able to search her mind, even if he had not bitten her.

Wrong, sir. We can't have that.

Again concentrating on the scattered atoms of his body, Rathburn rearranged them, this time with a different blueprint. Within a few seconds the transformation was complete, and he stood beneath the low branches in the shape of a huge gray wolf, his eyes a luminous green, his long claws razor sharp. He dropped his lower jaw, exposing his fangs, and uttered a deep growl that crept across the space toward Barnabas Collins like a living battle-ax.

Slowly, calmly, the caped figure turned, eyes blazing into the darkness until they met Rathburn's own, extending the challenge. By way of acceptance, Rathburn leaped into the open, landing directly in front of Barnabas Collins, who straightened and lifted his cane, ready to deal his aggressor a deadly blow. Rathburn growled again and rose on his hind legs, standing nearly as tall as his opponent. Throwing back his head, he loosed a shrill, ringing howl, sending a number of sleeping starlings in the nearby trees flapping away. Barnabas did not waver, but took a threatening step forward, brandishing his cane like a club, the silver wolf's head glinting in the moonlight.

Rathburn leaped, his jaws snapping at Barnabas's throat, his weight slamming full force into the other Vampire's body. Barnabas maintained his footing, smashing the head of the cane down on

Rathburn's back. An agonizing electric current shot down Rathburn's spine.

Silver!

He growled again, circling Barnabas on all fours, head lowered and eyes glaring. He lunged forward, slashing at Barnabas's throat with his front claws. Barnabas feinted and avoided the blow. Rathburn knew that in this form, with no means to pierce the other's heart, he could not kill Barnabas. His purpose now was to merely drive the other Vampire away.

Barnabas stubbornly held his ground, ready to lash out. Once again Rathburn howled, and at the corner of his eye he saw a light appear in one of the mansion's lower windows. Barnabas also saw it, and pointed accusingly at him with the end of the cane. Rathburn spread his jaws in a devilish grin and rose a third time, snapping at the cane with his fangs. Barnabas whipped it out of the way and slammed it down, again driving a firebrand of pain through Rathburn's spine.

The effort of maintaining the animal shape was beginning to take a toll on his energy. He had to finish this quickly. He made another circuit around Barnabas, staying well away from the reach of the weapon, growling low in his throat. From the direction of the stables he heard a dog's bark and the shuffle of approaching footsteps. A flashlight beam appeared in the distance, bobbing through the trees as its bearer rushed up the path.

Barnabas lowered the cane and glared murderously at the growling creature before glancing a final time at Victoria Winters's still darkened bedroom window. Then he spun on his heel, his caped coat swirling around him, and suddenly he was gone. A huge bat appeared above the spot where he had stood, and with flapping wings soared into the night, leaving Rathburn to watch after it on quivering paws, blood racing with exhilaration, knowing now that his suspicions about Barnabas Collins had proven correct.

The snuffling sound of the approaching dog and its master's footsteps in the dry leaves prompted him to spin around to observe the newcomer. He saw a figure in a long dark coat, carrying a rifle with a flashlight duct-taped to its barrel, the pit bull's leash wrapped around one wrist. For a moment the human looked for all the world like one of the Union soldiers who had rushed him on that final afternoon, and Rathburn greeted him with a deep roar. In the moonlight he recognized the man as Jake Stiles, the Collinses' hired hand. Stiles drew up short, aiming the light in the direction of the noise. Rathburn knew that the man would be able to see only a pair of luminous green eyes against the dark backdrop of the trees. Stiles drew back with a cry of shock, but kept the presence of mind to release the dog and chamber a round in preparation to shoot.

In a heartbeat Rathburn became mist and swept

across the lawn, leaving a furious and frustrated dog to sniff and circle the ground at the site of the duel. The shot never came, the target now lost, and Rathburn swirled rapidly and unseen toward the ancient beech tree. One thing was for certain: Barnabas Collins would be a force to reckon with, now angry and possibly enlightened as to Rathburn's true nature. For tonight, each had foiled the other's plans.

As Rathburn passed the great copper beech tree, in an abrupt flash he saw a snippet of the attack on his dear Elaine, the brutal murder of his son, again as if witnessed through the eyes of an observer at the scene. He cringed at her screams and the mad laughter of her assailants as they sated their basest cravings with her body, then her blood.

Could the eyes through which he continued to see the dreadful butchery of his family belong to Barnabas Collins?

Had this man—this creature—been the one to orchestrate the attack so many years ago merely to gratify some twisted aspect of his own blood lust?

He was undead. And certainly one of the old ones. The strong ones.

Why else would these images continue to beleaguer him?

Shaking his body as he had in wolf form, Rathburn regained his balance and his thoughts, confident he had learned the answer to at least one question.

The answer that means death for all of you.

He glanced back toward the mansion, then strode across the lower lawn and through the orchard toward the cottage, keeping his eyes peeled and his hearing sharpened in case a particular bat or other unnatural creature might present itself to him. He detected nothing nearby.

He pushed open the cottage's front door and slammed it behind him, then stood in the darkness, taking in the silence and the scents of dust and mice. He was exhausted, having expended a critical amount of energy in his transmutation. He would have to feed again soon to replenish himself.

In that regard, there was only one logical choice.

Yes, he thought, considering the implications of acting on such a choice. *It will do nicely. Very nicely indeed.*

chapter

11

When Thomas Rathburn awoke in the darkness of the cottage basement, he knew immediately that the sun still shone outside the sheltering walls. The jangling of his nerves indicated that someone had set foot within a certain radius of the cottage, and his sampling of the air did not register any familiar scent.

A stranger.

He rose from the old army cot he'd found in an upstairs closet and made his way up the stairs, noting with some dismay that several beams of brilliant sunlight filtered through the drawn blinds to form a blazing striped pattern on the dusty hardwood floor.

He kept his protective clothing—duster and wide-brimmed hat—as well as sunglasses, within easy reach for the very reason that his cottage lay in another's territory, one whose influence might extend to others who suffered no aversion to daylight.

He pulled on his coat, donned his hat and shades, then quietly went to the window that faced the front of the house. Squinting against the hellish rays of the sun, he saw nothing unusual. Several moments later a shadow slid into view, close to the front door. Someone from Collinwood he had not yet met? And when, after a full minute, no knock came, he knew this was not an innocent visitor.

Without making a sound, Rathburn went to the door and listened. Soft, rapid breathing. Someone was nervous. *Good.* He quickly drew open the door, startling a sandy-haired man in a gray sweater and dirty blue jeans.

"Argh!" the man grunted as he stumbled back several steps, his eyes growing huge. In one hand he gripped a long, crudely fashioned walking stick with a sharpened end. It shook visibly.

Rathburn regarded him curiously. Then he asked in his calmest, most commanding voice, "Something I can help you with, my friend?"

The man ran his free hand through his hair nervously. "I'm Willie Loomis," he stammered. "I, uh, work for Mr. Collins."

"Roger Collins?"

"No, uh, Mr. Barnabas Collins."

"If you're looking for Barnabas, I'm afraid he isn't here."

"Oh, I know, I'm . . . I'm not looking for Barnabas."

Rathburn aimed a piercing stare at the nervous young man. "Then, is there something you want with me?"

"Well, I, uh . . . I take it you're Mr. Rathburn?"

"That's right."

Loomis nodded to himself. He swallowed noisily. "Okay, well, I just came to deliver an invitation from Mr. Collins . . . Barnabas, that is. He'd like you to come over tonight . . . you know, for a drink."

Rathburn smiled knowingly. "That's very kind. I'd be happy to accept. Forgive me, but do you always deliver your messages in such a furtive manner?"

Loomis chuckled self-consciously. "I'm sorry. I, uh, just didn't know if anyone was here. I didn't want to disturb you if you were busy, or anything."

"Visitors don't disturb me unless they appear to be sneaking around the cottage."

"Yeah, okay. Like I said, I'm sorry about that."

"I guess you're not used to having a stranger living here, is that it?"

"Uh, yeah, that's right. It's kinda different, you know?"

"Of course. Anyway, tell Mr. Barnabas Collins I'd be happy to stop by. What time?"

"Anytime after dark is good."

"After dark, is it? All right. I can be there at seven."

"Yeah, okay. I'm sure that's fine. I . . . I'll tell him."

"Thank you, Mr. Loomis." With another cold smile, he rapped his knuckles against the door frame and leaned toward Willie. Willie took another step back. "And next time, just knock."

"I'll remember."

Loomis headed up the path to the road at a clip, clutching his pointed walking stick as if it might offer him some kind of protection. He glanced over his shoulder once, then hurried away as Rathburn raised a hand to wave at him. Closing the door, Rathburn took a deep breath, glad to be out of the painful glare. What a clumsy fellow Barnabas Collins seemed to have adopted for a servant. The best a town like Collinsport offered, perhaps?

He wondered if Loomis actually had a spare key to the place. Even if he did, he couldn't get past the dead bolt without forcing his way in, at least when he was at home. And Rathburn doubted that either Barnabas or Willie Loomis would want to leave any such evidence behind in the event of trouble.

Well, then. This evening the trouble would come to Barnabas, who might or might not have his own suspicions about his own nature, but could not possibly be aware of the kind of adversary he truly faced. Nor could Barnabas ever guess that, after all these years, vengeance for a foolish and wanton act of murder—one he might well have even forgotten—was about find him at last.

• • •

When Rathburn reached his destination, a drizzly dusk had fallen over the estate, though the thick boughs of cedar and white pine along the path had protected him from the worst of the rain.

The Old House, while not nearly as massive or imposing as Collinwood itself, made an impressive sight: a decaying white-walled, brick building with a row of tall Doric-style columns lining the facade. A single light burned in a window to the left of the front door; otherwise, the house appeared dark, with no cars or lawn equipment or such items in the yard that might indicate human occupancy. As he approached the door, he noticed one of the window shutters had fallen from its hinges and been carelessly propped against the wall. The cracked, peeling paint suggested it had lain that way for a long time. When he mounted the steps to the broad portico, the curtain of the lit window moved slightly as someone within looked out.

Standing at the front door, Rathburn rapped the circular brass knocker three times, hearing the sound within echo across seemingly vast distances. His host allowed him to wait for several long moments; only when he was about to knock again did he hear footsteps approaching from the other side of the door. When it finally creaked slowly open, the pale, nervous face of Willie Loomis appeared, his manner no more self-assured in his own abode than when trespassing on Rathburn's territory.

"Hello, Mr. Rathburn," Loomis said softly. "Uh, come on in. I'll tell Mr. Collins you're here."

"Thank you, Loomis." Rathburn stepped into the shadowy foyer, lit only by candelabra. With a shifty glance back, the handyman disappeared through a columned archway to his left. Directly ahead, a stairway rose to a landing that extended away into darkness. Beneath the landing a short hall led to an iron door with a barred window—the entrance to the cellar, Rathburn assumed. *What secrets hide in this house?* he wondered. Perhaps a few even more intriguing than those he might discover within the labyrinth of Collinwood itself.

Then, from the portal on the left, Barnabas Collins appeared, smartly dressed in white shirt and dark, patterned tie, a crimson velvet smoking jacket and neatly pressed black slacks. He smiled cordially and extended a hand. "Good evening, Mr. Rathburn," he said. "I'm pleased you accepted my invitation."

Taking the other's cold hand, Rathburn nodded politely. "I thought it might make for an interesting evening."

"So, you've decided to stay for a time?"

"Yes. I signed the lease to the cottage yesterday."

Barnabas raised an eyebrow. "I see. May I offer you a sherry, Mr. Rathburn?"

"Thomas, please. And a sherry would be just fine."

Barnabas led him into a cozy living room, furnished with antiques that even Rathburn found
impressive. A sparkling crystal chandelier hung
overhead, casting a warm glow over the otherwise
dusky colors of the room. The floor was covered by
a faded but beautifully embroidered Oriental carpet,
while a matching divan and wing chair, upholstered
in plush, rust-colored velvet, sat before a wide fireplace. Above the mantel hung an obviously recent
portrait of Barnabas, a modern reflection of the original painting that adorned the foyer wall of the main
house.

"That's a fine piece of work," Rathburn said,
pointing to it. "Who's the artist?"

Barnabas smiled, obviously pleased by the com-
pliment, as he walked to the sideboard in one corner
of the room, from which he produced a decanter of
sherry. "That was painted by Sam Evans, a local
artist." He poured a single glass of sherry and
handed it to Rathburn. "Here you are."

Rathburn took it, nodding his thanks. "Will you
join me?"

Barnabas shook his head. "I don't care for
sherry myself. But my guests often have remarked
on its quality. This is Amontillado, from Spain."

Rathburn lifted it to his lips and took a small sip
under Barnabas's scrutinizing gaze. To him, the fortified wine was basically tasteless, but he smiled
with pleasure. "Excellent. My compliments."

Barnabas's eyes narrowed as he watched Rathburn drink. "I may have misjudged you. I understand Willie Loomis met you earlier this afternoon. In daylight."

Rathburn nodded innocently. "Is that odd around these parts?"

Barnabas chuckled. "I only mean your eyes are rather red. I thought you might be an insomniac and needed to catch some sleep during the day. You see, I am sometimes troubled by that affliction."

"Ah. That can be most annoying."

"Indeed."

"Well, Mr. Collins. Your home is quite exceptional. I understand it's considerably older even than Collinwood."

"It dates back to the 1690s. In the late eighteenth century it was given to my ancestor as a wedding present, after the newer Collinwood was built." Barnabas's eyes took on a faraway look. "Unfortunately, the original Barnabas Collins was never able to find happiness here. Before his wedding could take place, his fianceé died tragically. And soon after, he went to live in England, never to return. I have always wanted to live here and hopefully find the happiness my ancestor never could."

"His fianceé. How did she die?" Rathburn asked, his curiosity aroused.

"A suicide. She leaped from the cliff at Widows' Hill. Her name was Josette DuPrès. My ancestor met her on the island of Martinique and brought her to Collinsport to be married. But there was only tragedy to be found here. Before the wedding, she ran away with Barnabas's uncle, Jeremiah Collins. And only a few days later she was dead. Despite my . . . ancestor's every effort, he could not save her." Barnabas had been ensnared by his own story, his eyes remaining fixed on some distant point.

"A terrible tale," Rathburn said, hoping Barnabas would continue.

Barnabas turned to look at him now, his cordial smile gone, his eyes blazing at Rathburn as they had during their duel the previous night. "I see Victoria Winters as being much like Josette," he said softly. "Young. Innocent. And strong. But not strong enough to face the kind of terrors that have visited this place before, and that surely will again. I will not let any harm come to her, Rathburn. I hope that has been made quite clear to you."

"Victoria?" Rathburn shrugged. "I've become very fond of her. You don't think I mean to harm her, do you?"

Barnabas said in a low voice, "I don't know who or what you are, Rathburn, or why you have come to Collinwood. But I assure you, it is within my power to find out. And I intend to."

The mention of Victoria had fired his blood, and Rathburn realized he again felt a deep, passionate longing for her. Strange, he thought, that another of the undead should feel so protective of this mortal woman, a woman who by rights should be seen as no more than satisfying prey to either of them. He sensed Barnabas searching his emotions, and he concentrated on erecting a psychic wall to keep the other out.

Rathburn didn't know how any of what he'd been told related to his presence at Collinwood. Yet he knew, instinctively, that it was important. His vengeance could wait if further truth might yet be divulged.

"You obviously have a strong feeling for Miss Winters," he said. "What makes her so special to you, Mr. Collins?" With a cold smile he added, "Other than the obvious reason any man might be attracted to her."

Barnabas looked at him thoughtfully for a long moment. "Come with me." He led Rathburn to the foyer and up the stairs to the next landing, where he went down another darkened hall, stopping in front of a closed door. Barnabas's features still bore the shadows of the tragic tale he had told. Whatever passions blazed in his blood, they were the powerful, soul-searing type that only a Vampire could know.

Barnabas opened the door, motioned for Rathburn to wait outside, then disappeared into darkness within. A moment later a warm golden glow appeared beyond the door, and Barnabas invited him to enter. When Rathburn stepped inside, he was greeted by the soft light of an oil lamp, which cast flickering shadows through the interior of the chamber. He found himself inside a large bedroom, decorated in a distinctly feminine style, its furnishings beautifully preserved, with nary a speck of dust to be seen anywhere. His glance was drawn to a baroque dressing table backed by a huge mirror; resting on it were a silver-handled hairbrush, several bottles of French perfume, a folded handkerchief embroidered with the letter J in Old English script, and numerous other women's toiletry items. The room also contained a huge, four-poster bed with a silken canopy, covered by an ivory quilt, and a screened fireplace with a mantel covered with unlit candles.

Barnabas carried the oil lamp to the fireplace. He held it up, slowly, the light revealing a large portrait of a beautiful, dark-haired woman in a flowing white dress. "This is Josette DuPrès," he said softly. "Such a delicate, exquisite creature. In her own way, Victoria Winters is very much like her." He added, as an afterthought, "Like she must have been."

"Very beautiful," Rathburn agreed, amused by the other's pretense.

Barnabas turned to face him again. "I have restored this room and kept it perfectly preserved, just as when it was Josette's. One day I intend that it belong to Victoria." He stopped, obviously waiting for a reaction.

Rathburn remained silent.

"Rathburn," Barnabas continued, "I do not customarily bring guests to this room. But I wanted you to understand that Victoria is as dear to me as Josette surely was to my ancestor."

Rathburn shrugged. "I am curious. If Josette was to marry the original Barnabas Collins, why did she run away with this Jeremiah—and then kill herself?"

Barnabas's face darkened with anger. "She was bewitched. By an evil, jealous woman who cast a spell on her, and Jeremiah as well, that made them become lovers. Josette's own servant, a woman from Martinique named Angélique, was jealous of the love between Josette and Barnabas. And when she could not make him love her, she used terrible, dark powers to see that Josette and he would never marry."

Angélique.

An unfamiliar name. Yet somehow the very sound of it filled Rathburn with foreboding.

"Go on."

Barnabas's face was a mask of pain and regret. His words faltered as he recounted a familiar, unbearable memory. "In a rage, Barnabas fought a duel with Jeremiah. He killed his own uncle, whom he loved very deeply. Josette . . . because of the witch, she was not herself. She committed suicide." Then, seeming to return to the moment, he looked back at Rathburn with calculating eyes. "There is more, and it involves Victoria Winters. Which is another reason that I will never allow harm to come to her. Tell me, Rathburn, do you believe in witch-craft?"

"Let's say I accept it as being within the realm of possibilities."

"I imagine you would." Barnabas smiled wryly. Then: "Not long ago an incredible event occurred here at Collinwood. There *are* spirits, Rathburn . . . spirits that struggle with each other in realms you and I could hardly imagine. Because of this, Victoria Winters was drawn back in time, back to the year 1795."

My God. Victoria had spoken of remembering flashes from "some other time."

Barnabas continued, "Victoria herself witnessed the events leading up to the death of Josette. She *knew* Josette, befriended her. I believe that she was meant to change history and save Josette's life. Yet, because of Angélique, Victoria was the one accused of orchestrating these terrible events. She was hanged as a witch."

Hanged! Victoria clutched her throat at the supper club, but I had no idea what it meant.

Barnabas saw Rathburn's incredulous look and nodded. "That act served to propel her back to her rightful time. But Rathburn, she was there. She lived through a part of history that should have been buried and forgotten forever." With a sigh, he said, "She learned many terrible truths."

Rathburn eyed Barnabas, gauging his expressions. And knowing now was the time, he said slowly, "She learned the truth about you."

Barnabas looked up at him sharply. The inner struggle raged in his eyes for several moments before he said in a soft voice, "As you have deduced, Mr. Rathburn, I am the original Barnabas Collins. Cursed by the same witch that destroyed everyone I ever held dear. For all Angélique did, I took her life. But before she died, she laid the curse of the undead upon me. It was when Josette learned what I was that she killed herself, rather than face an existence such as I had to offer her." Barnabas Collins looked close to tears. "I did love her so."

"So this is why Victoria fears you," Rathburn said. "But she doesn't remember the experience. Only disassociated flashes."

Barnabas shook his head. "She does not know the whole truth. But she suspects some terrible secret. If she is to ever learn this truth, it must be on my own terms."

"Angélique . . ." Rathburn said, again sensing a strange and disturbing pang of familiarity with the name. "She must have been an incredibly powerful sorceress."

"No one that crosses her path escapes unscathed. I have paid a terrible price for having known her. Her beauty was matched only by her evil. And she was able to conquer death. It may be that I will never be free of her. She is a monster. I fear she will reach out to strike Victoria as well."

His curiosity aroused, Rathburn said, "Do you have a likeness of her?"

Barnabas studied Rathburn for a moment, then said, "Come with me." He led Rathburn out of the room and down the stairs, through the living room and a pair of louvered wooden doors into a small library, its walls covered with dusty old tomes. Barnabas reached into the drawer of an old rolltop desk and withdrew a black leather folder. From it he took a faded color print, now crumbling with age, and handed it over. "That is Angélique Bouchard. Taken from an old portrait."

The print showed a beautiful, blond woman with luminous aqua eyes, her smile cunning, as if the secrets she concealed were dark ones indeed. And as Rathburn held the print, his nostrils were suddenly assailed by the scent of lilac, and the same whispery voice he had heard before suddenly fluttered in his ears, speaking the name, *Collins*.

A horrible image from the past again flashed before Rathburn's eyes; he saw his little boy being shot in the back, his beautiful Elaine raped by the trio of Union soldiers. As his vision cleared he thought he could faintly hear the sound of soft, feminine laughter. He noticed Barnabas regarding him intently, unsure what was happening in the mind of his visitor.

"Mr. Collins," Rathburn said as he handed the print back to his host, fighting with every fiber to keep control of his resurfacing rage. "I have reason to believe that we may have more in common than just Victoria Winters."

"Now it is your turn," Barnabas said ominously, slipping the portrait back into the drawer. "I have laid my cards on the table, perhaps more than I should consider wise. You will now tell me why you are here."

"To answer that, I must ask you one more question," Rathburn said icily. "Since you have seen fit to reveal your true identity, I want to know this: where you were during the War Between the States?"

"What do you mean?"

"Specifically, in the fall of 1864."

Barnabas chuckled dangerously. "I was rather seriously indisposed at that time, Rathburn. You see, after Josette's death, my father also learned the truth about me. He couldn't bring himself to destroy me, so he chained me in a coffin in the Collins family mausoleum, for what he thought would be eternity. There I spent nearly two hundred years in unbearable darkness and isolation. Can you imagine what it is like, to be aware of your own complete and utter helplessness, day upon day, year after year? It was a hell that Angélique never foresaw, yet must have had her howling with delight in whatever world of madness she existed. And there I expected to remain, until fate one day led Willie Loomis to my hidden chamber. So, here I am, Mr. Rathburn. And I am still waiting for an answer from you."

Rathburn gazed at his kindred with a new, building sense of horror. He had been certain that the sequence of events would lead to the revelation that, indeed, Barnabas Collins bore responsibility for the slaughter of his family. Yet, if his story were true, then he was quite innocent of that monstrous crime. Barnabas obviously knew nothing of his quest, and therefore had no compulsion to lie to him.

Why, then? Why have I been drawn to this place?

Now the beginnings of a terrible realization came to him, one so unthinkable that his eyes blazed with uncontrollable anger. Could it be that he was not at the center of a complex web of intrigue woven by some unfathomable, otherworldly spirit, but a mere pawn in a scheme that might very well have nothing to do with his own past? His visions—all lies. Lies concocted to lure him here for some other purpose entirely?

Rathburn looked back at Barnabas, whose own eyes had begun to gleam with crimson, his muscles tensing as if anticipating a possibly violent response from his guest. Rathburn backed away slowly, shaking his head at the other.

"I don't think it would be to my advantage to be quite so forthcoming," he said. "You might consider a similar tactic in the future, Mr. Collins."

"Indeed," Barnabas Collins said, his voice something between a whisper and a snarl. "But you might wish to reconsider your position. Otherwise, how can you possibly expect to leave this house alive?"

Barnabas raised his right hand, now holding his silver-headed cane, which had appeared as if from thin air. And as he thrust the tip toward Rathburn, with a sharp *click*, a twelve-inch-long, gleaming steel blade appeared from its end, its deadly point aimed directly at Rathburn's heart.

chapter

12

Whatʼs the matter with you, Miss Winters?"

Victoria looked down at David, who sat next to her at the large table in the library where, just moments ago, they had been studying the last days of the Second World War—Hitler in the bunker, Musssolini executed, Allies demanding a German surrender. David was frowning. "Iʼm sorry, David," Victoria said. "You were reading."

"Yeah, I was, but you werenʼt listening."

"But I was."

"You werenʼt. You were looking at the clock. Are you waiting for something?"

"No."

"For somebody? Miss Winters!"

Victoria had glanced again at the grandfather clock by the open door. It was nearly five in the afternoon. "David, I'm sorry," she said, turning to him again and letting out a long, silent breath. "It's been a long day."

"No kidding!" David said, thumping the book with his forefinger and rolling his eyes. "Long and boring. Why do I have to study this stupid stuff? Who cares who fought a war on the other side of the ocean? I don't! It's all over with."

"Well," Victoria said, trying to put on her best teacher expression and voice for David's benefit, although her mind was far from the library, "it's important to understand the past."

"But why?"

"Those who don't learn from the past are condemned to repeat it."

David grimaced. "You make that up?"

"No, somebody else did. But it's true."

"So if I learn about Hitler I won't have to fight him?" David teased sourly.

Victoria nodded. "Something like that, actually. It's a bit more symbolic, but . . ."

The gears of the grandfather clock turned, clicking and clacking quietly, and then the room was filled with five loud chimes.

"Miss Winters!" David lashed out his arm and sent the books, notebook, and pen flying from the tabletop to the floor. He jumped up into the seat of the chair and clenched his fist at Victoria's face. "Quit looking at the clock!"

"David!" Victoria stood and pulled David down by the arm. He yanked away and ran to the other side of the table. Victoria lifted her hands in a truce. "David, I'm sorry if I seem preoccupied. It happens sometimes. Now, sit back down. We haven't much more to do today."

"If I was in real school, I'd be done for the day," David whined. "I want to go to real school. I'm sick of having to learn at home!"

"You know that's not possible," Victoria said.

"Why not?"

"You know why not. You've been troubled at school. You've always felt you didn't quite fit in, and so your father decided home schooling was your best option."

"But I've learned from my past!" David smirked. "So maybe I won't repeat it!"

"Let's not get into this now. Please pick up those books."

"I don't want to!"

"Pick up the books and we'll stop for today, all right?" Victoria knew she shouldn't bargain with David; it was one of the laziest tactics a teacher could use. But in fact she was as ready to stop as David.

"All right," the boy said, his voice down a notch. He came back around the table and began to collect the scattered materials.

Victoria excused herself and left the library. It took a lot of effort to climb the stairs, and she held the banister as she went. Her whole body was heavy with fears and hopes.

He hadn't promised to come to her tonight. He had only said he enjoyed the previous evening with her. She had been the one to reassure herself that he would want to see her again. But that kiss. Oh my God, that kiss had been like nothing she'd ever experienced before. So passionate, so full of need and yearning . . . from both of them, a mingling of desires. There had been more than a physical bonding between them in that moment their bodies meshed and their lips touched.

It was still early. He might yet appear at the front door.

So why was she so despondent? Since rising this morning, Victoria had only been able to dwell on what seemed to her the pathetic impression she must have made on him at dinner last night. She'd suffered some strange spell she couldn't even remember, leaving her drained and upset, and no doubt looking like a fool to everyone who had seen her. Her anxiety had increased over the course of the day and now buzzed through her soul like a nest of hornets.

She went to her room and sat on the bed, facing the window and the world outside. *Come*, she thought. *Please come to me.*

She sat for a long time, staring out the window. She began to tremble. The sun lowered amid bold streaks of dark blue and red, dropping behind the trees to the west and drawing the light of the world with it. The copper beech tree seemed to glower contemptuously in the shadows.

Clutching one hand inside the other and biting the inside of her cheek so she would not cry, Victoria rode out the torment of night jitters.

Finally, the sun set. The Collinwood estate was swallowed up in blackness.

"Where are you, Thomas?" she whispered.

Dinner was served at six-thirty. Victoria tried to engage in the banter between Elizabeth, Roger, David, and Carolyn, but found nothing worth saying. Afterward, she asked Carolyn if she'd like to play a game of cards, but Carolyn laughed and told her she had somewhere she had to go and so she would just have to entertain herself tonight.

Entertain myself, Victoria thought angrily as she went back upstairs. *She thinks I'm incapable of a social life. She plays at generosity when she invites me to town with her, but she really thinks I'm boring.*

She stopped on the landing and said aloud to herself, "She's a member of the Collins family. And you, Vicki, are the hired help. Quit trying to fight it."

From below there came the sound of Elizabeth chuckling in the dining room, not a common sound, given Elizabeth's usual stoic manner, but one that was honest and pleasant. Victoria felt suddenly ashamed. "They care about you," she said. "You know they do. So who is being selfish now?"

Victoria didn't return to her bedroom, but wandered into the second floor gallery, a large chamber down the hall from her bedroom where the Collins family displayed their extensive—and treasured—collection of fine art. On the walls hung numerous portraits of family members dating back to the 1600s, as well as other commissioned and purchased paintings by artists ranging from obscure to the historically renowned. A huge, six-foot-tall portrait of the Madonna by Bouguereau dominated one wall, while opposite it, a landscape by the Victorian artist Charles Delaware Tate hung above the unlit fireplace, surrounded by the works of Corot, Courbet, and Gérôme. Overhead, where the vaulted ceiling joined the high walls, ivory-toned plaster masks of the poets Milton, Chaucer, Homer, and Blake glared down at her as if disapproving of her bleak mood. Yet the huge stained-glass window that overlooked the western lawn, now engulfed by pure darkness, seemed to reflect what she felt inside.

She went to the window and put her hands flat on the cold surface of the glass mosaic. She peered out at the night through one section of clear glass, looking northward, toward the spot where she knew Rathburn's cottage hid beyond the trees. Even though most of the branches were bare, she could not see any hint of light from that far corner of the estate. What was he doing now? Perhaps working in the cottage itself, cleaning, adding his own personal touches to it so that it might be a comfortable, pleasing abode for the duration of his stay—however long that happened to be. Was he out somewhere? Surely, not in the village . . . not in the Blue Whale.

No, he can't be.

The gallery was cold, and she pulled the sides of her wool cardigan together over her breasts and crossed her arms. From below, the distant chiming of the clock in the foyer crept softly up the stairs, marking the eight o'clock hour. It seemed like a signal to her, motivating her to leave the dark, silent chamber and go down the stairs to the more brightly lit foyer. But there, the portrait of Barnabas Collins stared moodily at her from its place on the wall, and though she had seen it hundreds of times, she felt a renewed stab of nervousness—the jitters. With a little grimace, she plucked her jacket from the rack beside the door, pulled it on, and stepped through the double doors into the brisk night air, briefly standing in the little island of light beneath the porte cochere before starting down the flagstone walk that led around to the back of the great mansion.

He won't mind if I stop in to see him, will he? Why should he? He'll be happy to have a break in the solitude. He'll be glad to have some company.

As she walked down the hill toward the darkness of the woods, she realized she should have brought a flashlight, but if she turned back now, she might change her mind. Above, a dense cloud layer hid the moon, diffusing its light into a uniform, pale layer of silver that dimly illuminated the landscape. Anyway, she'd taken this path so many times, surely she would have no trouble making her way.

Were these feelings that treaded the line between ecstasy and panic what it meant to fall in love? Or at least to be smitten by a man? Thomas Rathburn fascinated her, beyond his charm and good looks. He possessed a wisdom that seemed deep and hard-won, as if he'd seen and experienced more than was possible for a man of his years. He couldn't be over forty. Physically, he was beautiful. But while he possessed a good humor, he seemed to carry a darkness with him; a darkness that she wanted to explore, yet dreaded knowing. Traits that she had seen before, and closely, she realized, in another.

Barnabas Collins.

Any fascination Barnabas had held for her had vanished, however. In its place, only dread remained. But why? God, *why?* Barnabas had surely noticed the change in her feelings, and it must have hurt him. She hadn't wanted that—not for all the world. Yet she could not help herself. She knew that until she discovered the reason for it, her feelings would not change.

But did she want to resolve this through Thomas?

No, I'm not that shallow. I'm not Carolyn.

Yet he was so much like Barnabas. His eyes, so piercing, so hypnotic, able to compel her to release her own feelings without inhibition or qualm. His voice, smooth and low, so reassuring, so kind. Could it be that she equated Thomas's virtues with the qualities that had once drawn her to Barnabas?

It's not that simple, Vicki.

Now at the edge of the woods, she had to make her way carefully. Still, she could see no lights beyond the trees, and she began to fear this excursion would be in vain. She picked her footing deliberately, fearful of falling or getting tangled in the spindly underbrush.

Reaching the gnarled, barren apple orchard, she could see the outline of the cottage in the distance, dark and apparently devoid of habitation. But she still felt excitement at being so close to where he lived, as if his lingering aura were enough to bring her some sense of reassurance.

The car he'd leased was still parked in the drive. At least he hadn't gone into town. Crossing the gravel road and going down the walk toward the cottage, she wrapped her arms around herself, wishing he would appear at the door, or even call her name from somewhere nearby. Stepping up to the little porch, she paused a moment, gathering her nerve, peeking through the unlit window to make sure that some light didn't burn in one of the back rooms.

Nothing. Just darkness. She rapped solidly on the door, then stepped back and looked around at the neighboring woods, up the road that led along the northern edge of the vast estate. Only the soft moan of the wind and the distant whisper of breakers spoiled the silence.

No response. *Of course, silly. It's obvious he's not here.*

She trembled with frustration and cold. What if he had decided to call on her at Collinwood and simply taken the longer walk up the road to reach the mansion? Her first impulse was to turn and hurry back the way she'd come, to hopefully run into him as he returned, where she imagined his own disappointment at missing her would melt in a rush of excitement, just as hers would at meeting him. But then . . . no. If he paid a visit at Collinwood, he would almost certainly spend at least a few minutes with his hosts—or more correctly, his landlords—and perhaps have a drink with them.

Elizabeth and Roger were undoubtedly aware of her attraction to Thomas. Yet she felt awkward with him in their company, embarrassed and inhibited. So much better to catch him alone. But she didn't want to wait here in the thick darkness, which could easily become frightening if she dwelled upon it, regardless of her familiarity with the land. She started back up the gravel road that led around the northern edge of the grounds, an impenetrable wall of trees towering above her to the left, the mist-shrouded slope of the lower lawn climbing toward the distant mansion to her right. Her footsteps crunched solidly in the gravel and her breath came out in little wisps of steam.

As she reached the crest of the first hill, she could clearly see the huge, dark hulk of Collinwood several hundred yards away, its lower windows glowing warmly, a feathery gray plume rising from one of the chimneys. She could detect the faint scent of wood smoke from here, a pleasant, comforting smell, reminding her that nearby there were people she cared about, and who cared about her. Alone in the darkness, she felt strangely more at ease than she had inside, anxiously contemplating the night. Rather than turning toward the house, her legs carried her on up the road, as if leading her of their own accord, leaving her no choice but to go where they would.

Even as she moved farther from the house, she continued to watch the door, half expecting to see Rathburn emerge, casting his own eyes into the night in hopes of catching a glimpse of her. But he did not appear, and before she knew it she had reached the path that led across the eastern portion of the front lawn and into the woods, where it eventually ended at Widows' Hill. She stepped onto it. The ease she had felt being outside was draining away, replaced by despair and resignation.

He isn't there. He hasn't come to see me. He's off elsewhere.

Anyway, what was love between a man and woman? In her experience, little good ever seemed to come of it—or whatever passed as love. She was twenty-five years old and had never really known the meaning of true romance. When she'd first come here, she'd grown close to Burke Devlin, a somber man of wealth who had returned to Collinsport after many years away. It was an admittedly odd situation, for in his younger days there had been serious friction between him and Roger Collins, and Burke had initially called her a fool for staying with the family. Yet, eventually, he and Roger Collins had achieved something akin to reconciliation, and she was able to sustain a relationship with him that showed much promise for the future. For the first time in her life, she had felt a sense of security that someone *did* love her, and that she might be able to return it fully.

But before any of their plans could be fulfilled, Burke disappeared in a plane crash while on a business trip in South America. She had been devastated. It was then that Barnabas offered her his most devoted attention, supporting her in her grief, finally making it plain that he himself cared deeply for her. She had thought herself ready and willing to return his affection, until . . .

Until what?

Until the night jitters.

She thought of the other people in her life, the relationships they'd had. Elizabeth's husband, Paul Stoddard, had married her simply out of greed, and even attempted to embezzle the family's fortune—driving Elizabeth almost to murder. He had left Collinwood, probably forever; to this day, no one knew where he was. And Roger Collins's late spouse, Laura, now in her grave, but leaving Roger with no fond memories, only a lasting bitterness that he acted upon by forbidding anyone in the household to so much as mention her name.

So what is love, anyway?

A kiss. A momentous, passionate kiss that had thrilled her to the soul like nothing she had ever known. Not while in Burke's arms, nor in Barnabas's.

The excitement of a mere glimpse of the strange man from the South, the feeling of happiness just knowing that he was staying close by.

Will he ever kiss me like that again?

What if my feelings for him vanish as quickly and mysteriously as they did for Barnabas?

Victoria held herself tightly, pressing on along the path. The wind was picking up and the temperature dropping. The breeze rustling through the trees drowned the sound of the ocean waves, still a good distance beyond the woods and the bluffs ahead. At last she came to a division in the path. One branch led toward Widows' Hill, the other ended at the Old House. The thought sent a resurgence of anxiety racing through her. She stopped and looked back toward Collinwood, now hiding behind the intervening stands of locust and hickory trees.

This is far enough, she thought.

Just as she was about to head back, something caught her eye; something was moving off to her right in the direction of Widows' Hill. She turned her head quickly, hoping to see what it was, thinking it had looked like a light. Perhaps the beam of a flashlight.

Could Thomas be out taking a walk as well? she wondered. Her heart fluttered at the idea of encountering him out here, in the darkness, alone. But what if it wasn't him? More likely, so close to the Old House, it would be Barnabas.

"Oh, God," she whispered to herself. She tried to calm her nerves. He would never harm her. Consciously, she knew this to be the plain and simple truth. Yet on some deeper level, she felt she had reason to fear him. Should she hurry back toward Collinwood, exposing herself the moment she stepped out onto the open lawn? Maybe she should hide behind one of the nearby trees, for whoever it was would as yet have no clue she was here. If it were Thomas, she would see him first. She could surprise him—hopefully in an agreeable way.

Feeling a little foolish, she hid behind an old,

misshapen oak, peering out at the end of the trail where she'd seen the light. For several moments no one appeared, and she began to think that perhaps she'd only glimpsed the light from a ship at sea. But then, far up the trail, near the bluff, a pale luminescence slowly grew upon the trunk of a wind-bent scrub tree. It didn't look like the beam of a flashlight. Whatever was casting it remained out of sight, yet it slowly seemed to draw nearer, creeping through the darkness like a monstrous glowworm. As it drew nearer along the path, Victoria knew that in a moment its source would be revealed, and her heart leaped to her throat, pounding madly with both hope and alarm.

But suddenly the light vanished, and she found herself in complete darkness. She smelled a delicate, flowery scent—lilac, she thought. Fragrant, almost sickly in its sweetness. No sound rose above the wind, but she listened carefully for footsteps or other movement. Still nothing. But she was sure someone else must be nearby.

What is this?

She pressed against the tree, feeling a strange sense of déjà vu, along with the same sense of panic she'd felt at the restaurant the night before. Suddenly, the scenery around her shifted and shrank. It was less dense. *Less mature*. The tree next to her was now only a fraction of its former size, about a foot in diameter rather than three. The path was still here, yet it was more primitive, rocky.

She shook her head violently, trying to free herself from whatever force was at work. But she had no power against it. Abruptly, her wrists were grabbed from behind, and she was slammed against the tree. Her breath erupted from her chest with the impact. She tried to turn her head, but the back of her neck was seized in a fierce grip, preventing her from turning.

"Victoria Winters," came a deep, almost familiar voice. "I have you at last."

"What are you doing?" she gasped. "Who are you?"

"You thought you could escape. But you do not realize with whom you are dealing. It is time to put an end to the terror you have wrought upon the poor people of this town. You may have thought to escape, but you cannot escape me. I have you now."

The words brought back a flood of indistinct, jumbled memories. But this was impossible. This man could not be here, not now. *She* could not be here!

She felt a length of rope being wrapped around her body, pinning her to the trunk, the still unseen figure behind her pulling it tight so that she could not move.

"Who are you?" she cried. "What do you want?"

"I will give you one last chance to confess.

Repudiate the devil now and the Almighty will bring you salvation."

The figure stepped into view: a tall, black-haired man with piercing dark eyes beneath a heavy brow. He wore a black tunic, like a clergyman's, yet it seemed . . . *old*, like nothing anyone would wear in this day and age. As he peered at her, another rush of impossible familiarity overwhelmed her. In a flash she knew his name.

Reverend Trask!

She knew this man. But from where? How? When?

"Go away! You're insane," she managed.

"You make your own salvation very difficult," he said in a soft voice, never taking his eyes from hers. One corner of his mouth lifted in a vicious sneer.

"What are you going to do to me?"

"You will stay here overnight. You will remain tied to this tree—one of God's living creatures. If indeed you are guilty of witchcraft, the tree will be dead by morning."

"Please," she said, the words coming to her mouth as if by rote, "untie me and take me back to the house."

"You're afraid to go through with this test, aren't you?"

"I'm afraid to stay out here alone overnight."

Trask's voice rose with excitement. "It is the fear

of God you feel. The fear of being exposed as the witch you are." Turning from her, he put his hands together and raised his eyes to the stars above. "I adjure thee, O serpent, by the judge of the quick and the dead, by thy maker, and the maker of the world, by Him who hath power to put thee into Hell, that thou depart in haste from the flesh of this woman." Now he turned and laid a cold, dry hand on Victoria's cheek. "Go out, thou seducer! Go out, thou transgressor, full of deceit and vile. Enemy of virtue, persecutor of innocence! In the name of the Lord, I command thee to cast thyself back into the darkness whence thee came, and where thy everlasting destruction awaits thee!"

The man's eyes glinted with lust. He stroked her cheek with rough, dry fingers, his breath pouring hotly over her from his parted lips. She shook her head, trying to keep him from touching her, but to no avail. "Somebody, please help me," she whispered. Her voice quickly rose in panic as one hand lowered to her breast. "Somebody. Help me! Please!"

Leaning to whisper in her ear, he said, "You may scream the devil's words all you wish. But there will be none to hear you. None but the Lord."

Victoria struggled against the ropes. They cut into her flesh like knives.

She closed her eyes with the pain, opened them again and . . .

He was gone.

She gasped, caught her breath, and blinked.

She was free. No longer tied to the tree. Looking back, she saw it returned to its rightful size, the path again broad and worn. Her heart nearly exploded in her chest, her breath escaping in heavy sobs. *What was this? What was happening to her?*

Why did she know that man?

She realized then that the darkness of the woods had been pierced by a light. She could see her shadow outlined in white phosphorescence against the bole of the great oak. She spun around to face the source of the glare and was blinded by a congeries of blazing silver spheres, as if the moon and stars themselves had fallen from the sky and crashed to earth before her. The overwhelming scent of lilac swept over her, driving a spear of terror through her heart. She sensed a presence inside the light—one that knew her and meant to harm her. With a hoarse cry, she bolted up the path.

A few seconds later, Victoria found herself on the rocky precipice of Widows' Hill, overlooking an abyss of pure black, deafened by the crashing of waves against the rocks far below. She lurched to a stop, dropping to her knees, her lungs aching as she drew in one steadying breath after another. Glancing back, she saw that she was no longer being pursued. Whatever it was, it seemed to be gone.

"Oh God," she whispered. "What is happening?"

For several long moments she knelt on the rocks, trying to regain her composure. This could not be real. But if it wasn't, then it meant it was all in her mind. Was she going crazy? If anyone knew about this, they'd put her away. Maybe she *needed* to be put away!

No. Something had gotten inside her head, twisting her thoughts, her memories. Something *out there*. It was not her mind playing tricks on her. She was being assaulted, as surely as if someone had physically attacked her.

Who?

Her nerves finally began to steady, and she rose to her feet, brushing the dirt from the front of her jumper. She had to get back to Collinwood, try to recover her wits before she came completely unglued. But could she do it alone? No . . . this was too much. Who could she confide in? Thomas?

What if she went to him with *this*? Would he care enough about her to try to help, or simply turn away, unwilling to take on this kind of bizarre baggage? She wanted to believe that his feelings for her were genuine, but she didn't know for sure.

A single sob escaped her lips. "I just don't know," she said. "But I'll think this through, I'll . . ."

At the edge of her hearing, she detected something new—something more than the roar of the waves below. A deep rumble, like the very earth shaking. The leaves on the trees down the path began to quiver, whipping to life as a swift breeze swept through the branches. The rumble drew nearer, and above it there was a shrill, sirenlike cry: the shriek of a bitter, angry wind. As the whistling air rushed over her, she realized that something about it was unnatural.

Until now, the wind had been blowing in from the ocean.

Oh God. It's not over.

Like a giant hand, a sudden gust slapped her hard across the face and chest, batting her back toward the edge of the cliff. Gasping, she tried to recover her balance, only to find herself in some kind of fierce yet insubstantial grip, one that shoved her insistently toward the waiting precipice. The wind stank, like the breath of the grave. She tried to drop to her knees to keep from being driven any farther, but like a puppet on invisible strings, she could only writhe and struggle vainly, her body at the mercy of the hellish, unseen force.

"Stop, please!" she cried. "What do you want of me?"

In her ears, the rushing wind seemed to become a low, feminine chuckle, rising gradually into mocking, lilting laughter, unmistakably wicked and horribly familiar. Helpless, she could only watch herself being dragged backward, not knowing how many seconds remained before she would be hurled into oblivion by her otherworldly assailant.

She felt her body being shifted as the ghost-wind spun her around to face the vast darkness beyond Widows' Hill. Fear choked her. The wind sucked her breath away and she could not breathe.

Then she thought, *I can bear the torment no longer. Death will be welcome if it means the end to these terrifying visions!*

She faced the edge with open arms, and hung teetering. The ocean waves crashed and roared, seeming to beckon her into their violent, deadly embrace. She would never even know the truth about her own death—unless, somehow, the answers waited for her on the other side. She drew in a last breath and prepared herself.

And she felt the wind give her a final push.

chapter

13

Feeling the blade against his chest, Rathburn's spine stiffened and his muscles coiled. Though he was resistant to almost any injury, one lunge through the heart with his adversary's vampiric strength could spell the end of his existence. He considered a rapid shape-shift, but he might not be able to achieve it before Barnabas delivered a fatal stroke. And if he succeeded in escaping, his rival would not rest until he had hunted him down and destroyed him. Rathburn knew that here, on his home territory, Barnabas Collins might have resources that he himself could not foresee.

"That's rather drastic, Mr. Collins," he said softly. "And quite unnecessary. You overestimate any threat I might pose to you."

"That's hardly likely. And I am far more concerned about the threat you pose to Victoria Winters. It has been plainly evident from the beginning that you are no normal man."

"But then, neither are you."

"Regardless of what you have learned tonight, you still have little understanding of who and what you are dealing with. And you still haven't told me who you are, Rathburn. For all I know, you might be in league with Angélique."

"Nonsense."

"I've a good mind to destroy you here and now and be done with it."

"Without ever learning the real reason I have come here?"

"If you are dead, then that will no longer matter."

"Given the things you have told me tonight, Mr. Collins, I see I have no quarrel with you. And I have learned enough about you to know that you dislike being ignorant of all the facts. If you kill me, you will only be further haunted by what you still don't understand. Admit it."

Barnabas smiled knowingly, pressing the blade harder against Rathburn's chest. He turned his head slightly and called, "Willie!"

A moment later Rathburn heard a shuffling on the stairs, and a frightened Willie Loomis appeared in the doorway. "Yeah, Barnabas?"

"Let us have a look at him."

Loomis nodded reluctantly, and reaching around

the corner of the door, he produced a large, oval hand mirror. He stepped up to Rathburn, bolstered by the sight of the blade at his chest, and held the mirror up beside Rathburn's face.

Loomis gasped in surprise, and Barnabas raised his eyebrows, his expression slowly becoming a thoughtful frown. "Well . . . I had suspected as much. We do bear a talent in sensing other supernatural sources invading our territory. But then you exhibited a number of abilities that convinced me otherwise. You are indeed full of surprises, Mr. Rathburn."

"And you would like to learn some of them, wouldn't you." Rathburn did not pose it as a question. He glanced at the mirror, in which he cast no reflection. Then he looked at Loomis, who backed away with a grimace of fear.

"That will be all, Willie," Barnabas said. The servant turned and hurried out of the room with a look of profound relief. Barnabas then slowly lowered the cane, and with a *snap-click*, the blade disappeared into its hidden sheath. "You live dangerously, Mr. Rathburn. Despite your unusual powers, you are hardly invulnerable. For one in your position, arrogance could easily be your undoing."

"As I said, Mr. Collins, I believe we have more in common than just Victoria Winters."

Barnabas scowled at the inference. "Involving yourself with her may be the greatest mistake you've ever made, Rathburn."

Rathburn shook his head. Certain things had begun to make sense. Barnabas equated Victoria with his lost love, Josette. And given his own reaction to the portrait of Angélique, Rathburn was certain the same witch who had made Barnabas what he was had played a part in his own presence here. What had Barnabas said? *"For all I know, you might be in league with Angélique."* He remembered the ghostly shape he'd seen at Collinwood, and the scent of lilac.

So . . . was Angélique herself the source of his horrible visions?

Why?

And was Barnabas Collins truly innocent of the crimes for which he sought vengeance, even after so many years?

Then why had he been lured here? *Why?*

"Mr. Collins," he said at last. "As I said, I have no desire to harm Victoria. I will tell you this much: I still have questions of my own regarding my presence here. More than that you do not need to know."

"Your position is still precarious," Barnabas said in a low voice. "But I will admit that you interest me enough to grant you some time. Perhaps. Your secret of surviving in the daylight . . . I find that most fascinating."

"I'm sure you do."

Barnabas frowned. "Do not be glib, Rathburn, or my patience may not last. Perhaps you would deign to tell me just how old you actually are."

With a shrug, Rathburn answered, "I was born in 1825. And born again in 1864."

"I take it you have never been to Collinsport during your existence."

"Until a few days ago, the farthest north I've ever been was Boston. And I had certainly never heard of Collinsport."

"Yet now you come here under mysterious circumstances, and settle in on the Collins estate. You immediately begin a relationship with Victoria Winters and show more than a passing interest in both myself and Angélique. When I put those facts together, I see a rather dangerous scheme unfolding, Mr. Rathburn. And you confess to some degree of ignorance regarding the reasons for your presence here. So if this scheme is not entirely your own, then there are surely other forces at work. If so, you may not realize how vulnerable you really are."

"That remains to be seen," Rathburn said. But Barnabas had read him well enough. An astute man indeed. Of course, Barnabas was no more a man than he himself was. It was time to try a different tactic, as distasteful as it was. "You are obviously more familiar with such forces than I am. Maybe we can . . . help each other."

Barnabas's eyes narrowed and his lips drew into a snarl. "As yet, Rathburn, I don't see that I have as much to gain as I do to lose by any further exchange with you. I certainly have no reason to trust you. In fact, quite the opposite."

Rathburn spoke evenly, with an intentional hint of menace. "There is always Victoria to consider."

Barnabas reacted swiftly. He raised the cane again, pointing its tip at Rathburn. "Remember my warning," he growled. "I would suggest you stay away from Miss Winters. If you do not, your holiday at Collinwood may have a most unpleasant ending."

A knock sounded at the front door then, and Willie hurried back down the stairs, looking at Barnabas first to make sure he was doing the right thing. Barnabas nodded reluctantly. "Go ahead, Willie."

Willie opened the door. Carolyn Stoddard stood there with a brown paper bag in her hands. "Good evening, Willie," she quipped, stepping into the foyer and giving Barnabas a smile. When she saw Rathburn, her eyes at first flashed with excitement, then went cool, as if she'd just remembered that he had rebuffed her advances. "Hello, Thomas. I didn't know you'd be here."

"I was just having a pleasant visit with your cousin Barnabas."

"What brings you over tonight, Carolyn?" Barnabas asked, barely masking his frustration at her arrival.

Her face lit up again as she turned to him. "I was working at the antique shop today, and we received some wonderful items I thought you might be interested in." She held up the bag. "Several old books, a few silver pieces, and some other personal articles. They're supposed to be eighteenth century. Since I know how much you appreciate things like that, I drove right in from town to show you."

"That's very kind of you," he said. "I'd be glad to look at them. Later."

"But I thought maybe you could tell me if they're valuable or not. You know, I still wish you'd have a phone put in, Barnabas. I could have called first to see if it was convenient."

"Don't let me interfere," Rathburn said, retrieving his coat from the rack, preparing to take his leave. Though their business was far from concluded, at least another confrontation had been averted. Better to let Barnabas cool down, he thought. If he played his hand right, Barnabas could still provide much useful information. "Thank you for your hospitality, Mr. Collins. A most interesting conversation."

"Yes, Mr. Rathburn," Barnabas said, his eyes radiating daggers. "Most revealing."

Rathburn bowed slightly to Carolyn on his way to the door. "Nice to see you again, Carolyn. I hope you find some real treasure in there."

Her smile was glacial. "If anyone would know, it's Cousin Barnabas."

"Quite. Well, I'll see you all later." He nodded to Loomis, who stared sullenly back at him. "Willie."

As Rathburn opened the door he saw that Carolyn had moved close to Barnabas, the expression in her eyes all too obvious. Yes, he'd earlier sensed that she had been used by another. Barnabas had not summoned her, but she instinctively knew when he began to hunger.

"Good night, Mr. Rathburn," Barnabas called. "We will continue this another time."

Rathburn said, "Bon appetit," and returned the other's look of fury with an innocent smile. "Oh, and for God's sake, call me Thomas."

Rathburn stepped into the night and walked quickly from the Old House to the path that led toward Collinwood. A frost-edged chill had settled over the estate, and a low breeze whispered through the dark trees. The rain had stopped, but the wet ground had frozen, and Rathburn's footsteps crunched as he walked. A few stars gleamed in a hazy sky, the moon just beginning to creep over the eastern horizon.

What an exchange it had been. In many ways, he had learned more than he could have ever hoped, especially about Barnabas and his relationship to Victoria. But Barnabas's apparent innocence of the slaughter that Rathburn had been so ready to attribute to him disturbed Rathburn more than if his suspicions had proven correct. Because that meant that his visions and the burning drive to come here from Atlanta were not meant to enlighten, but to manipulate him.

Intolerable.

Like it or not, the most productive course would be to propose a truce, however uneasy, with Barnabas. For if the source of his own visions were indeed the spirit of a long-dead witch, then the force he faced would be formidable indeed.

Over his long lifetime, Rathburn had delved into much dark lore, ancient books of magic, even met other individuals who had dealt with eldritch powers he could barely begin to contemplate. If Angélique had once mastered such things, and somehow still existed beyond the barrier of death, then she could indeed have planted the subconscious images in his mind that she wanted him to see.

But why would she touch *him*? Surely, at no time in his life had he encountered her before; in no way could he have acted to incur her wrath, whether in life or in undeath.

It made no sense.

The wind picked up as he drew near Widows' Hill, and he could hear the ocean waves crashing against the rocky shoreline with unusual ferocity. Rathburn stopped and listened. The pounding and hissing of the sea seemed to call to him, to scream at him, yet in a voice harsh and indecipherable. He tipped back his head to sample the air.

The hairs at the back of his neck bristled. For a moment he caught the faintest scent of lilac, but then even stronger, over the salt of the waves and the frosted dampness of the earth, came the sharp odor of fear.

The terrified scent of one who had become so important to both his quest and his renewed, passionate longing.

He leveled his eyes, staring through the darkness, honing his vision in the direction of cliff's edge. There. A figure, writhing and crying, as if struggling with an invisible force in the air. And when he saw that a whirling, localized cyclone had seized her in its grip, slowly but surely propelling her toward the precipice, Rathburn's blood froze in his cold, undead veins.

Victoria.

chapter

⊛⊛⊛

14

*G*ive me the answer.
As I die, let me witness the truth!
The breath was sucked from her lungs in the turbulence, and she fell forward, her arms at last free enough from the cocoon of the wind to reach outward to her death.

"Victoria!"

She knew the voice but couldn't recall if it was one from this world or another. She closed her eyes, praying it would go quickly and painlessly.

"Victoria!"

Arms grabbed her around the waist and yanked her backward, her feet leaving the ground, her body crashing to the hard earth behind her with an agonizing thud.

She screamed as her arm was twisted behind her and red-hot lances of pain drove from her wrist to her shoulder.

"Victoria!"

She opened her eyes. There, hovering over her, was Thomas Rathburn. Stars swam in her vision; the pain in her arm squeezed her so hard she was unable to speak.

"What were you doing?" he asked, his voice quivering. He slid his arms beneath hers and lifted her to her feet, holding her tenderly. "You weren't going to jump, were you?"

Victoria shook her head. She grasped her throbbing arm and cradled it to her chest.

"Ah, dear, your arm," Rathburn said. "Let me see, will you?"

As gently as the most tender lover, he touched the arm, probing it carefully, stroking the length of it. The pain was still strong, but the intensity subsided. "It is not broken," he said, "but turned. Let me help you."

He pushed up the sleeves of her coat and sweater, exposing the chill-bumped skin to the night air. Then he bent and kissed the arm. Victoria felt the pain dwindle and fade, and a warm numbness take its place.

Is he magic? she wondered. *No, of course not, it would feel better on its own, being straightened out now. You only want him to be magic, for what romance there is in magic.*

He pulled the sleeves back into place, then touched her face. "What happened, Victoria? You could have fallen to your death had I been one second slower!"

The evil Reverend Trask, she thought. *I saw him, Thomas. And then something in the wind pushed me to the edge of the rocks. It wanted to kill me. It was aware of me, it knew me, and it hated me and wanted me to die.* She looked away from Rathburn's steady gaze. *I can't tell him any of that,* she thought. *It will only confirm what he may already think of me. No, God help me, I must deal with this alone.*

She managed, "I went walking and found myself here at Widows' Hill. I dared myself to stand on the edge to look over, as you have done, as Barnabas has done, as even young David has done, to see the sight from the clearest vantage. I'm not very brave, sometimes, and sometimes one must just face their fears to conquer them."

Thomas's head drew back slightly, and she could tell that he didn't completely accept this story. Yet he sighed and said, "Victoria, some fears should be conquered, but others are for our own good. The task is to determine which is which, and live accordingly."

"That sounds like good advice."

"It is."

He helped her to her feet. The wind had subsided. The only scents Victoria could detect now were those of dead leaves, sea brine, and the closeness of Thomas's body. She glanced at the edge of the cliff, and understood that if not for him, her skull would at this moment be dashed upon the rocks, her flesh food for the scavenging terns and rock-scuttling crabs.

They walked in silence back to the mansion, Victoria holding on to Rathburn's arm and her head against his shoulder. She felt the first stirrings of passion, as she had last night, finally blossoming in her core and moving in every direction throughout her body. If he would only reach for her now, she would let him make love to her. Her need was great; it was more than hunger or thirst. More than a need to sleep. It was insistent and demanding.

Don't think like that, she told herself. *You do not know how he feels about you.*

"Victoria?" he said as they walked, his face turning to hers. "Does the name Angélique mean anything to you?"

A sudden rush of dread killed the passion inside her. "Angélique?" She struggled with the name and the nebulous terror it conjured. But nothing she grasped in her thoughts was tangible, and the memory, if that's what it was, faded like a dream in the light of day. "I don't think so. No, Thomas, it means nothing."

"All right," he said. They continued to walk through the night, past the hooting of owls in trees and the scuffling of raccoons in the undergrowth. As they reached the mansion's driveway, Victoria took several steps toward the front door, but Thomas did not move. Still holding his arm, she stopped short.

"What?" she asked quietly, her brows furrowed.

He said nothing, but inclined his head. *Come,* his gesture said.

She knew what he wanted. *Yes,* her nod replied.

She went with him, around the corner of the great house and into the shadows behind it.

Desire returned, more intense now than before. It burned her fingertips and her lips. She could barely walk, but he held her firmly. Then he released her, removing his coat and laying it on the ground, seemingly oblivious to the chill. And turning to her, he lifted her effortlessly, laying her down upon the long, leather duster that smelled so sweetly of *him.*

Oh, yes, she thought.

He covered her body with his, the weight of it substantial and thrilling, the feel of his torso and limbs atop hers most welcome. She stretched her hands out to her sides, clutching the grass, wanting to cling to the earth, for she felt she might float away. She waited—longing to experience every moment of this seduction, aching to feel every movement of his desire.

His face was inches from hers, and he smiled. It seemed as if his mouth was full of white, sharp teeth, but surely it was the heat she was in, scrambling her sense of reality. She smiled back. His head lowered and he kissed her forehead and lips. She moaned and tilted back her head. He kissed the small of her neck.

His hands found the buttons of her coat and undid them one by one. She shifted to let the coat come off. He tossed it to the side and gazed down at her. His eyes sparkled in the darkness. Then he pulled open the cardigan and caressed her breasts through the fabric of her jumper. Victoria rose into his touch, arching her back. The caresses became firmer. Her nipples hardened and her face flushed.

She let go of the grass at last, and grasped his hair, holding onto him as if he were a lifeline and she a woman adrift at sea. Without thinking, she shifted her body, scooting the hem of the jumper up beneath her waist, and guided his hand to the space between her legs. His touch was electric, and she felt the massing of energy there, ready to burst.

Then Thomas's mouth came to her neck again, and she pulled it hard against her. His breath was rapid, frantic, and hers matched his in rhythm. Her heart joined in, beating faster than she thought possible. For the briefest moment she felt he was going to back away, but then there was no doubt he would not, could not, leave her in this moment.

Thomas, I love you, she thought.

There was a sound in his throat, almost a growl, and Victoria took it as his affirmation.

And then there was a pain in her neck, a sharp yet thrilling stab that made her gasp and arch backward, still holding his hair. Thomas's body came with her, his mouth pressed to her neck. Every nerve in her body screamed with exhilaration. Something warm coursed down her neck to her shoulders, and Thomas grabbed her face with both hands.

Hold me! Oh, God!

"Victoria," he said against the skin of her neck. "Victoria!" It felt as if her very spirit were flowing out of her and into him.

Yes!

Her body trembled, shook, then exploded in release. The contractions engulfed her, the most beautiful sensations she had ever experienced. She cried out, and the cry was cut short as Thomas put his lips to hers and kissed her deeply. His taste was briny and sweet.

The kiss was long, tender. She was aware of nothing but her lover as he fondled her cheeks, kissed her lips, then licked her neck and shoulders with determined, commanding strokes.

She no longer felt the cool grass nor the cold October air. She could not hear the call of the owl or the sudden howling of distant dogs. She could not smell the damp earth beneath her, nor see anything except the brilliant light that seemed to glow in Thomas's eyes.

She felt as if she were floating.

Time held no meaning.

Space had no sense.

Until the sun announced its return to the east by sending out tendrils of shimmering pink and orange through the trees.

Victoria found herself sitting up in the grass, her jumper back down around her legs, her coat buttoned up properly against the autumn chill. Thomas was standing, looking as pressed and dignified as he ever had. He held out his hand and helped her to her feet. Then, in a quiet voice, he said, "I must go."

And with a bow, he turned and strode away. Victoria blinked, rubbed her eyes, and looked where he had gone. He was no longer there.

"Thomas?" she called.

There was no answer.

She looked up at the brightening sky and shuddered. She was beneath the monstrous copper beech tree, the one that taunted her through her bedroom window at sunset. The dark, twisted branches were suspended over her head, like scythes ready to fall.

We made love under that devil's tree, she thought. She backed away, watching the angry limbs in case they did indeed decide to chop her to pieces. But the tree did not reach for her. The tree did not move.

With her head swimming and her eyes blurry, she made her way back to the front door of the mansion and let herself in as quietly as she could. As she hung her coat in the foyer, she could hear Elizabeth calling for her from down the long hallway.

Victoria straightened her jumper, ran her fingers

through her hair, and went to see what Elizabeth wanted.

And through the haze of her thoughts, she wondered if she had really made love to the beautiful Thomas Rathburn, or if the entire night—the vision of Trask, the demonic wind, the passion beneath the tree—was just a trick of an increasingly fragile mind.

chapter

15

A few minutes remained before the sun rose. Rathburn took his time as he walked across the lower lawn on his way to the cottage. Even having fed on Victoria, his blood still boiled with a singular desire for her. He had never tasted anything so sweet, so exhilarating, as the essence of her life; he had truly made love to her, in a way he never had with anyone since Elaine, when he was just a man. The sharing of their souls thrilled him so profoundly he could hardly imagine ever feeding on another. How incredible it would be to turn her, to make her his bloodmate. He doubted there would be any need for coercion. She would come to him willingly. And even if she didn't, once she had become his subject, he could transform her, *make* her be exactly what he wanted her to be. Just for him.

No wonder Barnabas Collins cared for her so deeply. Even if he had never taken her blood, he knew this woman's spirit, her desires, her pain. If she truly was anything like Josette, Barnabas must indeed long for her with all his heart.

In taking Victoria's blood, Rathburn had consumed so much knowledge of her, so much understanding of who she truly was. He could feel the shattering force of the displacement in time she had suffered. Fear and confusion, doubt and anxiety, all coursed through her mind and body with such intensity it was no wonder she had come so close to emotional collapse. Even for a Vampire, such a sensation of being caught between two worlds would have had a devastating effect on his psyche; as a mere mortal, she could easily be ripped apart by the sheer power of her own emotions. He knew that she still cared deeply for Barnabas. But her fear of him was so unfocused, yet so intense, she might never recover from it.

So much the better for me, Rathburn thought. Still, he could actually feel a certain, odd sympathy for Barnabas Collins and the turmoil of his existence. One thing was for certain—what he had done with Victoria would make procuring any assistance from Barnabas almost impossible; and Barnabas would know what had happened soon enough, if he didn't already. The next time they met, Rathburn knew he would be facing a furious adversary.

He cursed himself then for having allowed his own passions to override his reason. He had too much at stake here, and there was much he didn't yet understand.

Rathburn made his way through the apple orchard, the eastern sky now awash with bright gold. The skin on his hands began to prickle slightly, and his eyes started to tear. He felt . . . tired. He had expended a great deal of energy over the course of the night, and even having fed on Victoria's blood, he needed sleep to restore himself fully. If Barnabas had fed on Carolyn, he would probably be at his strongest by sundown tonight.

Stepping up to the cottage porch, Rathburn was suddenly taken aback by the sight of a glittering silver crucifix nailed to the front door. He growled in his throat, the holy symbol painful to him, yet hardly an insurmountable barrier. Much in the way he had developed a resistance to daylight, he could face such an obstacle without dire consequence, except when it was wielded by an individual with supreme faith in its power.

But anger at this transgression seized him, and he ripped the cross from the door, hurling it into the woods. Then he resolutely took his key from his pocket, unlocked the door and stepped inside, closing it quickly against the onrushing rays of the sun.

Now he saw that, at the two windows in the room, similar crucifixes had been placed on the sills. On the fireplace mantel, another. On the door of the coat closet. And in the kitchen, on the door to the stairwell. He hissed like a furious cat, going through the room and removing the offensive symbols, throwing them into the empty fireplace—except for one, which he thrust into his pants pocket in the event it might be useful later on.

Willie Loomis, he thought. The handyman must have a key to the cottage, and Barnabas had sent him to plant the crosses in hopes that they would be effective in keeping him from his place of rest. He glanced at the hatrack next to the front door, found his still hanging in its proper place, his shades still resting on the mantle. *Damn fool*, Rathburn thought. *If that idiot had any sense whatsoever, he'd have taken those as well.*

There was a rustling sound outside. Focusing his receptors on the area surrounding the cottage, he sought its source, scenting the air for a trace of the familiar—or the unfamiliar. *Yes*. There he was. The culprit was still nearby.

He reached for hat, put it on quickly, and donned his sunglasses. He opened the door and stepped outside, his anger far stronger than his aversion to the sun's irritating rays. He stalked unerringly toward a briar-tangled spot at the edge of the woods, finally catching sight of a crouching figure wearing a green sweater and mud-streaked black denim jeans.

Willie Loomis let out a terrified yelp and scampered into the woods, his fear spurring him on with surprising speed. But Rathburn caught him easily, grabbing him by the neck and jerking him rudely to a stop.

"Whoa, there, not so fast," Rathburn said, turning his victim around to face him. "I guess you must have misunderstood me when you were here last."

Loomis stared back at him in sheer panic, his lips trying vainly to form words.

"Settle down, let's just have a little talk. If I remember, I asked you to please knock when you came for a visit? Yes?"

Loomis nodded, sucking down deep breaths.

"Was there anything unclear about what I asked of you, Willie?"

The man shook his head, finally stammering, "It—It wasn't my fault."

"You apparently possess a key to the cottage. May I have it, please? I'd prefer that uninvited guests not let themselves in when I'm not home."

Trembling, Loomis reached into his pocket and removed a set of keys. He tried to separate one of them, but his fumbling fingers dropped the key ring into the leaves. Rathburn released him, scooped them up and pocketed the lot.

"That'll do. Thank you." He took a step toward the shaking handyman, who backed up against the trunk of a tall poplar. "You know, unintentional rudeness can be forgiven, at least the first time. But I would say you've gone beyond that, wouldn't you?"

"I was just doing what I was told!"

"I realize that. Let me guess. Barnabas told you to plant your little toys throughout my cottage, then wait and see what resulted. Did he really think, knowing what he knows about me, that I'd be seriously affected? Did *you*?"

"I don't know, Mr. Rathburn. But you know how it is. I—I just gotta do what I'm supposed to do. That's all. It ain't personal or nothing."

"I know that. But Willie, you would have been much wiser to at least vacate the premises after you'd taken care of your business. I think you have a fair idea of what can happen when you upset certain types of individuals. Don't you?"

Loomis nodded, his eyes widening with horror. "Don't hurt me, Mr. Rathburn. It—It wasn't my fault!"

Rathburn reached into his back pocket and withdrew the crucifix he had saved. He tossed it to Loomis, saying, "Catch." The man grabbed it with both hands but immediately dropped it. "Pick it up," Rathburn said in a low growl. "Now."

"Jesus, Mr. Rathburn. Please . . . please don't do anything."

"Pick it up!"

Loomis finally knelt and took the cross, holding it to his chest in terror-palsied hands. Rathburn took another step toward him, until his face was only a few inches from the Loomis's.

"Did you expect to see me cowering in fear, trapped out in the open until the sun caught me without any protection? Is that what you expected?"

"I don't know . . . I don't know!"

"Your Barnabas is going to be terribly disappointed in you, Willie." Rathburn then placed his hand directly on the crucifix, pressed it hard against Loomis's chest. Its cold silver began to warm in his palm. "Yes, it's true, some of our kind would find your little trinket a pretty painful sight. And God help them if they touched it. But I'm touching it right now, Willie. Do you see any particularly nasty results?"

Loomis shook his head, again speechless. He tried to back away farther, but the tree prevented him from moving.

"You are lacking in faith, my friend. For all you know about our kind, you still have no faith. How utterly embarrassing for you." He began to concentrate on the silver piece in his hand, focusing his will on its metal surface. "You want to know what it's like for some of us, Willie? Is this what you and Barnabas hoped would happen to me?" He then unleashed a burst of psychic energy, channeling it through his arm like an electrical conduit. The cross suddenly burst into golden radiance, a flare of white fire spewing from beneath Rathburn's palm.

Willie Loomis screamed in agony as the crucifix burned through the fabric of his sweater and found vulnerable flesh. Rathburn pressed it hard against him, sending the young man into a twisting paroxysm of pain, his jaw gaping in a terrible shriek that echoed through the woods like the cry of a wild animal. Finally Rathburn relaxed his grip and the cross fell to the ground, leaving a blackened, smoking imprint on Willie Loomis's breastbone. The handyman dropped to his knees, sobbing, hands clutching the terrible burn.

Rathburn knelt next to him and whispered in his ear, "Does that give you a better understanding, Willie?"

Loomis nodded between racking sobs. He finally looked up, his eyes streaked with tears. "I'm sorry . . . I'm sorry," he whimpered.

Rathburn rose to his feet, glaring at the man with contempt. "Pah," he spat. "If Barnabas told you to come back and try to drive a stake through my heart, you'd do it, wouldn't you? Anything for Mr. Barnabas."

Loomis leaned back against the tree, still clutching the burn on his chest. "I don't have any choice," he sobbed. "I gotta do what he tells me. I gotta. Don't you understand?"

"I understand," Rathburn said in a gentler voice. "But Willie, if you ever come around here again, that will be the end of you. Is that perfectly clear?"

"It may not matter," he whispered. "Barnabas will probably kill me anyway."

"No, he won't. You're the only one he has to protect him." He added mockingly, "He needs you, Willie."

"You don't know what he can be like."

"I have a pretty good idea. Don't forget, I could have killed you just now—quite horribly, if I'd a mind to. But I let you live. Perhaps Barnabas will be just as generous."

"God, it hurts," Loomis whined, his eyes still streaming. "What's he gonna do to me?"

"I doubt he will damage you to the point of being useless to him. Any more than you already are. Now, get out of here, Willie."

Loomis scrambled to his feet, backing slowly away from Rathburn. "He's . . . he's not gonna like this."

"Do you suppose I did? Just remember that next time I will not be so considerate. This time and this time only I have spared your life. What do you say?"

The stricken young man stared back, uncomprehending.

"You say 'thank you.' Wouldn't that be the polite thing to do?"

Willie nodded, now glaring back with a spark of hatred in his eyes. "Yeah. Thank you."

Rathburn stamped a foot and made as if to chase after him. "Now, git!"

With a cry, Loomis leaped away and scrambled out of the trees toward the gravel road, hugging his wounded chest with his arms. He ran at top speed toward the apple orchard without looking back. Rathburn watched him as he disappeared beyond the trees.

"Damn fool," he muttered, kneeling to recover the crucifix before turning back to the cottage and retreating to its cool, dim interior. He made sure the door and windows were securely locked, and hung his coat and hat back on the rack. Well, Barnabas had wasted no time making the first move against him. If Barnabas were already aware of his encounter with Victoria during the night, it was no wonder. And there might be more to come during the day. Rathburn knew that his early warning system would alert him in advance of any physical threat, but today he preferred uninterrupted sleep so that by tonight he would be completely rejuvenated. He still intended to approach Barnabas with the proposal they cooperate to solve the mystery that had brought him to this remarkable corner of the country, daunting though the task might be.

As he lay down on his cot in the cold, comfortable darkness of the cellar, Rathburn quickly began to drift into the deathlike sleep of the undead, even though certain senses remained alert for the approach of danger. And it seemed that no sooner had consciousness begun to fade than those senses suddenly jarred him awake, warning him that he was no longer completely alone in the darkness.

What the hell? No one could have gotten inside without his knowing it.

Gradually, he became aware of a distant sound; a light, feminine laugh, mocking in tone. The strong scent of lilac perfume assailed his nostrils, and he lay frozen, aware that some presence had entered the basement, something that could not be Barnabas, for outside it was daylight. He slowly turned his head to gaze into the total darkness, certain that *something* was there with him, slowly moving nearer.

There. At the far corner of the room a faint, luminous shape was emerging into the air, a silvery mist that swirled steadily toward him, finally coming to rest at the foot of the cot. Abruptly, the air went frigid, much as it had when he saw the ghostly figure the other night at Collinwood. The shape now rose over him, seemingly cognizant of him, studying him, as if seeking a means of *entering* him.

He did not move, for fear of driving this apparition away. But he focused his mental resistance, making sure the will that opposed his could not overcome him. The sickeningly sweet flowery perfume swept over him like a wave, and he knew beyond a shadow of a doubt that this shapeless thing was indeed Angélique.

He felt the spirit being attempting to reach into his brain, to find some opening, some weakness. Yes . . . if he had been taken unaware, as he had in Atlanta, it—*she*—could have insidiously affected his mind. He would never have expected such a thing, and thus been defenseless against it. Angélique must have expected him to be asleep now, and hoped to work some new spell on him that would shape him to do her bidding.

On that count, she would not succeed.

What he heard was not a voice; but words formed in his mind, in silky, musical tones that he knew came from somewhere beyond the barrier of death.

Thomas Rathburn, I know you.

His own thoughts traversed the spaces between them. *Tell me what you want.*

Thomas, let me help you. And in doing so you may help me. Don't you see he has lied to you, that you have fallen for his trickery? You came here for a reason. You must trust your feelings. He would tell you anything to turn you from your purpose.

How could he know my purpose?

He has made many enemies. He would speak the truth to no one. Especially one such as you.

Why would you come to me?

Because of the great power you possess, you alone can help me achieve what I desire. Tomorrow night, the veil between worlds grows thin. You must help me come through. I am the dream to be made flesh. Help me. And then deliver him into my hands. Give him to me, and I will see that you have the revenge you desire.

No. If he is guilty, then I shall destroy him.

The lilting, musical tones grew more melodious in Rathburn's ears.

But, Thomas, think of his anguish. How much sweeter will be your vengeance if he is destroyed by the one he fears most. What are you to him? Do you think he even remembers the death and horror he inflicted upon you in the past? No. Give him to me. In this way, his destruction will have meaning. For both you and I.

Then prove his guilt to me.

The truth is within you, Thomas. You have seen it. I have shown you what happened.

You have manipulated me. Why should I trust you?

Because you have no choice.

Suddenly, Rathburn felt a cold steel vise grip his heart, twisting, ripping. He cried out and jerked upright. And the silvery mist vanished, leaving him in a pool of frigid air from which the scent of lilac rapidly receded. It took several moments for him to completely recover his wits. My God . . . the power she wielded! Even from beyond the grave, it had shocked his sensibilities. Slowly, the air began to warm.

One thing was now perfectly clear. From whatever unearthly realm she inhabited, she had planted the precise images in his mind that would ensure he came to Collinwood. He could understand her desire for his help in achieving her goal of becoming flesh—to mete out a revenge of her own. But why should she help him?

No, he could not possibly trust such a being. But neither could he trust Barnabas Collins. Angélique had been quite right on one count: to a being such as Barnabas, revealing any truth posed a threat to his existence. Rathburn knew that better than anyone.

He lay back on his cot, trying to force himself to relax. Now more than ever he knew he would need all of his strength for the coming night. But he could not forget the disturbing touch of Angélique's cold hand upon his heart. The *pain*! What more might she be able to do to him should he refuse to aid her? After this experience, he could not doubt that Barnabas's fear and hatred of her was genuine.

But the thing that disturbed him most was that after the trauma he had just experienced, his foremost thoughts had turned to Victoria and his growing passion for her.

The very idea was maddening.

Had Angélique herself planted these feelings for Victoria in his heart?

When Rathburn awoke, the sun had not yet fallen below the horizon. But he knew he could not return to sleep, for his blood was still agitated, his spirit too restless. He checked his pocket watch: almost five o'clock. Less than an hour to sundown. Fair enough; he needed to prepare himself for another confrontation with Barnabas Collins. This time, Barnabas would be on the offensive, now that he would certainly know about his encounter with Victoria last night and his confrontation with Willie Loomis this morning.

He put on his protective clothing and stepped outside, intending to walk toward the Old House and wait for sundown, when Barnabas would just be rising. Willie Loomis would offer no opposition; if anything, the poor imbecile would probably be hiding somewhere, dreading the moment when he had to face Barnabas with his failure.

After the ordeal of this morning, Rathburn found the late afternoon sunlight pleasant. Clouds obscured the worst of its burning rays, and the colors in the west—brilliant violet and vibrant gold— brought back wonderful memories of those few autumn days he'd been able to spend with Elaine in between having to march with his regiment to fight the Federals.

Sweet Elaine. He would have sacrificed everything, even the new life he had found, to save her.

But now there is Victoria.

As he sauntered up the hill toward the hulking shape of Collinwood, he was surprised to see a solitary figure walking toward him, dark hair billowing behind her in a light breeze. Yes . . . it was Victoria, who would now be sensitive to him, and at least subliminally aware that he had awakened early. She approached him with a smile, her face a bit pale, eyes slightly fatigued. She wore a tight-fitting, black-ribbed turtleneck, trim blue jeans that flattered her long legs and perfectly shaped hips, and black suede boots with two-inch heels.

He approached her cautiously, barely able to trust his own longings. She was beautiful, and came to him intentionally seductive. His lust for her struck him with sudden ferocity, yet in the sunlight even his strongest passions were dulled and he was able to hold his desire in check.

"Good afternoon," he said to her as she came up to him and slipped into his arms, pressing herself against him and kissing him gently on the lips. She lowered her head and looked up at him with warm, beguiling eyes.

"I'm glad to see you," she said. "I was hoping to run into you."

"Were you?"

She nodded with a sly smile. "Last night was so special to me."

"I enjoyed it," he said, maintaining as much emotional detachment as possible. "You look wonderful."

"It's for you."

"Have you finished with David for the day?"

"Yes. I sent him to play outside until dinnertime."

"I see. I trust he won't cause any trouble if you're not watching him."

"Well, he might." She grinned. "But nothing I can't handle."

"I hope Roger and Elizabeth will see it that way."

"You sound like you expect him to do something terrible."

He smiled. "From what you told me, he's a regular hellion."

"He can be. He's restless. It's almost Halloween and he wants me to help him with a costume."

"Maybe that's what you should be doing."

She frowned at him, tipping back her head and arching one brow. "Aren't you happy to see me?"

"Of course I am. I'd just hate for you to fall into disfavor with Roger and Elizabeth."

"I can take care of David." She looked toward the great house with uncharacteristically cunning eyes. "I can take care of any of them."

He studied her with a concerned eye. His coupling with her had apparently affected her deeply. The bite of the Vampire often released the inhibitions of a mortal heart. Under other circumstances, he would find the idea of a more aggressive, unrepressed Victoria Winters delightful. But for now, he could not dwell on such a possibility. *Business first.*

"What do you want to do tonight?" she asked. "A night on the town? Or maybe a quiet night together—at your cottage?"

Knowing he must, he summoned his strength and said, "It would be best if we didn't see each other tonight. I have things I need to do."

Her painted lips pursed. "Like what? I thought you were on vacation."

He forced a smile. "Only to a point. I still have important affairs to look after."

"Can't they wait?"

"I'm afraid not."

"Thomas," she purred, again pressing close to him. "I want to be with you."

"I know," he said. "I want to be with you, too. But tonight is not possible."

"Are you going to the village?"

"I don't know. I may need to. For business."

"Do it tomorrow."

"Victoria, I can't."

She slipped away from him, disappointment shadowing her eyes. "I thought last night meant something to you."

"You know it did. And I will be with you again. Soon."

"When?"

"Perhaps tomorrow night."

"I don't understand."

Rathburn sighed. He knew that, ordinarily, she would never be so impatient, so distrusting. He should have waited. This was his own fault. "It doesn't matter. Look, I need to leave now. Why don't you go back to David. If I can, I'll stop and see you later tonight."

"After you've taken care of your 'business'?"

"Yes," he said softly. "If I can."

"Maybe you shouldn't bother."

He gazed at her. He could exert his will on her if he wished, mesmerize her, make her malleable in his hands. Yet the idea repulsed him.

"If you wish. I simply asked you to trust me, nothing more."

She seemed to consider the idea. With a melancholy look she finally said, "It's just that I want so much to be with you."

"Patience."

"You ask a lot."

"It's not that much. Now, be good and go see to David."

She glared at him now, obviously angered by his patronizing tone. "Why are you being this way with me?"

"I told you why," he said, as icily as he could manage.

"I see," she said, starting to walk away from him.

He looked after her without speaking, furious that he had let her affect him so deeply. How easy it would be to call her back. *Not now. Not yet.* "Good night, Victoria," he said with a forced note of finality.

She looked back at him, her face dark with pain and ire. Softly, she replied, "Go to hell, Thomas." Then she was gone, on her way back to Collinwood.

He watched after her with a sorrow he had not known in almost a century and a half. *What had he done?* He had allowed her to melt him. Disgusted with himself, he shook away his feelings of hurt, forced himself to focus on the more important issues at hand. Good Christ, his very survival might hinge upon what he did in the next few hours. If he let Victoria affect him so deeply, she became a liability. A potentially fatal one.

Just as she might yet be to Barnabas Collins.

He detoured around the northern end of Collinwood, taking the long way around the upper reaches of the front lawn to the trail that led to the Old House. He did not want Victoria, or anyone else, to be able to see him from the windows of the mansion. Above all, he wanted no witnesses to what might transpire at the Old House. His business with Barnabas Collins was intensely private, and he could afford no distractions.

By the time he reached its expansive portico, the sun was just falling below the horizon. Barnabas would be rising at any time. Rathburn mounted the stairs and knocked on the door, waiting for several long minutes before he heard a cautious shuffling on the other side. Finally, with a groan, the door opened just a crack and the nervous eyes of Willie Loomis appeared on the other side.

"Oh, no," Willie said. "You gotta get out of here, Mr. Rathburn. Go away."

"I've come to see Barnabas, Willie. Open the door and let me in."

"He . . . he ain't here. I don't know when he'll be back."

"Save it for someone who doesn't know the truth. My business here is important. If you don't let me in, Barnabas is going to be even angrier at you than when he finds out what happened this morning."

Loomis hesitated, but finally swung the door open and stepped aside. He stayed well clear of Rathburn, who removed his hat and coat and hung them on the rack without invitation. "Don't worry, Willie. Perhaps I'll put in a good word for you."

"About what, Mr. Rathburn?" came a voice from the darkened recess beneath the stairway landing. A moment later Barnabas Collins stepped out of the shadows, his wolf's-headed walking stick clutched firmly in one hand. "I'm surprised you had the nerve to come here tonight."

"Nice to see you, too," Rathburn said, his battle with his conflicting emotions now wholly forgotten.

"I thought we might continue where we left off last night. And I have a proposition for you."

"Finishing last night's business is indeed in order," Barnabas said, stalking forward with eyes glowing furiously. "You ignored my warning and went to Victoria. Well, Rathburn, that was a grave mistake. And it was the last one you will ever make."

chapter

16

"We missed you at dinner, Victoria." The voice was close, just inside the doorway. There was concern in the tone. "Are you feeling all right?"

"I suppose, Mrs. Stoddard," Victoria said without looking back. She was at the window, her forehead pressed to the cold glass, her eyes closed. Her fingers clutched a glass of Roger's brandy, something she was not accustomed to holding, but this evening it felt just right. She had shed the heeled boots but still wore the sweater and jeans, and the tight fabrics rubbing her skin reminded her of the desire she had yet to have sated. Her feet were bare. "I'll be fine."

There was a pause, and a shuffling sound as the matron of Collinwood took several more steps inside the gallery where Victoria had come to hide. "Would you like me to turn on the light? It's quite dark in here."

"No. Thank you," Victoria said.

"You sound angry."

"Do I? I don't mean to."

"Yes, you do. Is it David? Has he done something you don't want to tell us about? He can be more than a handful, and of course we've never doubted your ability with him. But if there is something Roger or I would need to say to him, something—"

Victoria spun around, brandy nearly spilling from the stemmed goblet. All day, every sight, touch, smell, and sound had been painfully amplified, and at this moment Elizabeth's voice was like a needle in her ear. "Mrs. Stoddard, I'm fine. Please, I need to be alone. I have done my duties for the day, I do my duties every day, so don't I at least deserve my time off?"

Elizabeth, always the epitome of control and reserve, flinched. Her eyes tightened. "I'm sorry. I don't mean to pry, I'm sure you know that."

"I know that." Victoria could hear the tone of her own voice, and it was unfamiliar, unsettling, commanding her to say more than she would want, and in a manner she would not have wanted. "But I don't know much else, do I? I should have learned much more about life than I have by now. I should know some of life's secrets."

"My dear, I don't know what you're trying to say."

"I'm sure you do. Everything is a secret, isn't it?

What is there of life that is not some dark, unspeakable secret?"

Elizabeth straightened, and one hand reached out for the small table by the door as if to steady herself. "What do you mean, Victoria?"

"How can I know what I mean? It's a secret, Mrs. Stoddard. Everything that matters is a mystery. Reality is the biggest and most dangerous mystery of all. It hides in the shadows, breeding, growing, twisting and festering. Light itself is illusion, meant to blind us to truth. Darkness holds the key to existence, only we are not allowed to touch it or understand it, are we? Tell me, is romance truth or an illusion?"

"I . . ." Elizabeth said. "Victoria, are you having one of your night problems that Carolyn has mentioned?"

"Tell me about you and your husband," Victoria said. "Tell me how you managed to cope, knowing he was trying to steal from you, to take your fortune?"

"Victoria!" Elizabeth shuddered, and her mouth remained open for a second. She looked then like a young woman again, vulnerable, anxious. "What are you asking me?"

"And you must have felt so alone after he was . . . gone. Did you look elsewhere for love, for solace? And if you found it, how long did it last? A month? A week? A night? But what about while you were still married to him? Even before Carolyn was born, maybe three years or so before. Did you ever look somewhere else for the companionship he couldn't provide?"

Elizabeth glanced away, to the floor, the hand now causing the table to shake violently, the other hand at her chest as if she was trying to push something back inside, something huge, something agonizing.

"Does love ever last, Mrs. Stoddard?"

"Please don't ask these questions."

Victoria took a step toward Elizabeth, who took a step backward. "I have no mother," Victoria said. "Who else can I talk to about such things? Who else will explain it?"

"What has happened, Victoria, that you would talk to me in such a manner?" Her voice was pleading now, and her eyes were rimmed with tears, something Victoria could not remember having seen before.

"Nothing has happened," Victoria replied. She shook her head, trying to rid herself of the venom that burned inside. She put her fist to her chest. The heart inside was beating, still beating in spite of Thomas's rejection. "I'm sorry. I have no reason to talk to you in such a way."

"Indeed," Elizabeth managed, her face rippling with emotion, her voice barely above a whisper. "Indeed."

"I have a headache, worse than I've had in a long time. I've taken something but it has yet to take effect. Please forgive me."

Elizabeth's sigh was long and heavy and full of unspoken answers. "I will leave you to your recovery," she said at last, "as you wish. Good night."

"Good night."

Good God! What is wrong with me?

Victoria took a long sip from her glass, wishing she'd brought the whole decanter in here. A drunken stupor was just what she needed to be rid of the feelings that boiled inside her.

Last night she had opened her soul, her mind, and her body to Thomas Rathburn. She had allowed herself to trust that this time the pieces would fit just right. This time she would have been right to trust, right to submit, right to love.

But it was no different from any other love story she'd heard or experienced. Love, like light, was an illusion, created by the mysteries of the dark to play havoc with the human heart.

"Stop it," she whispered. *It isn't like he crushed my heart and humiliated me. He said he couldn't see me tonight. That's all.*

Her blood burned like fire.

A dark bird with wide wings fluttered across the lawn, swooping down in search of insects or mice, then disappeared from view. Animals didn't fall in love. They didn't agonize over broken promises or broken intentions. It seemed to her that it must be wonderful to be an animal, a bird of prey, a cougar, a bat. Not to feel emotion. Not to hurt.

But . . .

"But it felt real," Victoria whispered to her reflection on the window. "It was real. I've never felt so totally real in my life."

She put her glass on a low shelf, walked to a chair at the corner of the room, and dropped into it. There were a few magazines in a chair-side rack. Art mostly, and some on New England history. Victoria picked one up, flipped through it, and saw nothing but blurred print. Thomas was a publisher, responsible for a successful magazine. He had much to do to keep it running smoothly, she knew. He would rarely have a rash of uninterrupted days, even while on vacation.

God. Victoria threw the magazine across the room, its pages flapping like wings of a great but dead bird. It landed on the floor, upside down.

The faces in the portraits lining the wall watched her intently, as if they had wisdom to impart, but they had been sealed behind paint and age and faded memories so long that even if she were able to cut open their canvas mouths, nothing would issue forth but stinking, incoherent hisses.

"Don't look at me," Victoria whispered to them.

It hurt so, that was the worse part. This aloneness cut down to the deepest part of her being.

She put her hand over her eyes. and immediately she saw herself back in the grass behind the house, with Thomas over her, kissing her, fondling her, and loving . . . yes, loving . . . her. His hands on her body, exploring with no hesitation, his mouth on her cheek, her neck. His breath taking in her own, making her lungs cry with trepidation and ecstasy, and she, fearful for a moment that they would never again draw air and then crashing back to earth with the sweetest rush of breath ever drawn. His breath. Her breath. One and the same.

Don't think this, Vicki, it will only make you feel worse.

His probing tongue, his demanding hands. Touching her where a woman must be touched, and taking her the way a woman must be taken.

The smell of the dead leaves, the taste of his skin, his eyes beholding her as if she was the most beautiful woman to ever have lived.

Victoria sat straight with a wail of anguish. *Don't think about it!* she told herself, but it was a useless order. Her body was inflamed with need for him. Her blood boiled in her vessels, demanding that she be with him.

She jumped from the chair and began to pace.

It's in your mind, Vicki. This is an emotional problem, not a physical one. Don't think about it and it will go away.

But her blood didn't believe her. It stung the

veins, it churned within the arteries. Every capillary writhed beneath the skin, crying out for Thomas Rathburn.

Thomas, I need you!

She shoved up the sleeve of her sweater and began to dig at the skin of her arm with her nails. She raked viciously, hoping to spill her own blood so that the burning might be cooled.

Stop it, Victoria!

I can't! Thomas, I need you!

The nails drew ugly red welts up on the skin, but it was not enough. Her fingers locked into claws and she dug harder. At last, a spot welled through the abused flesh.

Yes!

A small trickle began, and ran down to the crook of her elbow. But still it burned, still it cried out, still there was no relief. She dug deeper.

"Miss Winters, what are you doing?"

God!

Victoria pulled her sleeve down, and instantly felt the cooling of the blood beneath the fabric. "David, you scared me. I didn't hear you come in."

The boy stared at his governess, his arms crossed. "What were you doing?"

"I, ah . . . had an itch, David, what do you think I was doing?" *The little sneak, always creeping up on others. Someone should tie a cowbell around his neck.*

"Must be a really, really bad itch," David said.

"Never saw anybody scratch like that before."

"Poison ivy," Victoria explained. "It's hard to recognize in autumn when the leaves fall off. The stems are just as toxic, though."

"I know that," David said. He stared at her, his expression controlled, much like that of his aunt, Elizabeth.

"So what is it you want?" Victoria asked. "Lessons are long done, you've had dinner, and I don't feel like playing Scrabble."

"You promised me."

Oh, God, what now? "What, David?"

"You promised and you don't remember?"

"I'm tired. Give me a hint."

"My father says people remember what they want to remember. Guess you just don't want to remember."

Victoria bit the inside of her lip so she wouldn't scream. "I'm sorry David. I have a headache. That makes it hard for me to remember things."

David made a loud, exasperated sound, then said, "My Halloween costume!"

"Oh, yes, that."

"Yes, that! You promised me you'd help me, and Halloween is tomorrow night. I want to do it now."

"Not now, David. I can't."

"Not you can't! You won't! You don't want to and you won't because you're selfish!"

"I didn't say I wouldn't."

"You don't have to!" David glowered. "I can tell!"

"David, tomorrow."

"You're lying to me!"

"Of course I'm not!"

"It's him, isn't it?"

"What?"

"Ever since Mr. Rathburn came to Collinwood, you hardly pay any attention to me at all! You like him, don't you? Are you in love with him? When you look at him, you get all weird, all stupid-acting. It makes me sick!"

"David!"

He brushed past her and picked up the glass of brandy from the shelf. He stormed up to her, his mouth contorted. "What are you drinking? Now you want to be like my father, huh? Oh, great! This is just great!"

"It's none of your business, David, now put the glass—"

With that, David hurled the remaining contents at Victoria. It splashed on her sweater and ran down to her pants.

"David!" Victoria shouted.

Rage drew up her arm and drove her hand out and across his face with such a force that David was sent flying into the shelf and to the wood floor. He grunted once, then gasped, and looked up at her with horror.

David . . . !

David cried out, jumped to his feet and ran from the room.

"David!" she shouted. "Wait! Come back!"

He did not come back. Victoria heard his footfalls on the hall, and moments later a door slammed.

"David!" Victoria ran after him, and stopped before his bedroom. She knocked on the door, leaning her body against the wood to stave off the dreadful, dizzying sensation of guilt. "David, let me in. I'm so very sorry. Please let me come in and talk to you!"

There was no answer.

"I didn't mean to hurt you. I never want to hurt you! I was upset, but that is no excuse. David, please unlock the door!"

There was no answer.

"David?"

And then, in a soft voice, David called to her, "I hate you."

Victoria turned from the door, sobbing, wondering if she had at last lost her mind completely.

Before you do something you will certainly regret," Rathburn said, remaining steadfast before Barnabas's advance, "you might be interested to know that I had an unusual visitor early this morning."

"I'm aware of that," Barnabas said. "I will deal with Willie Loomis in my own way. In my own time."

"Why would I trouble you with that old news?" Rathburn asked. "I'm referring to a different visitor altogether. One with whom you have more than a passing familiarity. One not quite human."

Barnabas drew up short, casting a curious eye at him. "Just what are you talking about, Rathburn?"

"Perhaps you've heard the name Angélique before."

Barnabas Collins's reaction was immediate and surprising. His face grew pale and his shoulders tensed. The fingers gripping his cane turned bone white and he turned from Rathburn as if to hide the terrible dismay and fury that swept across his features.

"Are you saying that Angélique herself appeared to you?"

"Her spirit. Or something of the kind. Like nothing I've ever encountered before. But it was Angélique, without a doubt."

"So," Barnabas whispered. "She has returned."

"In whatever fashion. But, Mr. Collins, my reasons for coming to Collinwood have suddenly become clear to me."

Barnabas turned to face him again. "And just what conclusions have you reached?"

"As difficult as it is to admit, your assumption that I was an agent of Angélique was not altogether wrong. I can assure you, however, that it was entirely without my knowledge or consent. If you will remember, I told you I had no quarrel with you. That is now doubly true. If anything, I would say we have a common enemy."

"That is indeed an interesting statement. So, just what sort of scheme has Angélique involved you in?"

Rathburn studied Barnabas's eyes carefully. "You recall my asking your whereabouts during the Civil War. I was led to believe that a certain . . . incident during that period might have involved you.

Obviously it did not. As you yourself made clear."

Barnabas's face registered surprise. "She lured you here simply to take revenge upon me for something I supposedly did to you a long time ago? I cannot accept that Angélique would use you for so simple a matter, Rathburn. If killing me is what she truly wished, I expect she could manage it without plotting anything quite so elaborate." Barnabas turned and gazed toward the drawing room window. "No, Angélique has no desire to merely end my existence. Rather, she would torment me for the rest of eternity."

Rathburn said softly, "Which is why Angélique led me to Victoria Winters. To see that she was taken from you."

Barnabas now whirled and faced him with pure hatred burning in his red-rimmed eyes. "And for that I do not care if Angélique or any other is to blame. For that, Rathburn, I shall destroy you myself." Barnabas raised his cane. And again, with a metallic *snap*, the gleaming, deadly blade appeared from its tip. Barnabas pointed it at Rathburn and advanced quickly toward him. "You came here to die, my friend. And I shall be happy to oblige you." With a quick thrust, he drove the blade toward his rival's heart.

With lightning speed Rathburn's right hand shot forth and caught the blade just before it struck his chest. He turned the blade aside, but Barnabas then withdrew it, drawing a deep gash in Rathburn's palm. Cold blood streamed from the wound, dripping onto the floor of the Old House foyer. Snakelike, Rathburn hissed, and opened his hand to show it to Barnabas. Within a second the bleeding stopped and the laceration closed, leaving no trace.

"Your haste to destroy me can only work against you," Rathburn said. "The least you could do is hear me out."

Barnabas did not answer but thrust at his chest again. This time the sharp tip struck home, forcing him backward into the drawing room. Rathburn gasped in surprise and agony. He managed to pull himself free of the blade before it could reach the vital organ that preserved his life. Now, realizing there could be no reasoning with his enemy, he glanced around the room for a means to counterattack. *There*. At the fireplace. A poker.

He spun quickly and grabbed the poker from its stand, bringing it up just in time to deflect another blow with a metallic *clang*. He knew if necessary he could transform into mist, assuming he could gain a few moments to complete the process. But he could scarcely afford to retreat, simply postponing the inevitable. He must see his mission through, and somehow appeal to Barnabas's less volatile sentiments.

"Damn you, Barnabas," Rathburn growled. "This can serve no purpose. Listen to me."

Another lunge with the cane, another parry with the poker. The wound in his chest proved more difficult to heal, and the pain prevented him from making a counterstrike that might stun his opponent long enough to reason with him. Now, when Barnabas struck, the force of the blow sent the poker flying from Rathburn's hands. The long, glittering blade slashed right to left, slicing his shirt and finding flesh. Barnabas Collins's ferocity was amazing to behold, his rage fired by his own passion for Victoria Winters. Now, simply to preserve his life, Rathburn knew he might indeed need to transform himself.

Too late. The sword rocketed forward another time, heading unerringly for Rathburn's heart. In a flash his arm came up in a desperate attempt to avert destruction. He caught the blade in his hand, ignoring the bite of its razor-sharp edge, this time clenching it so tightly even Barnabas's strength could not free it. Summoning all his energy, he twisted his wrist and snapped the metal blade from the end of the cane. In a rage, he flung it back at Barnabas, a whirling projectile seeking his enemy's heart. Barnabas quickly sidestepped, and the blade slammed into the far wall of the foyer, its point driving several inches into the wood.

Then Rathburn reached into his pocket and withdrew the crucifix he had saved. He held it up to Barnabas's eyes, drawing a pained cry from the other Vampire's lips. Barnabas turned away from the gleaming holy symbol, his shoulders still shaking with fury.

Now, as Rathburn began to recover his composure, he said in a low voice, "Barnabas. Listen to me. I know that pleasant conversation is not your most ardent desire at the moment, but you must hear me out. As a token of good faith, I will put this away." When Rathburn slipped the cross back into his pocket, Barnabas slowly turned, raising his eyes to meet his rival's. They remained ablaze with crimson fire. Rathburn knew what he must now say, but could barely bring the words forth from his lips.

"Barnabas, if you agree to help me, I will free Victoria. She may become yours, if that is her destiny. Whatever her choice, it will be with no interference from me."

Barnabas glared at him as if unaffected by his statement. But by and by, his glowing eyes cooled and he lowered the cane, resting his weight upon it as if all his strength had finally departed. "You are indeed a force to be reckoned with, Rathburn. Say what it is you have to say."

"I believe the timing of my coming here is important. Tomorrow is Halloween. As trite as it may sound, in the old days, the devil's night was looked upon as a significant, fateful time, when the barrier between the worlds of the living and the dead becomes thin. When Angélique visited me this morning, I felt as if she were trying to enter me, somehow. At least that was her intention. I was able to ward her off. But what she revealed to me is important. To both of us.

"I believe that on All Hallows Eve she intends to try to come forth into this world—with my assistance."

Barnabas regarded him with shock, his features slowly reverting to his former rage. "Then that is all the more reason for you to be destroyed."

"Don't be a fool," Rathburn said, his voice a low, catlike growl. "Only together might we be able to stop her."

"You are the fool, Rathburn, thinking I would help you, that I would trust you!"

"I give you my word, Barnabas. If you help me, I will free Victoria."

Barnabas would not be swayed. "It would appear that Victoria is lost to me anyway. You've seen how she reacts toward me. Nothing I have done or can do is able to change that. And I still have no reason to trust you. For all I know, this may be a ploy to actually bring Angélique forth. Do you actually imagine the two of you could work together against me? I can promise you, if you do, then you will suffer every vile plague that she can visit upon you. That is her way." He glared spitefully at Rathburn's inscrutable face. "Can you even fathom her talents, Rathburn? She can tear you apart from the inside, leaving every cell in your undead body to scream in agony. She can haunt your mind endlessly, until you wish for the peace of insanity that will never come. If she wishes, she can take over your body and cause you to do her bidding, with no more mind than a mere puppet." He paused, tightened his jaw. "If, somehow, you were to free her, then at least I should enjoy a few moments of knowing the torture you would endure at her hands."

"Touché," Rathburn said. "But Barnabas . . . you don't believe Victoria is forever lost to you any more than you believe I'm telling you the truth. Admit it. But I know this: if you were to see Victoria taken from you to become my bloodmate, Angélique would win. And after that, if she actually is able to come forth, then she is, quite literally, all you have left."

Barnabas's shoulders slumped, his face darkening with defeat. *He knew.* Rathburn smiled triumphantly to himself. He was halfway there.

And now to lay the bait.

"I'm telling you, Barnabas. Because Angélique has manipulated me—and presents a personal danger to me—I will make every effort to stop her. To destroy her."

"You cannot destroy her," Barnabas said simply. "Regardless of how strong you might imagine yourself to be, Rathburn, she would turn that strength to naught with a flick of her hand should she cross over. The most one can hope is to keep her at bay on the other side—on the dark side."

Rathburn pressed on. "Then I will do everything I can to keep her there—to lock the portal doors between our worlds. And I believe I can. *If* you help me. If you do not, I will simply take Victoria away, and then whatever will be, will be."

Barnabas said quietly, "I am curious, Rathburn. What does it matter to you whether she returns or doesn't?"

"She touched me, Barnabas. She reached into me and nearly wrenched my heart from my body. I have no doubt that she can do it again, and complete that task if given the chance. That's why I need you. Your psychic ability, in addition to mine, will build a far more effective wall against her."

Barnabas regarded him gravely. "Do you understand the meaning of pure hatred, Rathburn? A hatred such as hers, one so deep, so consuming—so *timeless*—can only be a result of broken love. Yes, she once loved me. But love, for her, means possession. Having been denied that kind of jealous love, she has vowed to torment me through all eternity. And that vow is probably all that has preserved her spirit. If she comes back, I have nothing to look forward to but countless lifetimes of enduring hell."

"Then," Rathburn said softly, "I'd say that far outweighs whatever threat you perceive from me."

In a weary voice Barnabas said, "You leave me

little choice, Mr. Rathburn. But I want to tell you something. No matter what you feel about Angélique, the two of you deserve one another. I have existed this way for all these years, despising every moment of it, repulsed by every unholy thing I have been driven to do. Yet you revel in your condition. You thrive on the power. You sicken me."

"*C'est la vie*. Are you with me?"

"Only to stop Angélique."

"That's all I ask."

"You realize the only way to fight her is on her terms. Are you up to that task, Rathburn?"

"I am not entirely ignorant of the black arts. . . . You?"

Barnabas nodded. "But one fact I must reiterate. She must be kept on the other side of the veil between our worlds. Even from there she can wield power, but should she come even part of the way through, she might be able to affect our movements, our thoughts. Do you understand me?"

"I hear you."

Barnabas appeared to ponder the proposition for several moments, the turmoil cutting his features like a knife. At last he said in a resigned tone, "There is a room at Collinwood that may provide at least some of the resources we need. No one living there now knows of its existence. But Angélique once used it to work her own secret spells. The place is repulsive to me. It is full of her grimoires. Many of them are so arcane as to be beyond my comprehension."

"Then that is where we must go."

Barnabas took a step closer to Rathburn, his face still glowering dangerously. "Meddling with the powers of darkness is not something to be taken lightly, Rathburn. But then, I'm sure you know that."

Rathburn nodded grimly. Barnabas was right on that count. Having acquainted himself with certain books of magic and mystical lore, Rathburn knew that attempting to manipulate occult powers could as often as not backfire. The eldritch forces that existed in their unseen realms cared nothing for the motives of those who attempted to conjure them. Any black spell cast by a user was likely to return to him threefold; a terrible price to pay to bring down an enemy.

"Tell me," Rathburn said. "Is Angélique's body buried somewhere on the property?"

Barnabas nodded solemnly. "It is nearby. At least, I can lead you to the ground where she was first laid to rest. Whether or not there is actually a body there remains to be seen."

Rathburn could not suppress a shiver of cold dread. Playing Angélique and Barnabas against each other posed risks to him that he could not foresee. Yet it was the only way to resolve the problems at hand.

Yes, Angélique, I will help bring you forth. You may

have your precious Barnabas. But then we shall see what happens to you as well.

"By showing you this," Barnabas said, his voice echoing as he led Rathburn down the stairs to the cellar of the Old House, "I am putting more faith in you than I believe you deserve. If you betray me, nothing Angélique could ever do will prevent me from seeing you destroyed."

Rathburn followed two steps behind Barnabas as they reached the dank, earthen-floored cellar of the ancient mansion then crossed a pitch-black room to what appeared, even to Rathburn's ultrasensitive eyes, to be a blank stone wall. Reaching up to a particular spot, Barnabas pressed his palm against the stone, and a panel in the wall swung slowly inward with a rough scraping sound. The opening revealed a dark passageway that disappeared around a curve in the distance.

"During the Revolutionary War," Barnabas said, "my family built a number of secret passages and chambers, to hide ammunition and supplies. Then during the War of 1812, new ones were added and joined the old, forming a complex network around the estate. From here we can get into the cellar of Collinwood, and then into the closed-off areas of the house without being seen or heard."

Rathburn went after him into the passage, running his hand along the wall to help guide him.

"Intriguing. You know, I've always wanted a place like this."

Barnabas said nothing more, continuing down a long, narrow corridor that descended gradually for what Rathburn guessed was at least two hundred yards. Here, the crudely hewn walls were damp, and overhead, the roots of trees had pushed their way through the ceiling and anchored to the walls like frozen, tangled serpents. Eventually the passage began to rise again, finally ending at a three-way fork. Barnabas chose the path to the right, and pointed to the others. "The left one leads to a cave near Widows' Hill. The other leads to death for any human unlucky enough to stumble into it. Stay close to me, Rathburn, for it is not the only one that could prove to be a dead end."

The passage divided several more times, and at each junction Barnabas unhesitatingly chose his path. Even with his keen senses, Rathburn found himself hard-pressed to determine the exact direction they were heading and the distance they had covered. Finally, they came to what appeared to be a featureless stone bulwark; and as before, Barnabas located the precise pressure point that would open the secret door. This one swung slowly inward, and from the darkness issued the odors of human habitation—or at least traces of it, from things moldering in the darkness that had once belonged to countless unknown individuals.

The cellar of Collinwood.

As they made their way carefully into the light-less space, they were forced to avoid stacks of old boxes and bundles that contained the last remaining articles of long dead generations, both the owners and their valuables mostly forgotten. Rathburn sensed the presence of minuscule lives around them—spiders and roaches, a few mice, perhaps rats. When Barnabas finally came to a wooden shelf of old storage jars and metal cans, he reached behind it and flicked a hidden dead bolt. The shelf and a portion of wall slowly opened, revealing a narrow stone staircase leading up into blackness so thick even Rathburn's attuned eyes were sightless within it. But Barnabas proceeded silently through the aperture, and Rathburn tenaciously followed, all the while wondering if he himself were being led into some kind of trap.

The staircase wound upward for several flights, the stone steps finally giving way to wooden ones. At several points Rathburn saw featureless walls that must open to various rooms in the house, or at least other passageways. Barnabas came to one and opened it silently, taking them into a room with a single window, through which moonlight gleamed faintly. When Barnabas closed the panel, Rathburn saw that, from this side of the wall, the door appeared as a mere blank wall, with nary a seam to betray what hid behind it.

"Where are we?" Rathburn asked softly.

"An old cabinet room in the west wing. The door to the hall has been plastered over. We will not be disturbed."

Rathburn looked around, seeing that the walls of the chamber were lined with tall shelves containing hundreds of dust-covered, moldy books. When he brushed the dust from some of the spines, the moonlight revealed their titles: *The Spheres Beyond Sound*, *The Marrow of Astrology*, *Linton Witch Stories*, and *Phrenology Amongst the Todas*, among others. All were certainly over a hundred years old.

"Angélique's?" he asked.

Barnabas chuckled dryly. "Hardly. These would belong to certain other family members whose tastes favored the esoteric. Angélique would have found these merely amusing."

Now, Barnabas went to a tall wooden cabinet against the wall adjacent to the window. Again, releasing a hidden catch, he pulled the cabinet open to reveal yet another small opening into a dark chamber. Both of them had to stoop to enter the room, which was a small cubicle with only the narrowest glass slit to admit a few rays of moonlight. And Rathburn could scarcely refrain from gasping at the sight of this hidden "library." Several shelves of ancient tomes lined one wall, while another cabinet contained rows of glass vials and flasks, some stained by the mud-colored residue of various unknown substances. *How many of them might still be potent?* Rathburn wondered, picking up one, opening the glass stopper and sniffing the contents. A whiff of something acrid, a sickening combination of vinegar and sulfur, wafted from the container.

Studying the titles of the ancient books on the shelves, Rathburn could hardly repress a shudder. Indeed, the tomes found here could be possessed only by one deeply ensconced in the occult. Some of them he had seen before. Others he knew only by their reputations—reputations foul indeed, even among other members of the undead. The most innocuous of them were a John Dee translation of *The Key of Solomon*, the *Tibetan Book of the Dead*, a collection of anonymous writings on West Indian *Voudoun*, and, interestingly, a number of journals by Cotton Mather, the infamous seventeenth century witch hunter. But prominent among the dread works was a thick, leather-bound volume entitled *Al Azif*, by one Abd al-Azhred; a rotting copy of Olaus Wormius's *Malleus Maleficarum*; and a painstakingly handwritten transcript—probably by Angélique herself—of le Comte d'Arsenault's *Les Cultes des Morts Vivants*. Rathburn had never been certain that some of these truly existed. Now, facing him from their shelves, they seemed to exude pure, odious power that dared him to so much as peer at their contents.

"Well," Barnabas said, studying Rathburn's

gloomy expression. "Here they are. Can we accomplish what you intend with these?"

Rathburn nodded slowly. "I fear we can."

"An apt way of putting it."

Carefully removing one of the books from the shelf, Rathburn opened it and studied the contents. Latin. Another was in French. Yet others in Arabic, some Hebraic. But in examining a number of the charts, symbols and English notes on some of the spells, he knew that these were indeed the keys he would need to engage the spirit of the long-dead witch.

"My Latin is rather rusty," Rathburn said. "A lexicon wouldn't hurt."

"In the cabinet room," Barnabas replied. "I think you will find what you need in there."

Rathburn went out through the low entrance to the larger room, leaving Barnabas to peruse some of the terrible grimoires for himself. Rathburn ran his eyes up and down the shelves but did not immediately discover what he was looking for. Going to a large bureau in one corner of the room, he opened a few of the drawers, finding numerous papers, envelopes, notebooks, and ledgers. And then his eye was drawn like a magnet to it: an ancient, yellowed envelope addressed to a Mr. Edward Collins, lying atop others in the bottom drawer.

The postmark read: December 1864.

Almost afraid of what the contents might reveal,

Rathburn gingerly opened the envelope, finding within a letter written on the back of a strip of wallpaper—which was oftentimes one of the few writing materials to be found in the war-torn country of those days. The return address indicated the writer lived in Baltimore, Maryland.

The letter read:

Dear Edward,

I don't know when this letter might reach you, as postal delivery is sporadic at best under the current conditions of war. This is the most shameful admission I could ever make, yet I cannot hide what facts I know simply because they are unbearable. But I am certain you would want to know, for you and he were close in age and in friendship.

My son, your cousin Andrew, has been court-martialed and executed for terrible crimes perpetrated during his service to his country. I do not know the complete story, for the army refuses to elaborate further on the circumstances. I am not well enough to travel, and of course, your Aunt Anna has been gone for over a year now. It cuts me to the core that my son had no family to stand with him even when the sentence was handed down.

All I have been told is that he and a number of men from his company deserted their ranks and committed the most heinous murders imaginable, taking the lives of a young Virginia woman and her child, only because they were rumored to be the family of a Confederate officer.

You and I both knew Andrew to have been an honorable, God-fearing young man, and it shocks and pains me to relate how he could have been guilty of these vicious and horrifying crimes. But I know that war changes people, and I can only believe that poor Andrew himself must have suffered unspeakable hells to be driven to such depravity. I know that forgiveness is the commandment of the Lord, and it is my deepest wish that, one day, I shall indeed be able to forgive my son for these acts that caused him to be taken from the world in such a disgraceful manner.

I pray that God will have mercy on my son's tormented soul.

> *Your loving uncle,*
> *Gordon Collins*

"Oh, my God. My God," Rathburn whispered. For a moment he felt strangely dissociated, almost faint. Here it was: the proof of the Collins family's involvement in the murder of his wife and child. The proof he had hoped to find from the moment he arrived here.

But for one thing.

It was not Barnabas.

The implications were staggering, shocking. Barnabas Collins, innocent of those murders; yet

Angélique had without hesitation placed the blame on him.

Simply to ensure his own cooperation?

She had lied to him. What else might she be lying about?

But he had already assumed she could not be trusted.

This must change nothing.

A moment later Barnabas reappeared in the doorway. "I believe this is what you're looking for," he said, reaching for a volume on a shelf directly in front of Rathburn. Seeing Rathburn's dazed expression, he studied him with a wary eye. "What is it? What's wrong?"

Rathburn could barely speak, finally managing, "I think I just walked over my own grave."

"What do you mean by that?"

He shook himself, trying to throw off the terrible mantle of shock and disbelief that had enveloped him. "Nothing," he whispered, more to himself than Barnabas. "I'm all right. Just felt a chill. I have a feeling Angélique will know what we are up to." That much was true; he thought he could sense a presence in the chamber, as if they were being watched.

He took the book that Barnabas handed him, still under the other's scrutiny. It appeared to be an acceptable Latin-to-English dictionary that would certainly help him translate any number of instruc-

tions for the upcoming rituals, if not the spells themselves. He could read the French, and most of the
Hebraic and Arabic texts would be used only for
symbols that might need to be rendered at the site of
the witch's grave.

"Let's take what we need and get out of here,"
Rathburn said, eyeing Barnabas with renewed cold-
ness. "You were right about one thing—it is a repulsive place."

As the two of them collected the materials from
the arcane library, Rathburn felt confident that
within these ancient volumes the means for working
the spells he desired could be discovered and utilized. But he knew that he and Barnabas would need
to pore over them thoroughly until the coming of
dawn, and that he himself would need to continue
and rehearse his own special part over the course of
the following day. Which meant that by the coming
of nightfall he would be weary.

And worst of all, hungry.

chapter

18

When Victoria opened her eyes, she could see hazy sunlight through the shades at her window. When she sat up, her muscles ached and her head felt heavy. It must still be early, she thought; but upon looking at the clock on her nightstand, she received an unnerving jolt. It was well after ten in the morning. But she never slept so late on a weekday. What was she going to do about David's lessons?

The incidents of the previous evening came flooding back with terrible clarity, and her heart sank as she remembered David's last words to her: "*I hate you.*" She had slapped him. Hard. Probably bruised him, enough so that his father would wonder what had happened to him. David had annoyed and upset her terribly, but that was no reason to strike him. She had never laid a hand on him before. He would surely be angry with her, but worse, afraid and distrusting. For a boy with such a volatile temperament, that was a dangerous combination.

She pulled herself from bed, feeling dizzy and wrung-out. She'd had a couple of drinks the night before, but not enough to affect her like this. At least the terrible burning in her blood had subsided, seemingly dissipated by the light of day.

You just needed a night's sleep, she told herself. *Now you'll be calm enough to make amends with David. And you and he will make the best Halloween costume in the whole of Maine if it takes the entire day.*

She pulled on her housecoat, glancing over at the sweater, jeans, and boots she'd left on the bed-side chair. Had she actually gone out in those? She felt instantly embarrassed.

I don't want to think about it.

She slipped into the hall, heading for David's bedroom. His door was open, and looking in, she found the room vacant. A tremor of fear shook her. If David had gone to Roger to tell him what she had done to him, quite a serious reception might be wait-ing for her downstairs.

Gathering her courage, Victoria went down the silent hall to the landing that overlooked the foyer. No sound came from the lower floor except the soft ticking of the grandfather clock in the corner. Going down the creaking stairs, she crept to the drawing room door and peeked inside, finding it empty, much to her relief. She would have to explain her tardiness eventually, but better to do it later, if possible. Right now, she hardly felt like seeing anyone, least of all David; yet she knew he was the one she needed to see most.

She turned down the hall to the dining room, passing Roger's study, the main floor library, and Elizabeth's office, all of which were unoccupied. Roger would be at the plant, but it was rare for Elizabeth and Carolyn to be out at this hour. If they'd gone on errands, that suited her fine. But where was David? It was unlikely they would have taken him along—not without consulting her first, for they would expect her to have his day planned out.

The dining room was similarly empty, and in a last good-faith effort, she went through to the kitchen, where she discovered Mrs. Johnson wiping down the countertop with a wet rag. When the housekeeper saw her, she gave Victoria one of her typical scowls. "Ah, there you are," she said softly. "I was wondering if you were sick, since you didn't come down for breakfast this morning. Missed dinner last night, too."

"I'm not feeling all that well," she admitted. "Have you seen David?"

Mrs. Johnson shook her head. "He skipped breakfast, too. I saw him an hour or so ago, in his room. He didn't have a word to say, though. Must be in one of his moods."

"I guess he is," Victoria said. "We had a little disagreement last night."

"I see."

"I think it's better if we take the day off."

"I see."

Mrs. Johnson's mouth formed a tight line and her tone changed. "David is a little ruffian who doesn't deserve a day off from his schoolwork to appease a disagreement, Victoria."

"Oh, but we'll make up for it tomorrow," she said. "First day of November and we begin a whole new series on geometry and civics."

"I'm sure you know best. But if you want anything to eat, get it now. I'm about to mop in here."

"I'm not hungry, but thank you. By the way . . . are Carolyn and Mrs. Stoddard home?"

"Mrs. Stoddard had an early meeting with Mr. DiCenzo, the lawyer. She should be back soon, I suppose. And I think Carolyn's still here, somewhere. Probably in her room."

"Thanks," Victoria said, turning to leave.

"You look peaked," Mrs. Johnson called after her. "Are you sure you don't want anything to eat? Or a cup of coffee?"

"Nothing, thank you. Eating is the last thing I want to do," she said, her stomach lurching at the thought of so much as a drink of water.

"Maybe you should go back to bed."

"I'm sure I'll feel better in a little while." She headed back toward the foyer, leaving Mrs. Johnson clucking like a mother hen. Just as Victoria started to mount the stairs, the front door opened and Elizabeth stepped in, wrapped in her heavy winter coat.

"Ah, Vicki. Goodness, it's gotten cold out," she said, at first smiling vaguely, but then frowning as she saw Victoria in her housecoat. "Are you feeling ill?"

"I'm afraid I might be coming down with something."

Elizabeth slipped off her coat and hung it on the rack. "I thought as much, after last night. You were not yourself, Vicki, and I must say it gave me some concern."

God, yes, I think I said some terrible things. I don't remember clearly and don't think I want to. But Elizabeth's face says enough. What's wrong with me? "Yes, well . . . Mrs. Johnson recommended I go back to bed."

"You do look pale," Elizabeth said, touching Victoria's forehead with the back of her hand. "But you don't have a fever. In fact, your skin's rather clammy. Carolyn comes down with the same symptoms once in a while, but she seems to get over them quickly. Do you have any aspirin in your room?"

"I think so." Then, in what she hoped sounded like a matter-of-fact tone, she asked, "Have you seen David this morning?"

"No, I haven't. Am I to take it there's no class for him today?"

"I thought a day off might be nice for a change. Tonight's Halloween and all. Not quite a national holiday but I figured—"

"That's fine," Elizabeth said. "I'm sure Roger has no problem with an occasional break for the boy. But, Vicki, last night—I thought about it, about what you said and how distressed you seemed, and I'm wondering if working with David has become too much for you?"

Victoria's mouth dropped open. "Oh! No, absolutely not! Please don't ever think such a thing!"

"Then perhaps living here, at Collinwood? It is quite isolated. Roger and I, Carolyn and David, are used to living a life of frequent solitude away from others, but you . . ."

"No, no," Victoria said. "You misunderstand. It is nothing like that, I assure you!"

"Or if not David or Collinwood, perhaps it was something else entirely."

"What do you mean?"

"Although Mr. Rathburn has only been here a short time, I've noticed your interest in him. It hasn't been hard to detect. And it is obvious that he, too, is drawn to you. So with your harsh words to me last evening, I thought perhaps something might have happened between you that—"

"Mr. Rathburn? Oh, no, you're mistaken. I've no interest in him whatsoever. He was pleasant company for several evenings, nothing more." She tried to smile. It hurt her face.

Elizabeth nodded, not clearly convinced but willing to let it go. "Very well. If you need anything, just call. I can have Mrs. Johnson bring you up something to eat, if you'd like."

"No, no, that's all right." Victoria started up the stairs, aware that Elizabeth was watching after her with a resigned expression. Victoria couldn't begin to explain what had been happening to her. She couldn't even be sure that any of the frightening things she'd experienced were real. To believe it was would be to admit that forces she couldn't understand were attempting to take hold of her . . . to hurt her. Yet the alternative was just as disturbing, if not more so.

I can't be losing my mind! I won't, I refuse!

"Well," she said to herself as she reached the top of the staircase. "Thank God David hasn't said anything to Elizabeth about what I did to him. But, on the other hand . . ."

If he hasn't told anyone, he must have something in mind to get back at me.

When she reached her room, the first thing she saw was a familiar-looking black sheet lying on her bed. David's Dracula cape. But as she picked it up, she found it had been torn to shreds. And then, on her dresser mirror, written in crude letters, with red lipstick: LYING BITCH.

"Oh, no," she whispered, tears suddenly burning in her eyes. How many times had she promised to work on his costume with him? He'd been so looking forward to trick-or-treating in Collinsport.

There wasn't much to his outfit. How much of her time could it have possibly taken? *My God*. Going back on her word was, to him, probably even worse than hitting him. As she stared at the awful words on the mirror, she felt her heart rise to her throat, and sobs that she could not quell began to rack her body. David could be rancorous and even cruel, but he had never been so openly vulgar with her.

He had to have done this in the brief time she was downstairs. At least he was in the house. Hurrying back to his room, she found it still empty. She didn't want to call out for him and risk alerting the others in the house to the problem. She went down the hall, room to room, looking in the gallery, the second floor study, the storage rooms . . . everywhere. Except for Carolyn's room, the door to which was closed. Hesitantly, she stepped up to it and knocked softly. A moment later Carolyn called, "Come in."

The young woman was at her bureau brushing her hair. She was dressed in expensive jeans and a blue cashmere sweater. "Hi, Vicki," she said, glancing at her in the mirror. "What's up?"

"I'm looking for David. Have you seen him in the last few minutes?"

"When are you not looking for David?" Carolyn laughed. "No, I haven't seen him."

Victoria wondered if she should confide in Carolyn—at least about her argument with the boy. The two of them were close enough that they could trust each other with at least minor secrets.

Carolyn put the brush down and turned to look at Victoria fully. "Hey, you don't look good. What is it? Something's wrong."

Victoria blurted, "I've done a terrible thing. I got upset with David last night and I slapped him."

"Well, well, Miss Self-Control finally lost it!" Carolyn said with a conspiratorial grin.

"Carolyn, I'm serious. I hit him—hard. And now it seems he's hiding from me."

"If you slapped David, I'm sure he deserved it," Carolyn said. "But of course he won't think so. He never does."

"No," Victoria said adamantly. "He didn't. This time it was my fault. I'd promised to help him with his Halloween costume and I kept putting it off. He got upset, but I completely lost my temper. Now it's too late, he's . . . he's . . ."

Carolyn stood up. "God, Vicki. Something's really wrong, isn't it?"

"Come with me." She led Carolyn to her room and showed her the torn cape and the crude message on the mirror. "He just did this a few minutes ago. But I don't know where he is."

"He really is pissed," Carolyn said.

"I'd rather not tell your mother or Roger, if it can

be avoided," Victoria said. "I need to work this out with him myself."

"Yes, I think you do." Carolyn glanced at her watch.

"When do you go to work today?"

"Not until this afternoon," Carolyn said. "Why? You said you needed to work this out with David yourself."

"True, but I have to find him first."

Carolyn rolled her eyes. "Vicki, you chased him off. I think you should find him. It's not my job."

Victoria grabbed for Carolyn's arm. She didn't care how desperate she might sound or how much Carolyn's reference to her job hurt her, for at times she thought she and Carolyn were truly friends. "Please! You've known David longer than I have. You know how he has little control over his temper. I'm afraid he might be planning something dangerous, to himself or to others! I need help finding him."

Carolyn pondered this, her face showing traces of irritation, then worry. Then she said, "All right. I'll help you look for him."

"Would you?" Victoria said gratefully. "Thanks."

"He could be anywhere. He may even have gone into the closed-off wings. Is Mother home from her meeting?"

"Yes."

"Okay. I'll look in the east wing. You want to try the west wing?"

"Yes, anything."

"Don't worry, we'll find him. Get dressed. I'll go ahead and start looking."

Victoria nodded and went back to her room. She hurriedly pulled on jeans, a knit shirt, and her well-worn suede loafers, which she hoped would allow her to step softly on the ancient, creaky floors of the deserted west wing. Just as she was about to leave her room, she stopped, recalling that there would be few, if any, working lights in the closed-off corridors. She had not been into that wing in ages. Even at the best of times it seemed like an entity separate from the rest of the house, its closed doors concealing a past peopled with the figures from the many oil portraits throughout the house and filled with their countless secrets, dark secrets she felt were best left undisturbed. Taking a small flashlight from her nightstand, she set off down the hall, dreading what she was about to do, but dreading even more leaving David to carry out whatever vindictive scheme he might have in mind for her.

The door to the west wing lay at the end of the hall beyond her bedroom. Elizabeth had locked it years ago, but David had jimmied it so many times that the lock gave with only a firm twist of the old brass knob. Now, as Victoria pushed it slowly open, she saw a long, dim corridor before her, from which a stale, musty odor crept like an invisible fog. In the distance an alcove with a single window provided the only light in the hallway, murky as it filtered through the dusty, cobwebbed panes. All of the doors on both sides of the passage were closed. Most of them probably had not been opened since the wing had been shut off, long before she ever arrived at Collinwood.

Except by David, perhaps. If anyone knew what lay behind these mysterious barriers, David Collins did. He could get anywhere. He knew this place was frightening to her, which was exactly why he might decide to hide there.

Switching on her flashlight, she moved ahead, her footsteps causing the hardwood floor to groan despite her best efforts to walk softly. Shining the light downward, she saw that the dust covering the floor had been disturbed, but it was still so thick she could not tell if it had been this morning or a month ago.

She tried the knobs of the first few doors. Each was locked, but knowing David could often find a way around petty inconveniences, she paused at a couple of them and listened, half anticipating some movement to come from the other side. She heard no sound but the low murmur of settling boards— nothing she could not attribute to the normal sounds in such an ancient structure.

Thank God, she thought, almost hoping she would not find David in this near-forgotten corner of the Collins family's world.

The next door she tried did open. Fanning the light beam about, she realized she was staring at what must have once been an opulent bedroom, either for a family member or some distinguished guest. The arched ceiling rose high above, plastered in faded blue, decorated with small, gold-painted stars. A huge, web-shrouded canopy bed occupied the better part of the chamber, its mattress exposed and moldering. A few chairs and a table were covered with yellowed, mildewed sheets, but an exotic lamp and a couple of Romanesque statues stood on an uncovered oak desk in one corner. Through the filthy, undraped bay window a few sickly rays of sunlight tried to push their way into the gloom, all but halted by the barrier of cobwebs across what might once have been recognizable as panes of intricately etched glass.

For a second she thought something in the room moved—a shadow! "David?" she whispered. But then she realized that beyond the window a tree swayed slightly in the breeze, disturbing the ghostly light that played through the web-frosted glass. Turning back to the hall, she closed the door too quickly, and it slammed loudly, the sound echoing through the corridor like a gunshot. She moved on, shuddering involuntarily, her remorse at having struck David tempered by her irritation at being forced to explore this unpleasant portion of Collinwood.

Something nearby went *clunk*. She froze.

She was standing next to a long section of unbroken wall, a space between two doors that seemed too large for only the rooms behind them. She held her breath, waiting for the sound to come again, leaning against the cold plaster wall to keep from shifting her balance and creaking the floor. For several seconds nothing further disturbed the stillness, but as she let one hand run along the wall, she felt a rough ridge beneath her fingertips. She followed its contour, which ran vertically up the wall.

A door. There was once a door here, now plastered over.

Something on the other side of the wall shuffled . . . something heavy. She backed away, staring at the smooth, pale surface.

It must be David, she thought. *He must know some way into whatever room is behind that wall.*

She went to the next door—the last one on this side of the hall—which also opened easily. This was little more than a small cubicle, which appeared to have once been a study or private library. A single, tiny window opposite the door overlooked the lower lawn; the other walls were lined with shelves, empty but for a few worm-eaten books whose covers were completely illegible. An old hurricane lantern stood on a crooked wooden desk, both layered with dust and cobwebs. The only other furniture was a rickety wooden chair, which looked as though it would fall apart beneath any weight.

"David?"

She saw no door to connect with the space between here and the bedroom she'd left. In parts of the house, she knew, there were hidden panels leading to passageways behind the walls; perhaps one of them was here. She cautiously made her way inside, gingerly touching one of the shelves, finally grabbing hold of it and shaking it to see if it might betray a secret doorway. It seemed sturdy and did not so much as jiggle. With her knuckles, she rapped softly on the back panel. Solid. Apparently a permanent wall.

She thought she heard another shuffling sound somewhere, and stood completely still, cocking her head to listen. Then: a low, whispery hiss, rising and falling, slowly, rhythmically.

Breathing?

"David?" *Oh, please be you, David!*

The sound seemed to come from close at hand, as if its source were in the room with her. She backed toward the door to the hall, her pulse quickening. This could not be any of David's doing—could it?

The dim sunlight began to fade. The flashlight beam faltered. And then a thick darkness began to fill the room, a liquid, animate ebony swirling from the corners, swallowing everything it touched. Victoria stumbled into the hall, unable to look away. Her heart pounded. She could not catch her breath. The blackness rolled silently, at last devouring what little light poured in through the window and changing the room into a hellish, ebony void.

What is that void?

At the edges of her hearing she detected distant, soft chirping sounds, chaotic and layered erratically, but strangely articulated. Almost like . . .

Like inhuman laughter. Like the evil merriment of a she-demon.

"No, not again," she whispered. "Leave me alone. Don't do this to me now."

The odor. Sweet perfume. Flowery. Lilac. And then a faint voice coming from close to her ear. *All Hallows is coming, my dear. And what delicious treats I have in store for someone you love. . . .*

"Who do I love?" Victoria gasped.

The air went suddenly frigid, and she turned and ran down the corridor the way she had come, desperate for the relative safety of the halls and rooms she knew, the warmth of the inhabited part of the mansion. No longer caring how much noise she made, she bolted through the waiting portal to her own hallway, grabbing the handle of the door and turning to slam it shut. As she did she could not help but look back into the darkness, only to find herself facing an unexpected sight. In place of the inky blackness that had poured like smoke from the chamber, a pale, glowing mist seemed to be trickling over the hardwood floor, swirling and coalescing into a cluster of eerie, phosphorescent spheres that danced just above the floor like fantastic fireflies.

Something is watching me. Someone has spoken to me! Who is it?

Biting back a cry, she threw herself against the door, pushing it shut, leaning her weight against it for many long moments while she caught her breath. Would she never be freed from these horrifying assaults, whatever they were?

"Vicki!"

Praying she could hold herself steady, she turned to see Carolyn rushing toward her from the door to the landing. Carolyn's frown was irritated, and she shook her head in exasperation as she drew up before Victoria.

"I just saw David. He ran outside before I could catch him. I called him, but he disappeared in the trees."

"Oh, no," Victoria whispered, trying to shake free of the image of the thing behind the door. She shivered, and hoped Carolyn didn't notice. "So he wasn't in here." *Then what was it?*

"No. I was just coming out of the east wing. He

must have been hiding in the cellar. What's the matter? You're shaking."

"It's . . . it's nothing. I'm still just upset. Did Elizabeth see you?"

"No. I think she's in her office. Come on. If we split up, we can probably figure out where he's gotten to. We know most of his hiding places."

"Yeah," Victoria sighed, and hurried after Carolyn to the landing and down the stairs. *Anything to get away from this place.*

They paused at the door to grab their coats, then went out into the chilly, drab autumn morning. A gray cloud cover stretched from horizon to horizon, and a low breeze swept through the trees, causing their branches to rustle ominously. If David had left without a jacket, he probably wouldn't stay outdoors very long. Victoria glanced back at the huge mansion, the place she had come to think of as her home. But it was also a house of nightmares, and for a moment she felt a powerful urge to start running and just keep running and never come back, to go somewhere—anywhere—that offered her a reprieve from the terror that had come to overshadow her whole existence.

"I'll go toward the greenhouse and the swimming pool," Carolyn said. "You look in the stables and in the woods around the Old House."

"Why don't you take the woods," Victoria said

softly, feeling a twinge of premature night jitters. "I'll look at the greenhouse."

"Well, okay, sure." Carolyn began walking toward the stable building, far to the right, then called over her shoulder, "I'll check Rose Cottage, too, it's right on the way."

Victoria nodded. "If you find him, just get him back to the house. As quickly as possible."

"God, Vicki, you do look bad," Carolyn said with a shake of her head. "But don't worry. And I'll try to keep Mother out of it, all right?"

"Thanks, Carolyn."

"It's nothing we can't handle. We're the adults, right? And David's just a kid."

"Right."

Victoria took off toward the distant greenhouse on the northern edge of the property, thankful that the late October air seemed to have a revitalizing effect on her. At least she could catch her breath, and the air didn't smell of dust and things long dead. But when she reached the gravel drive that led to the greenhouse, something deep inside her began to shake again. *Careful, whatever's trying to get at me, it doesn't seem to make a difference whether I'm inside or outside, whether it's day or night.*

And what if David is also in danger?

She looked down the hill toward the lower lawn and the northwest cottage, hidden behind the trees in the far distance. An image of Thomas's face suddenly replaced all else, and her fear evaporated like a drop of water in a fire, replaced by a terrible yearning for him. She needed him almost more than the air that coursed in her lungs. Where was he now? After the way they'd last parted, he probably wouldn't want to see her again. He might never love her again, might never run his fingers over her body, kiss her, hold her.

Victoria pressed the tips of her fingers into her face, trying to stop the insistent sensations.

Thomas, what have you done to me? Is all of this somehow of your making?

Then she remembered: Just before he arrived, Barnabas had warned her of an imminent danger. *He* seemed to have known, or suspected, that something terrible was going to happen.

Or . . . had Barnabas somehow *made* it happen?

Oh, no! Maybe my fear of him really is justified. Maybe there is no one I can truly trust!

She forced herself to walk on, coming at last to the crumbling latticework of the old greenhouse. It had long ago fallen to ruin, and David had been warned countless times not to play here. That, of course, was no deterrent. Nor for keeping him out of the old natatorium a short distance ahead. Behind the buildings the woods grew thick and impenetrable, ending only when they reached the main road, a mile or more away. How could they really hope to find David out here? There were only two of them, and there was just too much ground to cover. David could even double back and get inside the house without either of them knowing it.

Gazing at the glass and steel structure from which trees sprang and vines curled like predatory tendrils, she called, "David! David, are you here? Please come back. I want to talk to you. I want you to know . . . I'm sorry. I'm so sorry, David."

A few distant crows cawed mockingly in reply.

She continued toward the old swimming pool building, a dilapidated brick structure so overgrown that only the Doric-columned facade could be seen from the road. *No way I'm going in there,* she thought. She didn't care if that's where David was hiding, she wouldn't set foot in that dark, dangerous place.

Once again: "David! Please come back. Everything will be all right. I promise."

And can you believe my promises, David? Will you ever again?

Tears burned her vision, then spilled down her cheeks in twin columns. But with all the determination she possessed, she wiped them away with her fist and forced herself onward down a shallow culvert that led back toward the eastern lawn and the woods beyond. From there she could glimpse the roof of the

Old House far in the distance above the trees. And a few moments later a small figure emerged from the woods, and Victoria briefly dared to hope that it was David, finally come to his senses. But then she saw that the figure had long blond hair.

Carolyn.

The younger woman walked desultorily toward her, indicating that Carolyn had had no more success in her search than she. As Carolyn approached she glanced at her wristwatch, shaking her head worriedly.

"Vicki. It's almost noon, and I've got to go to work."

"No luck?"

"Not a sign. He might have gone back to the house by now."

"I know. I guess I'll go back and look again."

"I'm sorry."

The two headed for the mansion. Carolyn sighed. "He's got to come back eventually. Why don't you just let him wander back in his own time?"

"You don't understand. He's so upset, Carolyn. I'm afraid he's going to do something rash. Suppose he gets hurt?"

"I see your point. But he's run off so many times. He knows how to take care of himself. And you still look pale. You should get some rest. I've got to get ready to go. If you find him, call me at the shop, okay?"

"I'm going to look a little longer, and I'll call. Thanks, Carolyn."

Back inside, Victoria checked the drawing room again. Still empty. Back down the hall, to the dining room, the kitchen; no one. As she returned to the foyer, she heard hurried footsteps above and saw Carolyn rushing through the hall door and down the stairs. Her blue eyes were filled with dismay.

"I took a chance and looked in David's room and then yours. He's been back! This was on your bed." She handed Victoria a scrap of paper with a hastily scrawled note on it:

BY THE TIME YOU GET THIS I'LL BE FAR AWAY.

Victoria clutched the note in her cold fingers. On a whim, she looked at the coatrack by the door. David's coat was missing.

It had been there before . . . hadn't it?

"He's not fooling around, is he?" Carolyn said. "Look, I can't stay. I'm, uh, kind of on thin ice at work as it is. I have to go."

"Go. It's all right."

Carolyn laid a hand on her shoulder. "Maybe you should tell Mother. I'm sure she'll understand."

"No!" Victoria said quickly. How could she explain about David without having to go into the rest of it? In a barely controlled, softer voice, she said, "No. This is for me to work out."

"All right, Vicki." Carolyn went out the door, giving her a last hopeful glance.

There was only one thing to do. Start over again. She could not let David just take off like this. Above all else, she was responsible for him. Leading her on a wild goose chase might be exactly what he wanted, but she could not just sit and do nothing. And she could go to no one else for help.

No one.

Allowing herself to catch her breath for a few minutes, Victoria went back out into the frosty daylight, pulling her coat tightly around her. She saw Carolyn's car heading slowly up the drive toward the main road, her friend obviously watching for any sign of the boy as she drove. Victoria felt a pang of sadness seeing her go, for right now Carolyn seemed to be the only one in the world who could even begin to understand her feelings.

Certainly, Roger Collins would never understand. If he ever found out she had hit David, that would be the end of it. She'd be relieved of her position, probably sent back to New York on the first available train.

Maybe that's what David wanted.

Could he really be that angry with her?

Why not?

As she set out to start the search anew a small voice in her head began to harangue her—one that became more and more difficult to block out.

Maybe being sent away would be the best thing that could ever happen to you.

"Be quiet!" she said to the voice. "Be quiet and leave me alone."

But it would not.

chapter

19

Sundown at last.

Rathburn arrived at the Old House carrying a leather valise with the materials he required for the upcoming rites. A queasy feeling like he'd never known in his present life churned in his stomach, and his blood raced with both pure excitement and cold dread at the prospect of what he was getting himself into. As he rapped on the door a sudden gust of wind whirled through the trees and over the porch, whistling eerily as if to warn him away from the course he had set for himself. It seemed an age before footsteps on the other side of the door came in answer to his knock.

Barnabas himself opened the door, already in his caped coat, with obviously old, hand-cobbled leather boots on his feet, his hand clutching his wolf's-headed walking stick. He stepped out without greeting, doubtless determined to have this task over and done with as quickly as possible. "I trust you have everything we need," he said, pointing to Rathburn's valise.

"I hope so. If I've forgotten anything, it will be a bit difficult to run back to the house and get it."

"Very well." Barnabas closed and locked the door, then led Rathburn around the back of the house to the beginning of a trail that led into the woods, roughly paralleling the rocky cliffs that overlooked the Atlantic. "Eagle Hill cemetery is on the other side of South Beach Road, not far from here. A large section of it is reserved for the Collins family." He gave a mirthless chuckle, his eyes radiating his abhorrence for the place. "I spent an inordinate amount of my existence within its confines."

The trail had seen little use, and was choked with dying brambles and fallen branches. Rathburn had come dressed for such a trek, wearing denim jeans, tough leather boots, and his usual long duster. Through the branches above, the rising gibbous moon cast only a pale light over the path, creating long, menacing shadows that seemed to writhe and twist of their own accord, like restless spirits angry at those who might attempt to trespass into their domain. With a sharp *caw*, a huge crow startled by their passage suddenly took flight, circling among the trees ahead of them, pacing them for several minutes before finally whirling out of sight. The voices of distant whippoorwills echoed mournfully through the woods, their cries resonant with fore-boding.

Once the pair had crossed the deserted road, the woods thinned and the ground inclined steeply ahead of them, leading up to an iron rail fence, beyond which Rathburn could see the tops of several tall grave markers. As they drew nearer, Barnabas veered to the left and took them around the northern edge of the cemetery, where a portion of the fence had been knocked down countless years before and never repaired.

Inside the graveyard, Rathburn saw that this particular section appeared all but forgotten, the markers obscured by thick weeds, the tree limbs that overhung the graves gnarled and spidery. He noted some of the names and dates on the stones, many of which went back over two hundred years: *Daniel Collins, 1785–1840; Millicent Collins Forbes, 1775–1833, Edith Collins, 1813–1897; Judith Collins Trask, 1841–1917; Edward Collins, 1843–1912; Jamison Collins, 1886–1946.* And to the south, beyond an expansive stand of pines and oaks, he could see a large mausoleum with the name "Collins" sculpted in bas-relief above the entrance. By the way Barnabas avoided so much as glancing at it, Rathburn gathered that this, truly, had been the site of his two-hundred-year, half-living interment.

Continuing south and eastward, they came at last to a dark, secluded corner ringed by dense maple trees, marked by a conspicuous absence of gravestones. And here, the trees grew in weirdly contorted fashion—particularly one enormous but diseased black oak tree. From its twisted trunk sprang numerous clusters of bent, skeletal branches upon which nothing appeared to grow, for the ground beneath them was barren of dead leaves, unlike the surrounding area, which was fairly choked with fallen foliage.

"Here," Barnabas said, indicating the base of the great tree. "Two hundred years ago her remains were buried in this ground."

Rathburn regarded the sinister tree standing sentinel in the earth where the body of Angélique had been laid to rest. "No marker."

Barnabas lifted his cane and hung it on the limb of a nearby maple. "My family had no desire to see her remembered by so much as a scratch upon the ground."

Rathburn set down his valise and opened it, removed a sheaf of papers upon which he'd copied the necessary, complex incantations, and handed it over to Barnabas. He then took several sticks of incense, which he placed in a circle around the old tree and lit with wooden matches. The fragrances of sage and sandalwood wafted over the site, and the nearby woods fell deathly silent, as if even the night creatures sensed impending mortal danger. Rathburn produced a flask of orange powder he had taken from the secret room at Collinwood and carefully poured it in a circle roughly six feet in diameter, directly in front of the great tree.

"This will be our protective ring," he told Barnabas. "Once the ritual begins, we must stand within it. And under no circumstances, no matter what happens, are we to step outside of it. If either of us do, then the protection for us will vanish. She will be able to command us."

"I understand," Barnabas said.

From the valise, Barnabas removed a small silver bell, a wooden bowl, and a sharp, unadorned athame—a ceremonial knife—while Rathburn, guided by Angélique's grimoires, poured more of the orange powder around the perimeter of the circle in the shapes of intricate magical symbols. Once these were complete, he stepped back to regard his handiwork, satisfied he had completed them as prescribed.

"Are you ready?"

Barnabas nodded, stepped into the circle and drew himself up, gazing at the tree as if facing an ancient nemesis. Rathburn joined him, knowing that he had reached the point of no return.

"Well," Rathburn said softly, "let's get it done. And done right."

There will be no second chances.

Barnabas turned to him a final time. "At least I can be assured of one thing," he said, glaring deeply into

Rathburn's eyes. "If this is some trick on your part, whatever happens to me will also happen to you."

Rathburn shrugged as nonchalantly as he could.

Barnabas seemed to accept it as a sign of understanding. "You are either very courageous or very foolish."

"Angélique must be vanquished," Rathburn said.

The other Vampire nodded knowingly, turning from Rathburn to face the tree again. "All right, then . . . Thomas. Let us begin."

Now, in accordance with the instructions for the ritual, Barnabas rang the silver bell three times in succession, the total silence capturing its peals like a ravenous predator. As the thin echoes drifted away in the distance, he placed the bell on the ground in the center of the circle and turned to face westward, while Rathburn turned to the east.

Rathburn intoned loudly, "Guardians of the watchtowers of the East, powers of the air! I do summon, stir, and call thee up to witness this rite and guard the circle. Be here now!"

Barnabas followed with: "Guardians of the watchtowers of the West, powers of water. I do summon thee to guard the circle. Be here now!"

Rathburn then turned northward, Barnabas to the south.

"Guardians of the watchtowers of the North,

powers of fire. I do summon thee. Be here now!"

"Guardians of the watchtowers of the South, powers of earth. I do summon thee. Be here now!"

Then, together, they called to the night, "Spirits of darkness preserve those who seek to lighten the four corners of thy domain."

The silence of the night remained complete. Then, shortly, a distant rustling of wind crept toward them through the trees, until a low, rushing whine surrounded them. Yet not a single branch or leaf stirred with the faintest breath of breeze. Rathburn gave Barnabas a nod of satisfaction, then knelt to take up the wooden bowl and athame he had placed at their feet.

While Barnabas held the bowl, Rathburn pulled back his sleeve and slowly drew the sharp blade across his inner forearm, opening a thin slit from which a stream of cold crimson poured into the bowl. After a few seconds he willed the wound to close, then exchanged the athame for the bowl. Barnabas repeated the procedure, slicing his own vein so that his blood mingled with Rathburn's. Once the bloodletting was complete, Rathburn placed the bowl at the edge of the magic circle; he then took a vial containing a thick, charcoal-like powder and emptied the contents into the bowl.

"If anything," Rathburn said softly, "the blood of a Vampire will increase the potency of the spell."

Now, Rathburn called out, *"Iä! In nomine domini nostri Azahoth magnus, patris et materum et daemonus sancu, santa trinitas et inseparabilis unitas te inuoco, ut sis mitu salus et defensio, et protetio miyoris meae!"*

Barnabas then chanted, *"Iä! Dans l'appelle de la chèvre noire du forêt avec les milles jeunes."*

As Barnabas's voice echoed through the night there was a sharp *crack*, and a flare of white light erupted from the bowl of blood. A bitter-smelling smoke rose from it in a thin plume. Once the smoke had dissolved into nothingness, Rathburn took the bowl and poured the now pure black liquid on the ground outside the protective circle. He dropped the empty bowl, which rolled slowly toward the tree and settled against the trunk as if drawn by some strange magnetism. As he watched, the dark pool was quickly absorbed as if the hard earth were greedily consuming it, until, moments later, not a trace of it remained.

For a full minute all was quiet but for the low groan of the wind which disturbed not so much as a hair. Rathburn knew that *something* was happening, though; his sense of danger had awakened anew, standing the hairs of his arms on end and cutting a path beneath his skin. Then, seemingly from deep within the earth, a rumbling sound rose above the moaning of the wind-voice, and Rathburn could feel heavy vibrations beneath the soles of his feet. Barnabas glanced at him questioningly, as if unsure all

were going as expected. Rathburn nodded reassur-
ingly.

*But were these truly the appropriate results of the
incantations they had voiced?*

He would know the answer in a scant few
moments.

Then a new, distant wail joined the sound of the
wind, this one distinctively human; low, melancholy, and feminine. Still, nothing stirred nearby.
Rathburn's senses reverberated with a warning so
strong that under ordinary circumstances he might
have transformed into mist. Barnabas appeared
equally alarmed. Yet both stood firm in their resolve
to see the ritual through to its climax. Finally, above
the scent of the incense, Rathburn detected the
aroma of lilac perfume.

Above the gnarled black oak tree in the dark
blue sky, a congeries of luminous, aqua spheres
appeared, swirling and dancing in the air like enormous, deranged fireflies. The sparkling mass slowly
descended toward them, accompanied by a deepening of the rushing wind-sound. As the fireworks
touched the branches, each tip burst into white
flame like a blazing magnesium flare, sending up
columns of gray smoke that swirled madly into
miniature, shrieking cyclones. Finally, the coalescing, fiery mass wrapped about the trunk of the tree
and poured down it like an incandescent liquid. As
the unearthly thing began to reshape at the base, the

feminine voice rose to shrill shriek: the voice of the witch Angélique.

The shriek became a lilting, chilling laugh.

Above, the tips of the branches blazed but were not consumed. Rathburn ironically thought of Moses and his encounter with God at the burning bush; yet the power he now faced filled him with a greater dread than would the Almighty Himself. Here, there was no possibility of mercy or of reason; only pure, unadulterated hatred.

The fireball seemed to split again into a swarm of madly warping spheres until, spent at last, the flames faded into a swirling plume of greenish smoke, from which two pinpoints of angry red light glared like animalistic eyes. Slowly, the smoke began to take on a recognizable form: a hovering female body, wrapped in a pale, feathery raiment that billowed around it as if blown by a ferocious wind. New tongues of fire roiled over and around the figure, whose long blond hair swayed and swirled Medusalike around her beautiful face. The power in the hypnotic eyes seemed invincible, and Rathburn found his resolve wavering. *She is lovely, so very lovely.* Suddenly, he found himself being tugged toward the rim of the circle, this time saved only by Barnabas's strong hands, which pulled him back to its center.

"That," Barnabas said in a low, fear-laden voice, "is Angélique."

The glaring eyes shifted back and forth between Barnabas and Rathburn, and the cruel, lilting laughter washed over them. The apparition's lovely lips parting in a wicked grin. She was incredibly beautiful, perhaps the most beautiful creature Rathburn had ever seen. He wanted to touch her. To be with her. To become one with her. To submit to her. To offer her his own blood. What had they thought in wanting to harm her? The glory would be in becoming one with her.

"No, Thomas," Barnabas whispered furiously in his ear. "Resist her! Resist now!"

Rathburn shook himself. *God, the temptation!* Her power was as unchallengable as her beauty. So this was the true terror of Barnabas Collins!

The same creature who wanted to bargain with me.

Facing his enemy, Barnabas narrowed his eyes, tightened his jaw, and began the final part of the banishment ritual. He called out, "*Iä! Iä! Dans l'appelle de la chèvre noire du forêt avec les milles jeunes! Je vous command rendre à l'abîme d'eternité, par la commande des tous pouvoirs de la pègre, maintenant! Maintenant!*"

The glaring eyes released Rathburn from their hold and turned to focus solely on Barnabas. He instantly seemed to lose all cognizance, his willpower drained by the terrible phantasm before them. He took a step forward.

This was the moment. Rathburn reached for

Barnabas's arm as if to hold him in the circle. Instead he shoved the other Vampire forward—outside of the protective ring.

Angélique laughed. Her spectral arms flew wide in joy, and insane peals of delight issued from her lips, lifting skyward to stir the cyclones of smoke dancing at the tips of the unconsumed tree branches. The stench of brimstone suddenly overwhelmed the scent of lilac, as if it had billowed through an open door to the Underworld.

Rathburn had altered the rites of banishment so that they only held at bay the forces *preventing* Angélique from entering the world.

It was Halloween night. The witch would have her way.

Barnabas regained his balance and spun to face Rathburn with eyes glowing red and his fangs exposed. "You!" he growled with the sound of an angry wolf. "You've betrayed me!"

Rathburn shook his head, seeing in his mind his little boy being lifted by the force of the minié ball and slammed to the floor, his blood gushing onto the floor from the wound in his back. He heard Elaine's desperate pleading as young Andrew Collins slid the knife into her heart, ending her life in a moment of horror.

Somewhere deep inside, he heard his own voice.

Barnabas was not the killer.
But it was a Collins.
Barnabas is innocent.
No. He is dead.

"Vengeance is mine," Rathburn said, turning to face the eyes of the regal, floating figure that had now turned to gaze at him.

chapter

<svg>—∞∞∞—</svg>

20

*S*he'd been walking for hours, going in circles, her legs aching and insisting that she stop, but her mind demanding that she go on. Several times she'd ventured near the Old House—but never so close that she could actually see its front doors through the trees. If David had any idea how badly the place had come to frighten her, he would probably hide near it; surely, though, he would not be brash enough to sneak inside, not with Barnabas and Willie Loomis living there.

"Or would he?" she asked herself and the crow who sat on the gravel in front of her, its little head tilted and its black doll-eyes shining. David was a child riddled with anger and insecurities, many his father didn't understand. The boy did not know how to control his impulses. He held a deep resentment toward Barnabas, who had moved into what had once been his favorite playhouse. David might have gone there to hide, hell-bent to prove another point.

Victoria stood at the eastern edge of the property, near the entry gate to South Beach Road, her teeth chattering, trying to ease her breathing. In spite of the cold air, she was sweating. She felt clammy and dirty. Her hands had been caught by the thorny fingers of brush and were scratched and raw. Her eyes were blurred with tears that had flowed off and on over the course of the hours— tears of fear, rage, and confusion. Her face was covered with the residue of anxiety.

She had forgotten to put on her watch, so she couldn't be sure of the time. But it was getting late. She'd lost track of the day, as afraid to go back inside Collinwood as she was to continue wandering outside with the approaching nightfall.

Caught in a spiral, she thought. *A downward spiral that I'm too weak to fight. God help me.*

And then, in the distance, she saw Roger's car turning into the drive, headed for the mansion. She ducked behind a nearby tree, in case he happened to glance in her direction. He was, quite literally, the last person on earth she wanted to see right now. How could she show herself back at the house? If David had not come home, there would be questions she could hardly answer honestly. And if David were there, waiting to tell the story of what she'd done to him, she might as well *stay* gone.

She made her way through the barrier of tall pines that edged the main road and came out a few hundred feet south of the entrance to the estate. She walked a ways on the rough pavement, again feeling the urge to just keep going until she arrived somewhere—anywhere—away from the pain and terror. She told herself that she was still hoping to find David; he occasionally stole away to play in the cemetery some distance ahead, on the other side of the road. He'd been strictly forbidden to go there, but like any edict, it was largely ignored. The note he'd left suggested he might go farther afield than usual. He *could* have come this way.

That was what she told herself.

That was what she clung to.

The road curved to the left and began to rise as it meandered toward the bluffs north and east of the Collins property. Through a break in the trees ahead she could see the dull surface of the Atlantic. As she continued up the road, she could see the dark, distant hump of St. Eustace Island protruding from the center of a shadowy inlet; and beyond that, a few lights from the village on the misty horizon.

It was already getting dark. Back through the trees the sun broke through the low banks of clouds, but only in time to drop slowly behind the distant ridges in the west. As the landscape began to submit to the veil of twilight, Victoria felt the beginnings of a burning sensation somewhere deep inside her body. She stopped on the road and clenched her fists, preparing for the first rush of irrational dread that came with night jitters.

And the rush came.

But it was not night jitters. Not this time.

No. Tonight, it was different. It was a strange burning of her blood, like she'd felt last night, when she'd almost clawed the skin from her arms just to free herself from the feverish blaze.

Oh, God . . . Thomas . . . I need you . . . !

She began to sob, bending at the waist, holding herself tightly. How could she have been so brusque with him, so distrusting? What if he really didn't want to see her again? She could hardly blame him.

She stood up straight and shook her head. Her jaws clamped and her breath came in hissing gasps through her teeth.

No, it was his own fault! He got what he wanted, then turned cold. Wasn't that how it was with men?

The burning was worsening. Victoria wrapped her arms around herself and began walking faster, hoping to outpace the sensations. Ahead, across the road, she could see a few grave markers at the top of a long, wooded hill.

Eagle Hill Cemetery.

At dusk.

On Halloween night.

Trick or treat.

"What am I doing?" she whispered to herself.

The closer she walked to the cemetery, the hotter her blood burned. Barbs of heat clawed at her nerve endings, chewed at the flesh from within. She needed Thomas Rathburn. She needed him *now*. Only he could extinguish this fire.

It is for him, isn't it? He is the reason for it.

So why did she feel so drawn to keep going? Thomas wouldn't be anywhere near here. And the chances of finding David now were slimmer than ever. She *was* still looking for him, wasn't she?

Why should I? The little monster can leap off Widows' Hill, for all I care.

No!

"Stop it," she pleaded with herself. "Don't think like that." But it was true. All the time she'd been looking for David, what kept her going was fear of the consequences to *her* if he wasn't found, not any genuine concern for him. Shame burned along with the raging fire in her blood, and for a moment she saw David's face, the look of hurt when she'd dismissed him time after time, and how shocked he'd been when she hit him.

"I hate you!"

"I'm sorry, David. I'm so sorry."

She stepped off the road and hurried up the weed- and vine-choked hillside toward the graveyard, for a second feeling she was on the right track, that she was going exactly where she was supposed to go. Something in the air. A scent . . . ?

Smoke.

Yes, she'd detected a faint whiff of smoke in the air. Not uncommon this time of year, for fires would be burning in countless fireplaces all over the area, even at Collinwood. But there were so few houses bordering the Collins property, and it didn't smell like wood smoke. It was sharper, more noxious. *Like brimstone.*

Good God.

When David was younger, he'd been known to set fires, especially when he was upset. Had he come to the cemetery and set something on fire— something that smelled like sulfur? Fighting back trepidation, she walked unsteadily along the fence rail that bordered the graveyard, dragging her fingers along the iron bars for balance, breathing heavily against the pain in her blood, coming at last to a broken-down section where she could enter. The nearest headstones gleamed pale in the gathering darkness; beyond them, shadows from the crouching, skeletal trees swallowed the graves. Above, the clouds had begun to break, and a rising moon cast its ghostly light upon her as the breeze moaned softly like a chorale of restless dead.

Something flickered in the distant sea of blackness. *A fire! David* must *be here.*

Victoria moved to her right, trying to catch another glimpse of the faraway blaze. If only she had a flashlight to help her pick her steps on the treacherously rough ground. All she needed now was to trip and crack her skull on a jagged gravestone. Wouldn't *that* suit David just perfectly?

Her feet moved automatically now, taking her farther and farther into the land of the dead, her wits beyond rebelling. She could only follow the unseen force that drew her inexorably onward. Whatever was to come would come.

Seeing the dark shape of the Collins family mausoleum, she froze, caught in the paralyzing fear that had gripped her with the onset of twilight. But it was overshadowed quickly as she again caught sight of a flash of flame in the distance, filling her with a whole new, different dread. The flames were high.

If David set a fire, oh, my God, it's gotten big!

The smell of sulfur was stronger now. A terrible, evil smell.

And why . . . *why* was she suddenly filled with concern for Thomas Rathburn?

Of all people, he was the last one she should be worried about.

Ahead, someone was shouting. A strange voice, it seemed, the words unintelligible.

Suddenly, the odor of brimstone dissipated, washed away as if by a cleansing rush of sea breeze. And the sounds in the distance were smothered by an unnatural wall of silence that consumed even the whine of the wind. Her footsteps no longer crunched in the dead leaves; no sound at all reached her ears as she pressed on. Had she been stricken deaf?

No. The silence was *too* complete, too heavy. There was a pure *deadness* in the air; not within her ears or mind, but from *out there*.

A sudden, furious wind whipped over Victoria, stinging her eyes as it struck, throwing her hair back in disarray. A wind thick with the scent of sickly sweet lilac.

chapter

21

The terrible laughter was hypnotic, mesmerizing.

Outside the circle, Barnabas stood transfixed, his wrath at the betrayal now drained by Angélique's overpowering will. The floating figure glared at Rathburn with eyes intermittently pale aqua and flaming red. The sultry lips parted, and for the first time he heard her actually speak, a voice seductive and sorrowful, as if uttered by Elaine herself.

"That is only half the bargain, Thomas. You must continue. Open the way."

Rathburn focused his mental eye on the alien lines that he had painstakingly inscribed in his brain over the hours since dawn. These were the most difficult, the language being that of the underworld, taken from books of power that had presumably been transcribed by Angélique's own hand some two hundred years ago. This was risky, but he

needed to test the effectiveness of the rites—the part
only *he* knew. Drawing a deep breath, he began.

*"Iä! Kaddai n'ghayash im vraig'yim im zhappat.
N'gar ag-sohoth, iod g'mir zulei hem f'taghn. O, shamir
el n'yig, el gai-shin quiteh azahoth na. Ag-sohoth, y'mir
na f'taghn. Y'mir na f'taghn."*

The figure of Angélique suddenly drifted backward, as if struck by the invisible hand of the wind.
Her face twisted with pain and anger. Her eyes
again blazed like hot lava before cooling to pale
blue-green, her face taking on an expression of
rebuke.

"Do not even think of resisting me, Thomas.
Remember what I can do to you!"

Rathburn felt a sharp, wrenching shard in his
chest—as he'd experienced when Angélique visited
him at the cottage.

Damn it!

Still within the ring of protection, by force of his
own will, he cast the pain away. But, as if in conces-
sion, he nodded to the apparition. He called out,
"You shall have your desire." Then: *"Iod, el-rhajh
nyich. Ahg adry'el azhyad im estu f'taghn, ag-sohoth im
n'yarl o'hoteph, ich shaggoath el Hali kaddai. Ich shaggoath el Hali kaddai."*

Like smoke entering a glass mold, the floating,
ethereal figure began to take on a more solid form,
the features of the long-dead witch assuming the
beauty of true flesh and blood. A look of uncon-

cealed delight passed over her face, and her pale
eyes turned to Rathburn with a seductive gleam.

"I knew you would understand," she whispered, her voice slithering like a serpent across the
distance between them. "Vengeance, however, will
not be yours. It will be mine."

And suddenly Rathburn's body was seized in
the icy grip again, freezing his limbs, the very words
in his throat. Her body still enveloped by a green,
supernal fire, Angélique turned to face Barnabas
and said, "Now. Break the circle!"

The caped figure stepped forward, his eyes
regarding Rathburn's with seething hatred. Surely,
Barnabas was aware of his own plight, yet, outside
the protective boundary, he was unable to resist
Angélique's complete and dreadful authority. He
went to the tree where he had hung his cane,
removed it from the branch and walked toward
Rathburn, grasping the stick from its lower end and
brandishing it like a club. But instead of striking
with it, as Rathburn half expected, Barnabas lowered it and swept it across the ground, wiping out a
portion of the orange powder that formed the protective ring.

No! I cannot let this happen!

Rathburn tried to utter the command he knew
that he must, his lips contorting with the effort, yet
the words hung before they could reach his lips.

Barnabas again swung the cane, the wolf's head

destroying several of the symbols Rathburn had painstakingly drawn. Then Barnabas stepped back, still under Angelique's complete control, but with features radiating satisfaction.

Rathburn felt razor-sharp, invisible fingers seep through his chest and clutch his heart. He dropped to his knees with a silent scream as terrible pain arced through his body, knowing that, *somehow*, he must complete the final portion of the rites he had designed. He had not counted on the circle being broken, at least not this soon.

"Oh, Thomas, I'm so sorry," came Angélique's musical voice. "But you could not possibly know the true reason I needed you here. You possess greater power than any of your kind on earth. Your presence here proves to me that I made the right decision. And when I am done with you, nothing and no one will ever stand between Barnabas and me again. I shall have him forever." Her glowing aqua eyes turned to Barnabas. "And you, my love . . . you will have me. I swear it!"

The wind-sound suddenly became a deep, subterranean rumbling. The icy grip on Rathburn's heart tightened, and he felt as if his very spirit were being wrenched from him. Angélique lifted a hand to him as if demanding he kiss it. He could see the tips of her fingers quivering as she drew his vitality from his body. A gossamer, swirling tendril crossed the air between his body and hers—his life force.

"All that is yours will be mine," she said in a lilting whisper. "Your energy will bring me through the door. And all your strength will be mine to use. Imagine . . . the powers of the undead at my command, but without the liabilities. To take whatever form I wish, my body unbound and immortal. I will be more than I ever was, or could have dreamed of being—until I found you. For that I owe you a debt of gratitude, Thomas."

He had to stop her. But he could not move, or even speak. His vision had become a sheet of red, the aqua eyes of the witch blazing through it like brilliant jewels.

"Now," came her voice. "We must finish this. Rise and come to me. Take my hand. And bring me through."

Rathbun felt his limbs begin to move, though he did not will it. He staggered to his feet, feeling as if his body were suspended and manipulated by invisible wires. He lurched forward, raising a hand to the outstretched arms of the waiting figure, whose eyes continued to blaze with the power of absolute command. He saw his fingers reaching for hers . . . and he could invoke nothing within himself that would call them back.

Then, from behind, a panicked scream drowned the rumbling of subterranean thunder. For a moment the red haze vanished, and he turned his head to see Victoria Winters, her face chalky white, standing beside a gnarled cedar tree, transfixed by the sight of the radiant avatar from the other side of death. Victoria fell against the trunk, one hand clutching a limb for support, the other rising to her mouth as if to stop the screams that came in an unbroken flow from her lips.

The aqua eyes of Angélique also turned to regard the newcomer. In that moment Rathburn saw Barnabas's eyes flash with rekindled light, renewed resolve. Victoria's presence had shattered the witch's total control for the barest moment. Summoning all his remaining energy, Rathburn cried, "Now, Barnabas. Throw it now!"

Barnabas Collins lifted his hand to reveal a flask containing a seething, smoking potion the color of onyx. Upon seeing this, Angélique uttered a cry of horror, and a sudden thundering vibration rumbled through the earth as if its crust were about to split and swallow them all. With a look of triumph, Barnabas hurled the potion at the phantasm before them, but the flask fell short, shattering not on her form but on the ground beneath her. White flame and black smoke erupted like a blossoming flower around the figure of the witch.

Fire! According to Barnabas, the thing that Angélique feared most. Perhaps it worked. Perhaps this is enough to destroy her.

From within the roiling flames a horrible, agonized wail arose. Rathburn staggered back from the inferno, his limbs still reluctant to support his weight. Leaning against the trunk of the great black oak, he saw Barnabas moving toward Victoria. She gazed transfixed at the raging pyre, her eyes so wide with fear that the whites showed completely around her dark irises.

Suddenly, from within the flames, the figure of Angélique reappeared—miraculously unscathed, a self-assured smile on her lips. She strode forward with raiments trailing like the wings of a firebird, the flames licking at her body but failing to touch her. As she lifted a hand, the lapping tongues dwindled, as though bowing down before her.

"Thomas," came Barnabas's voice. "You must complete the rite to send her away. Do it now!"

With an angry glance at Barnabas, Angélique hissed, "No, my love. The rites *have* ended." She lifted a finger, and Barnabas spun away from Victoria as if struck, dropping to one knee with a look of shock. Rathburn, once again, was struck mute.

"So, the two of you attempted to trick me," Angélique said with a thoughtful expression. "But I will forgive your transgressions, Barnabas. And you will come to understand that everything I have done was for you. It's *always* been for you." Then she turned to look at Rathburn. "Insolent creature that you are," she said to him, "you shall suffer, Thomas Rathburn. You shall suffer every torment of hell for the rest of eternity. What my beloved Barnabas has suffered shall be but a trifling compared to yours."

Then, to Rathburn's horror, she took a step toward Victoria. "But first you, my dear," Angélique purred. "I have no further need of you. I could have finished you the other night on Widows' Hill. But it's so much better now, for you to die in front of both Barnabas and your new love."

Victoria cringed, unable to speak, shaking her head in disbelief. She tried to retreat, but found the way blocked by trees. Angélique lifted a hand like a queen demanding to be attended by her servants, her body still surrounded by a flickering aura of flame. Victoria's hand suddenly went to her throat as if she were choking.

"Remember how it felt, my dear? Remember the hangman's noose around your neck? How it felt for life to depart from your body, ever so slowly? You were spared once. But this time, your life is mine to take."

"No!" Barnabas cried. "Killing Victoria can't change anything. Do you think that simply eliminating anyone who stands in your way will bring us closer together? Open your eyes, Angélique. This is madness!"

"I think not," she said in a soft voice. "It is you who don't understand. As you have suffered, so have I. This is the only way for our suffering to end. We will be together, Barnabas. We *must* be together." Turning from him, she focused her eyes on Victoria again. And this time, when Angélique's hand rose, Victoria's body arched in a spasm of agony and she fell to her knees, her eyes rolling upward in their sockets.

Rathburn felt a sharp sting in his leg—the ancient pain of his flesh being pierced by a bayonet. Even as a man, he had once summoned strength from within to overcome impossible odds. Drawing up everything he had left inside him—and more— he rose . . . and lunged toward Angélique. He struck her body, knocking her from her course, throwing his arms around her increasingly substantial form with all his might. Flames still danced at her feet, licking at her body like playful kittens, as if waiting for an opening; an opening Rathburn now made sure they would find.

He held her in his embrace as if preparing to pierce her throat with his fangs. Instead he leaned close to her ear and whispered, "*Ag-sohoth, y'mir na f'taghn. Y'mir na f'taghn, el Hali kaddai.*" Then: "*Dans l'appelle de la chèvre noire du forêt avec les milles jeunes. Allez vite à l'abîme . . . ma chèrie.*"

"Return quickly to the abyss."

Angélique's features twisted into a grimace of hatred. "No," she whispered. "You cannot do this."

Rathburn felt icy daggers again piercing his heart. He released Angélique, pushing her away with a snarl. He fell, crumpled, to the ground. His strength gone, he could only lie and watch, and hope that he'd completed the ritual in time.

The flames around Angélique began to grow. "No," she whispered, her eyes turning to meet Rathburn's with an expression of dreadful realization. "No, you cannot have succeeded. You cannot stop me. You cannot!" But the deep rumbling in the earth rose again, as if some monstrous door were being forced open. Just beyond the black oak tree a flower of sparks appeared in the air, swirling and spinning as if assuming some kind of form—until they outlined the mouth of a great vortex, the heart of which gradually became visible. As Angélique watched, the flames surrounding her finally appeared to touch her body. She cried out in anguish, casting Rathburn a look of unutterable hatred.

The silky raiments she wore quickly blackened and withered away, though Angélique's flesh was not consumed. Her feet left the ground, her flame-shrouded figure naked and translucent, her long blond hair again writhing as if with a life of its own. For a brief moment Rathburn's heart ached at the sight of her beauty; so stunning, yet so horrifying in her full splendor. She began to thrash, her lips widening in a silent scream, the deep thunder in the earth now the only sound Rathburn could hear.

From somewhere beyond his field of vision he heard Barnabas's voice: "Oh, my God."

Within the vortex, seemingly an infinite distance away, something took shape . . . something that only vaguely resembled a human figure ... something tall and impossibly thin, wrapped in a mantle of pure gold, its features indistinct within the whirling circle of sparks. As if having crossed some vast, otherworldly gulf, a thunderous voice swept through the vortex, calling:

"Ythirr! Ythirr!"

Angélique's eyes took on a new look of terror. "No! Diabolos!" she cried. "You cannot have me! You must not take me back! Allow me to stay ... please!"

But the flames denied her. Her body became an indistinct, swirling mass of golden tongues that began to drift toward the opening of the vortex as if drawn by an invisible hand. Rathburn could only stare mutely, as much stunned by the apparition beyond the opening as by Angélique's struggle. Barnabas also gazed enraptured, fascinated, attracted and repulsed. He had once loved Angélique, at least in some fashion, Rathburn thought. Yet love had turned to hatred along the way, for both of them. Barnabas could now scarcely hide his torment, as if at having done what he had to do. For a second Rathburn's heart moved, full of compassion for this kindred soul, this *man* who had suffered so much at the hands of the witch, now rapidly diminishing before them.

As all that remained of Angélique passed through the door between worlds, the ground shook and, within the heart of the spinning portal, the indistinct, distant figure in gold wavered and dissolved into nothingness.

Gradually, the rushing sparks began to slow, and the rumbling in the earth softened until it again seemed a low breeze that did not so much as stir the tree limbs. Like hot ashes blown by the wind, the last remaining traces of the vortex vanished, leaving the night air still and silent. Above, the blazing tips of the tree branches began to wink out, leaving behind uncharred, pristine wood, as if no spectral fire had ever touched them. And finally, the odor of brimstone faded; in its wake Rathburn smelled only the loamy, delicious scent of the autumn woods— the clean, empty air of a Halloween night as it was meant to be: a night void of all true wickedness, a night for happy children and trick-or-treating and the joy of youth.

Rathburn tried to move, but found his arms and legs pinioned to the ground by a great, invisible weight. His energy had departed, and his heart still ached from the stabbing touch of Angélique's ghostly fingers. Consciousness ebbed and flowed, making him feel as if he were bobbing on a great, black sea. As he explored the sensations in his body, the true impact of what he'd experienced dawned on him.

Then he heard Barnabas utter a low curse, and Rathburn painfully turned his head and forced his eyes to focus. He saw the caped figure standing over Victoria, lifting her in his arms and touching a hand to her cheek.

With a look of purest grief, Barnabas turned to Rathburn and whispered, "She's not breathing."

chapter

∞∞∞∞

22

Victoria lay motionless in Barnabas's arms, her features etched with disbelief and terror. Rathburn fought the pull of oblivion and dragged himself across the coarse grass to her side. He touched her wrist and found it cold. But there was a faint pulse. *Thank God.* Angélique had not succeeded. He squeezed her hand, willed her to recognize his touch. Victoria was still bonded to him. He *must* be able to save her.

Barnabas's eyes regarded him, cold suspicion breaking through his mask of grief. "Will she live?" he asked.

"I think I can save her," Rathburn said, his voice just above a whisper. "Leave us for a few minutes."

Barnabas growled. "After what you've done, how can I dare?"

"I did what I had to do, Barnabas. You know that."

"You sought to destroy me!"

"No . . . I did not. You're still here, and Angélique is gone. Listen to me. Decide now whether you want her to live or die. I will save her if I can."

Barnabas lingered, his eyes tortured with indecision. But finally, gazing at Victoria, he nodded slowly. "You have only a short time. Use it wisely." He gently lay Victoria with her back against the tree, her head lowered to her chest; then he turned and melted into the shadows.

Rathburn pressed one hand tenderly over Victoria's heart, praying to whatever benevolent force that might be listening that it would keep beating. Then, with one fingernail, he sliced the skin of his wrist until a few beads of blood came to the surface. He dabbed his thumb with blood and touched it to her lips, whispering softly, "Awaken, my love. I command you. Cast out the pain, and take in the breath of life. Awaken to me."

After a moment, Victoria's chest heaved and her mouth opened to draw in a gulp of air. He touched her chest again, and found her heartbeat stronger and faster. Her breasts began to rise and fall rhythmically as her breathing returned to normal. Rathburn gently pulled her collar down to look at her throat.

It was bruised, as if a noose had encircled it and been murderously tightened.

Again, he whispered, "Awaken now. Victoria."

At the sound of her name, her eyes fluttered open, and she gazed at Rathburn uncomprehendingly. For a long time he could see nothing in those beautiful, dark irises but his own reflection. But finally a new spark gleamed in her eyes, and she whispered, "What happened to me?"

"You don't remember?"

Confusion clouded her lovely features. "I was looking for David. I saw flames . . . oh, Thomas, there was a fire."

He shook his head and placed one finger over her lips. "Everything is all right now."

She watched his eyes, a new concern growing on her face. "You . . . what's wrong? Are you hurt?"

He shook his head. "I will be fine."

"No," she said, looking with mounting dread at his haggard, sallow features. "You're in pain. What happened to you, Thomas? Please tell me."

"I cannot. I only want to make sure you are safe. I believe you are now."

She took one of his hands in hers. "I don't know what happened," she whispered. "But you saved my life. You did, didn't you?"

He did not answer right away. "I only did what I had to do. I could not let anyone harm you."

"Who . . . who wanted to harm me?"

"It is best you do not remember," he said, and again put a finger to her lips to stop her protest. The effort of moving brought a grimace of pain to his lips, and she gazed with a look of understanding.

"I know what you need," she said. "As you saved me, let me save you."

She tilted her head to expose her neck to him. "Take me," she whispered longingly. "Let my blood restore you."

But he shook his head.

All the blood in the world would not save him now.

He did not have much more time. Angélique had ripped everything in his heart from him. He looked at his hands, then down at his body. This shell was all but empty. His every instinct told him it was beyond restoration. Even the idea of taking blood repulsed him now.

A footstep crunched nearby, and Rathburn looked up to see Barnabas standing by a tree, watching them in amazement. When Victoria looked over at him, her eyes registered warmth, reassurance. The fear Rathburn had seen before was gone now.

"Barnabas will help you back to Collinwood," Rathburn said. "Do you hear me, Vicki? Is that all right?"

She again looked to the solitary figure in the darkness beneath the trees. "Yes," she said. "That will be all right."

He leaned close to her ear and whispered, "There is no need to fear him. He will never harm you."

She glanced at him, as if she expected him to

explain himself further. But when he said nothing more, she bowed her head against his chest. Rathburn saw Barnabas watching them intently, as if he could scarcely accept the words he'd just heard. Then he came to them and knelt next to Victoria.

"You did save her," he whispered.

"There is but one more thing for me to do," Rathburn said. "After all . . . I gave my word."

He opened his shirt, and with the nail that had sliced his wrist, drew a long cut across his chest from left to right. Blood poured from the laceration, streaming down his chest and over his shirt and coat in a symbolic gesture. He felt his energy fading further with this assault, but he grit his teeth and tensed his muscles, forcing himself to remain aware.

"Victoria Winters, I free you," he said. "Our blood is no longer joined. And in time you will forget me. Until then, may your memories be only sweet. Now . . . sleep."

He touched her forehead, and her eyelids fluttered, then her head nodded. Rathburn motioned for Barnabas to support her. He no longer had the strength.

Barnabas lay Victoria back against the tree.

She would have been a wonderful bloodmate, Rathburn thought. *So much power within her, waiting to be released. She could have made a masterful hunter . . . a companion to me . . . the soul with whom I desired to spend the rest of eternity.*

None of these things could happen now.

"Rathburn," Barnabas said softly. "You lived up to your word. You surprise me."

Rathburn put his hand to his head, struggling against the slow, downward spiraling of his soul. "Barnabas," he managed, "when we planned this, I couldn't tell you what I required of you. I needed you to be outside the circle. Just as it protects those within, it would have prevented the potion from working against her. And you had to be the one to wield it, because I knew Angélique would not actually kill you—not with her feelings for you. I was trying to protect you from within the circle, but she was too strong. Once you broke the ring with your cane, nothing could save me."

"I had no choice," Barnabas said.

"I know. But I had to allow Angelique to cross far enough into the world of the living for the potion and the spells to finish her. I had to make her think she had turned me against you. But I could never have convinced you beforehand. You would have thought I intended to hand you over to her. And now . . . after all that, we did not succeed in destroying her. She exists still, in some world beyond our own. What incredible power . . ." He felt his own voice fading away.

Barnabas shook his head with something resembling sympathy. "And now you have learned that for yourself. What a curious creature you are, Rathburn. You came here for revenge against me. But now you free the woman you love so she can be with me."

"No. I have freed her to make her own choices."

"Indeed," Barnabas said with a thoughtful nod. "Tell me. Would you have truly killed everyone at Collinwood for those crimes against you, such a long time ago?"

Rathburn nodded. "I would have . . . once. But . . . they are *her* family. I could no longer take that away from her. Now that I . . . "

"What?"

"Nothing. Take her home, Barnabas. Tell her that I have left. Tell that to all of them."

Barnabas nodded in understanding. He leaned down to Rathburn and softly said, "Do you have any other last request?"

Rathburn tried to shake his head. "I think I must have been mad. I could have simply destroyed you at the beginning, and left with Victoria. But I suppose Angélique would never have allowed that."

"If you were mad, then your madness has made you more than what you were."

"And what was I, Barnabas?"

"No less evil than Angélique herself. A creature devoid of compassion. A mere walking hunger."

"If you believe you are so different, you're fooling yourself."

"Perhaps. Yet the only thing that stops me from taking one last step into the sunlight is the hope that one day I may be freed from this curse so that I might be like other men. But even to the end, I know that could never have been for you."

"No ... it could not. Tell me, Barnabas." He gazed at Victoria's sleeping figure, which seemed to shimmer as his eyesight grew weaker. "You could have her, if you wanted to. For all time, she could be with you, and make your existence bearable again. Why not make her as you?"

"It would be meaningless. When my dearest Josette saw what her new life was to be, she killed herself rather than face eternal horror. How could I inflict such evil on the one I truly love? Victoria can only take the place of Josette in my heart if it is of her own free will. Surely, you understand *that*."

Rathburn nodded with effort. "Victoria's fear was of Angélique's making. Perhaps things will be different now. But Barnabas ... what if you are never able to become mortal again? What if you lose Victoria forever?"

Barnabas gazed into the darkness, his gaunt face shadowed with sadness. "Then that will be my destiny. And hers."

"You must face the fact that, in all likelihood, you are what you are, and always will be. That is how I have lived, Barnabas. I have always accepted that reality."

"You merely surrendered. It is easier to embrace the darkness than fight against it. I know this too well, Thomas. So many times, I have surrendered myself." He grimaced. "Every time the hunger comes."

"It is a terrible thing."

"But tonight, something new was born inside you. Or something old was reborn."

A sharp dagger in Rathburn's chest sent him writhing. He clenched his teeth against the pain. Barnabas backed away in surprise, his eyes concerned.

"Go away," Rathburn whispered, once the spasm had passed. "Go away. I don't want you to see me die."

Barnabas nodded thoughtfully. "As you wish . . . Thomas. I will take Victoria home now."

"Goodbye, Barnabas."

He turned his head to watch Barnabas lift Victoria into his arms. Without another word, the caped figure slowly walked into the darkness and disappeared. Rathburn could no longer hear footsteps beyond his field of vision.

He lay on the cold ground, alone, his heart a spent ember from Angélique's touch. He could not even move a finger, the remnants of his life energy seeping away as if through a gaping wound. The sounds of the night—the frogs, the nightbirds, the few insects that still chattered in the cold—these things were a welcome accompaniment to the silence that surrounded him. He had not contemplated his own demise for a long, long time. When he had, he'd concluded that he would probably die like so many of his kind, hunted by some fanatic he had wronged, and having a stake driven through his heart.

This is better, he thought with a wry smile. Perhaps there was honor—of a sort—in what he had done. A long time ago, as a soldier in the Confederate Army, to die with honor meant everything to him.

How things change.

As he lay there, he thought he heard a distant whisper—perhaps the wind, he thought at first. But after a time he determined that it was something else altogether, and feared some hidden doorway was about to open again, admitting a vengeful wraith from the dominion beyond death; that everything he'd sacrificed tonight had been in vain. But the scent of lilac he expected, and the sound of lilting laughter, did not come. Instead he caught a whiff of something sharp, acrid . . . *gunpowder*? And he heard what he thought was the sound of marching feet, the call of an officer sending his troops into battle. For a few moments Thomas Rathburn was uncertain whether he lay in a deserted graveyard outside some small, New England village, or on the

battlefield in Virginia where his company had met a
valiant but meaningless end.

"Thomas," came a soft, distant voice. "At last
we will meet again."

"Phillip," he whispered. "Phillip O'Conner."

"Yes. A long time ago, I gave you a gift. You
called it a curse. Tell me what you think now."

"It was neither. It was only what I made it
to be."

"I will see you soon, old friend."

Thomas Rathburn was unaware of the passage of
time. The sounds of the night became a long, endless
song that soothed him, the scents in the air a sweet
perfume that reminded him of his childhood, of
those carefree days when death was but a meaningless word and darkness was only the time after the
sun had fallen. He remembered his precious days
with Elaine, all too brief though they were . . . the
birth of his son, the precious little boy whose life had
been taken before it could even be lived.

Perhaps he would see them again, too.

He was aware of the ground beginning to warm
around him. The midnight-blue sky took on a
golden hue in the east, and the stars that speckled
the sky through the barren tree limbs began to fade
into a brighter backdrop. He could hear the morning
birds begin to sing, and somewhere far away he

heard a cock crow. The world was coming to life again.

As the sun climbed above the horizon, casting its light through the trees, brightening the gravestones and crypts of the Eagle Hill cemetery, Thomas Jackson Rathburn had no choice but to cross the threshold that waited for every mortal who walked upon the earth. When the brilliant rays found him, he was beyond all pain, and with a momentary burst of energy that came like a gift from an unknown benefactor, he raised his arms to greet the onrushing specter of death with resolve, understanding, and even a measure of fear.

He was, after all, a man. Nothing more, and nothing less.

23

She awoke with a start, her back arching and her hands clutching to her sides. She could not see, but it was not blindness; no, it was the darkness, the living, pulsing darkness, that had swallowed up the room at the far end of the west wing. It had come for her at last and was wrapping her in its cold black wings like a horrid, unearthly lover, ready to pull her into the void and have its way with her again and again until there was nothing left to take.

My God!

The air was foul, heavy, smelling of crow feathers and burning earth. There was a creaking, snapping sound, and although she could not see in the blackness, she knew it was the copper beech tree, reaching for her with its cruel branches. She tried to scream, but in a void, screams are killed in the throat of the screamer.

No no no no!

And then her eyes opened to the darkness.

Another darkness. Not that of the void, but the darkness of drawn curtains and late morning.

What . . . ?

It hurt to move, but she turned her head on the pillow and saw a form that looked like a chair.

She shuddered, and coughed. She stared. "I know that chair," she said aloud.

It was the chair that always held the position near the closet door. Her closet door. To its right was the low-topped vanity with its mirror. Then another wall, and in the wall, a window with curtains pulled tightly into each other.

"My window," she said. "I'm home. I'm . . ."

Safe?

As carefully as she could to assuage the aching of her muscles, she slid her feet off the mattress and placed them squarely on the floor. Then she forced herself upward and stood, swaying, breathing against the ebb and flow of her star-specked vision until it cleared and she knew she was indeed awake. She *was* home.

With shaking hands she pushed the curtains aside to reveal a bright, glittering November morning. The light stunned her eyes and she covered them for a moment until the thin slices that pierced the space between her fingers had become tolerable, then lowered her hand again. A few starlings and sparrows hopped across the grass of the lawn, pecking for seeds and insects. The sky was nearly white. The copper beech tree had not moved, and stood as it had the moment a young and naïve Victoria Winters had first set eyes on it when she had arrived from New York to be governess for Master David Collins.

Then am I safe?

She ran her hand along her face, tracing what she was, and who she was. She was Victoria Winters, and she was safe.

But there were scratches on her face; she could feel their irregular, tender lines. And her hands were also sliced and laced with dried blood. Where had these come from? Where had she been?

And then the smell of blood flooded her nostrils, and around her was a deafening crackle of fire. She stumbled from the window. Voices cut the roar of the flames, voices she knew.

Thomas Rathburn.

Barnabas Collins.

Chants, shouts. And then a woman's furious and agonizing shriek.

Victoria dropped to the bed, her face in her hands. From where were these images coming? They were too strong to be remnants of a nightmare. She curled up on the bed, drawing her legs beneath her and covering her head with her arms. She trembled uncontrollably. She drew breath through her lips, fighting the bitter odor of smoke. Something had happened to her, but the impressions were scattered, disjointed, and even as she pressed her skull as tightly as she could with her forearms, they would not come together. They made no sense.

She felt sick and she felt sickened.

Just like the illness I suffered months back, when I began to distrust Barnabas. Why can't I remember?

"But do I want to?" she whispered.

She put her arms down and stared at the window. *Remember!* she told herself. *Victoria, remember! You heard Barnabas's voice, you heard Thomas's voice. There was a scream. There was fire, smoke. What happened?*

It was as though Collinwood was toying with her again. The great estate was manipulating her for its pleasure, its entertainment, or something darker and much more menacing. She had long believed the place was a world unto itself. A world with secrets, with its own rules and its own terrible powers.

Remember, Victoria! Don't let it have you so totally! Fight it!

The scent of fire faded, replaced by a smell of dried leaves. The chants were chased into the recesses of her mind, replaced by the echo of another voice . . . a lone voice, buffeted by cold winds and echoing down a long, night road. Her voice. Calling.

David, where are you hiding? David, don't do this!

David was missing.

Yes, she remembered that, and her heart

clenched. No matter what disorientation played with her concentration, she recalled that David was gone. He had disappeared, angry with her for slapping him.

I have to find him!

She got up quickly, ignoring the residual pounding in her head, and pulled a pair of jeans from the dresser. Her shoes were by the closet, and she noticed several leaves stuck to the bottom. Yes, she had gone outside looking for David, but more than that she couldn't remember.

Angry tears welled. *It doesn't matter that I can't remember. I'll start over again. I'll start and I'll find him.* She was sure everyone knew by now that she had hit him, but she wouldn't let them think that she hadn't done all she could, all she was capable of, to find him.

Victoria quickly put on the knit shirt that had been left draped over the back of the chair. She remembered wearing it yesterday, remembered the west wing and the blackness. But none of it mattered. Nothing but finding David.

She touched her chest, felt her heart slamming beneath her fingers. Aloud, she said, "I'll find him if it's the last thing I ever do at Collinwood!"

"Good morning!"

Startled, Victoria looked at the door. Carolyn stood there, smiling.

"Carolyn!" she said. "I can't believe you let me

sleep so late. My alarm didn't go off, something happened, I don't know, but we have to find David!"

Carolyn laughed.

Victoria's jaws came together and her eyes narrowed. "How can you laugh at a time like this!"

"Vicki, take it easy," Carolyn said. "David is home."

"He is?" Victoria dropped the shoe she was holding.

"He is indeed." Carolyn shook her head, her laugh incredulous. "You really don't remember, do you?"

"I remember looking for David in the house. I remember I was outside, near the road, I think, but . . ."

"You must have had quite an evening. You were out pretty late, and came back with Barnabas, looking quite the mess but not upset by any means. In fact, from that dazed little expression on your face, I'd say you were rather satisfied. So, I take it you and Barnabas are over whatever friction was between you?"

Victoria shook her head. "Is David really here?"

"Yes, he came back while you were out, and was home when I got in from work. Mother and I told you he was back, tucked safely in bed. You don't remember, do you?" Carolyn peered at her with questing eyes, as if expecting an admission of drunkenness.

Victoria closed her eyes and sighed. Nothing remained in her memory of last night but the now-faint fragments of chants and vague scents of something burning. Her imagination, perhaps; tricks of the ancient place, likely.

"Did Barnabas say anything to you?" Victoria managed. "Did he say where we'd been or what we'd done?"

"Oh, come on, Vicki," Carolyn said with a raised brow. "You must really be upset. You apparently broke Thomas's heart, for him to have left so suddenly."

Victoria sat on the chair, her head tipped. "What?"

"That's what Barnabas said—that Thomas went back home late last night."

Still disbelieving, she repeated, "What?"

"He said Thomas needed to return to his business affairs much sooner than he planned. I guess he just didn't want to face you."

"Thomas is gone?"

"Earth to Vicki. Yes, he's gone. Didn't he tell you he was leaving?"

"I don't remember. Maybe he did."

"Wow." Carolyn came into the room and put her hand on Victoria's shoulder. "How much *did* you have to drink last night? I've never seen you like this before. Maybe you need another day off or something. Maybe a couple days?"

Victoria rubbed her forehead, then stood and slipped into her shoes. *Thomas is gone. He's left. I'll never see him again.* "This shirt is filthy."

"Yeah."

She found a fresh sweater in the closet. As she pulled her arms into the sleeves, she said, "Elizabeth must be furious with me. Roger must be even more so. Facing them is going to be incredibly difficult. I have no excuses for any of it."

"Uncle Roger brushed it all off as David being David. But Mother, well . . ."

"Well what?"

"It's been a long time since I've seen Mother so upset."

"She's going to fire me, then."

"No, not upset about David. About you."

"What do you mean?"

"By dinnertime everyone knew David was missing. Roger had Jake go out and drive about the estate, but when he got back, David was home. David didn't say anything about you slapping him. He didn't say anything at all except he was hungry and wanted to go to town to trick-or-treat for candy, with or without a costume."

Victoria shook her head.

"Of course, Uncle Roger said David wasn't going anywhere for running off, that he could have some leftover dinner if he wanted but he was going to go straight to his room for the rest of the night and to hell with Halloween."

"Really?"

"David, his usual dour self, took a chicken leg and went upstairs. But Mother was all edgy about you, seemed to think something was terribly wrong. She asked Jake to drive through the estate again, and he did. When he came back, he said he'd gone clear to the entrance gate but didn't see hide nor hair of you. I could tell he didn't really want to look all that hard. Maybe he thought Thomas would punch him for ruining a romantic moment, or something. But you weren't with Thomas after all."

Victoria's head was pounding harder now. She looked out the window at the bright and misleading innocence of the morning.

Thomas is gone.

"Mother went into her office," Carolyn continued, "and told everyone to leave her alone. She closed the door and was there a very long time. When she came out, I could see she'd been crying. If I'd gone missing I wonder if she would have cried for me? Sometimes I think she would drink a toast to my absence."

"Nonsense," Victoria said. "She's your mother. Mothers never stop loving their children."

"Maybe. But I've given her a lot of stress over the years." Carolyn chuckled, but the sound was laced with sadness.

"Just knowing that is in itself a good place to start."

"Perhaps, perhaps. Well!" Carolyn tossed her hair and smiled. "I'm going into town. I'm going to be a good cousin and see if I can find any leftover Halloween candy on sale at half price for David. The drugstore has to have a couple bags of candy corn and some of that eyeball bubble gum. Want to come?"

"I can't."

"Why?"

How could she explain to Carolyn the utter despair and depression that had settled on her? Carolyn could never truly understand. No one could. "I just can't. Thanks. Have fun."

"Okay, sure! I'll see you later!"

I don't think you will, Carolyn. "Sure, see you later."

With a flash of golden hair and a click of expensive heels on the bit of hardwood floor by the hall runner, Carolyn turned and was gone.

The air was silent. Even the birds outside the window could no longer be heard arguing over territories.

Victoria looked around her room. Her room? No. It did not belong to her. She owned only her clothes, her books, a few trinkets she'd collected over time. What did she have to show for her time at

Collinwood? Nothing but odds and ends, broken hearts, and haunting visions.

"I can't stay here," she said to herself. It had become intolerable. There was no one in whom she could confide, no one to whom she could completely belong. "I must go." Her voice cracked around the last words, and a fresh tear cut down along the side of her nose. *I must go.*

Her two scratched suitcases were inside the closet. She put them on the bed and folded her clothes carefully inside, slipped the little bit of makeup and jewelry she had inside a liner pocket, then snapped the suitcases shut. Other items—a scarf Carolyn had given her that hung on the mirror's edge, a collection of seashells she'd bought at a small gift shop in town the week she'd arrived, a mother-of-pearl-topped perfume bottle Elizabeth had presented her on the first anniversary of her employment—these she would not take. Collinwood had to be stripped from her mind. It had to be drained from her blood. Somehow.

Then she spied the music box on the shelf by the window. It was a gift from Barnabas, back when she and he were falling in love. Back when she had trusted him.

Victoria went to the shelf and picked up the delicate antiquity. She lifted the lid, and the sweet, poignant melody began to play. Barnabas. The music spoke of his care for her, a caring she had pushed away. She no longer felt distrust for the gallant, mysterious man. She only felt guilt at the way she'd treated him, the way she had avoided him. As carefully as if she were holding his heart in her hands, she opened one of the suitcases, rolled the music box in a blouse, and shut the case again.

Downstairs in the foyer, she quietly set the suitcases by the door, then hesitated. Elizabeth was home, somewhere. Mrs. Johnson was, too. And David, where was David this morning? Could she really leave without saying a word to anyone? Which was easier: to escape without having to face their questions, or to face the tormenting questions they would demand of her in her dreams to come?

Slowly, Victoria walked down the long hallway. She hesitated outside Elizabeth's office, and peered inside the dark room past the half-opened door. She had rarely been inside the office; it always had an atmosphere that spoke of stern duty and cold business. When Elizabeth was here, she was working, and when she was working, she was totally absorbed and unreachable.

On a small drop-leaf table by the bookshelf, a single candle glowed, half melted to its base. The shadows it cast across the otherwise lightless room were fuzzy and shimmering. It seemed out of character for Elizabeth to leave an unattended candle lit when she was not in the room. She was a careful person, and an unattended candle could set the whole of Collinwood ablaze.

That notion had no doubt crossed Elizabeth's mind, Victoria thought. She knew that her mistress had the same reservations about the mysteries of the old place as she herself did, and the same fear of it as well.

Victoria pushed the door farther open and walked in. Believing she heard a sound outside, she paused, but it was only the echo of footsteps from the kitchen, traveling the length of old floorboards. Intending to blow out the candle, she moved to the table, then stared at the arrangement she saw there, the backs of her hands prickling.

The candle was in the center of a circle defined by glass beads. Within the circle were a handful of feathers, several cloves of garlic, a gold cross on a chain, and a small pouch, tied shut. There were also dried leaves Victoria could not identify, a scrap of paper with unrecognizable symbols drawn in ink, and a knotted length of string. All these, she was certain, were intended to ward away an evil; items from various traditions, meant to protect.

But the object she found most arresting, lying amidst the others, was a small, white baby's cap: a tatted lace christening cap with satin ribbon woven through its fabric.

Victoria slowly reached out toward it.

"I light the candle once a day when no one else is about."

She pulled her hand back, and spun around toward the voice, and saw in the far corner of the room, near the drape-shrouded window, a figure.

"I keep it covered otherwise. No one notices. Even Mrs. Johnson in her cleaning leaves it untouched. It has been this way for many years."

Victoria had recognized the voice. It was Elizabeth, who now emerged from the corner and crossed the floor to stand beside her. In the candlelight, the creases in her mistress's forehead were more defined, the lines of care at the corners of her eyes pronounced and deep.

"I—I didn't mean to come in uninvited," Victoria stammered. "I know my place—I was just concerned about the candle."

"I knew you would be, Victoria." Elizabeth moved away and sat down on the chair behind her desk. She put her elbows on the wood and folded her hands beneath her chin.

Victoria frowned. "Elizabeth, I don't understand. You wanted me to see this?"

"You mentioned secrets the other night," Elizabeth said. "Yes, secrets, dreadful secrets, are in this house, visited upon certain members of this family. Secrets so powerful that if they were ever uttered, great disaster would follow."

Victoria looked back at the candle. At the baby's cap.

"Some things can never be spoken, Victoria."

Elizabeth's voice began to tremble, but then she caught itself, and her words became steady, clear. "But I want you to understand. People sometimes do what is against their nature because of stronger, unnatural forces set to work."

"You want to protect a baby," Victoria said. "What baby?"

Elizabeth said nothing.

"Someone cursed Carolyn as a child? David?"

Elizabeth said nothing.

"Then there was another child? Elizabeth? Who was this baby?"

Elizabeth turned to gaze at Victoria.

"A child who died?" Victoria asked.

The older woman's expression said no.

"Then a child who lived? A child you could not acknowledge for fear of its safety?"

Elizabeth stood abruptly and went to the door. "Blow the candle out, Victoria. And put the cloth back over it all. It's on the desk."

"Elizabeth—"

"You said a moment ago that you know your place," Elizabeth said. Across the dim space of the room her eyes caught Victoria's, and the expression was one of resignation, pride, regret, and hope. And love? "I do not think you did, my dear. But now I believe you do. You know, Victoria."

"I . . ." Victoria began.

"Some things can never be spoken," Elizabeth

said, "for the dark and unrelentless threat of curse. And curses, at Collinwood, must never be ignored."

"What do you—"

"I bid you good morning."

With an odd little bow, Elizabeth left.

Victoria stood without moving for many minutes. Then, slowly, she blew out the candle. She draped the small cloth over the shrine. Her heart was beating so rapidly she could hardly stand.

My place, she thought. *The cap was mine.*

The child was clearly born without the family's blessing. It had had upon it a supernatural curse. Perhaps Elizabeth had sought solace in the arms of another when the truth of her husband's greed had come to light. Perhaps she had borne a child, a child that Paul had threatened with a curse if it was not gotten rid of.

And she was the child.

She was the banished one.

Elizabeth was her mother, and had brought her back home at long last under the guise of a governess, a ruse only she would know but one that would have to be good enough, so she could be near her other daughter.

But fear of the mysterious curse remained, and the shrine was maintained.

Victoria understood. Her own speculations on the riddles of Collinwood were surely as powerful and as controlling. Secrets, terrible and most powerful secrets, held this place in their grasp, and the grasp was as alive as the copper beech tree and as immortal as time, as silent as the graveyard on the hill.

Victoria went into the hall. Elizabeth was gone. "Some things can never be spoken," Victoria said to the floor and the walls. Her lips were dry and her voice not much more than a whisper. "I won't, Elizabeth. I won't."

She walked on shaky legs to the kitchen. She needed to sit down for a moment. She needed to think. But there she found one lone boy, hunched over a bowl of cereal, stirring the soggy mess disconsolately.

She watched him for a moment from the doorway. And then she said gently, "David?"

David dropped the spoon into the bowl and looked at her with a frown. "Go away," he said.

And then she knew she didn't have to think.

She didn't have to wrangle over whether to leave or to stay.

If she left, she would be abandoning this child whom she had worked so hard to befriend and teach. This child who represented a new generation of Collinses, who might be the only hope of breaking the curses someday and scaring the family secrets out of the dark shadows and into the light.

"All right, David," she said kindly. "But not far. Only down the hall and perhaps up the stairs. I'll never be far, don't you forget it."

David scowled. But Victoria repeated in a whisper, "Don't you ever forget it."

She walked slowly back to the foyer. She could hear shuffling upstairs, Elizabeth maybe, moving around in her bedroom, or Mrs. Johnson, scouring a lavatory in her diligent way. David mumbled back in the kitchen. Victoria's own footsteps caused the hall floor to creak. Outside, the fist of a late autumn wind banged against the front door, wanting to be let in, perhaps; perhaps just telling the family that it was there.

Sounds that were part of Collinwood. Sounds that had always belonged to her.

I didn't know. Now I do.

At the foot of the staircase she picked up her suitcases from the floor and put her foot on the first step.

What difference will it make? she thought. *I can never speak of it. Elizabeth will never speak of it.*

She looked up at the stained-glass window above the landing. The colors this morning were brilliant, startling.

"I suppose time will tell," she said aloud. "But only one thing matters now. I'm here." There was salt in her mouth, and only then did she realize that tears had made their way down her face.

She started up the stairs, then put the suitcases on a step and went back down to stand beneath the portrait of Barnabas. She gazed at the deep-set eyes beneath the heavy brows.

Barnabas.

"I'm here," she said. "It looks as if I'm going to stay."

And for a moment the gaunt, sad face in the portrait seemed to smile at her.

Epilogue

H ow close I was! So close I could have touched him, wrapped him in my arms, held him forever, to be mine . . . mine!

What could have gone so wrong?

Thomas Rathburn had been the right one. She had no doubt of that. He had fulfilled her every expectation; he had taken Victoria Winters, just as she'd anticipated; he had made Barnabas fear that Victoria was lost to him forever—until the end. Rathburn had understood, but then resisted her, just at the moment when he could have ushered her into the world she so madly desired. She had underestimated his strong will, his cunning mind.

And Barnabas lived still.

Yet . . . I still love him. I still want him. I MUST have him!

Even now, among the black flames, she could not give up hope. She had been driven back but not destroyed. *They* could never destroy her! What laughable conceit, to think they could banish her forever. Yet, there were those who *could* destroy her . . . and she remained in their domain, still at their mercy. Somehow, she must escape. She *had* to escape, before madness became her whole existence.

She would have to again follow the threads of power that led through this abyss. Seek again some portal opening to the land of the living, where she might again touch one of them . . . influence them . . . manipulate them. . . .

Someone at Collinwood. Yes. She would work her will on one of them, make him bring her over. Someone weak of will but influential . . .

Yes.

The master of the house. *He* would do nicely.

But for now, she was trapped here. And the dark masters were so near. So near, and so terrible. But so silent. She belonged to them, and they would not want her to escape. Here, she had nothing to offer them. Yet, if only they would let her serve them again, to live in the world of the flesh, she would work to please *them*, to carry out their desires upon the living. . . .

I must be free.

Get me out of this.

By all the powers of Satan. Lucifer. Diabolos . . .

Set me FREE. . . .

There is no answer. There is nothing.

How I despise you, Barnabas Collins.

How I love you. I have always loved you so. . . .